"Come back s

Shay said. *Like tomorrow. And the next night. Every night.* "If I'm not at work, I'm usually here."

His only response was a faint smile as he shifted into gear.

"Easy?"

He looked at her.

"Does this trip into town mean that you're not going to hole up out there forever?"

"No, it means—" Second after second ticked by before he finally answered. "I wanted to see you." Then, before she could respond, he backed up and drove away.

Pleasure bubbled up inside her as she watched his taillights disappear around the corner— pleasure and pure, sweet need. Maybe she was a fool for falling for him all over again. But she couldn't turn away—not from him or her feelings for him. She couldn't stop hoping, and Easy was her best hope.

Always had been. Always would be.

Dear Reader,

Welcome to another month of fabulous reading from Silhouette Intimate Moments, the line that brings you excitement along with your romance every month. As I'm sure you've already noticed, the month begins with a return to CONARD COUNTY, in *Involuntary Daddy,* by bestselling author Rachel Lee. As always, her hero and heroine will live in your heart long after you've turned the last page, along with an irresistible baby boy nicknamed Peanut. You'll wish you could take him home yourself.

Award winner Marie Ferrarella completes her CHILDFINDERS, INC. trilogy with *Hero in the Nick of Time,* about a fake marriage that's destined to become real, and not one, but *two,* safely recovered children. Marilyn Pappano offers the second installment of her HEARTBREAK CANYON miniseries, *The Horseman's Bride.* This Oklahoma native certainly has a way with a Western man! After too long away, Doreen Owens Malek returns with our MEN IN BLUE title, *An Officer and a Gentle Woman,* about a cop falling in love with his prime suspect. Kylie Brant brings us the third of THE SULLIVAN BROTHERS in *Falling Hard and Fast,* a steamy read that will have your heart racing. Finally, welcome RaeAnne Thayne, whose debut book for the line, *The Wrangler and the Runaway Mom,* is also a WAY OUT WEST title. You'll be happy to know that her second book is already scheduled.

Enjoy them all—and then come back again next month, when once again Silhouette Intimate Moments brings you six of the best and most exciting romances around.

Yours,

Leslie J. Wainger
Executive Senior Editor

Please address questions and book requests to:
Silhouette Reader Service
U.S.: 3010 Walden Ave., P.O. Box 1325, Buffalo, NY 14269
Canadian: P.O. Box 609, Fort Erie, Ont. L2A 5X3

MARILYN PAPPANO

THE HORSEMAN'S BRIDE

Silhouette®
INTIMATE™MOMENTS®

Published by Silhouette Books

America's Publisher of Contemporary Romance

SILHOUETTE BOOKS

ISBN 0-373-07957-5

THE HORSEMAN'S BRIDE

Copyright © 1999 by Marilyn Pappano

Visit us at www.romance.net

Printed in U.S.A.

Books by Marilyn Pappano

MARILYN PAPPANO

After following her career navy husband around the country for sixteen years, Marilyn Pappano now makes her home high on a hill overlooking her hometown. With acreage, an orchard and the best view in the state, she's not planning on pulling out the moving boxes ever again. When not writing, she makes apple butter from their own apples (when the thieves don't get to them first), putts around the pond in the boat and tends a yard that she thinks would look better as a wildflower field, if the darn things would just grow there. You can write to Marilyn via snail mail at P.O. Box 643, Sapulpa, OK 74067-0643.

To the Friday afternoon bunch:

Laura Altom, who's so much like me, it's scary. We *could* be twins. Hey, it's just a *slight* age difference.

Meg Reid, who answered my questions—some of them twice—without getting impatient, and who gave me such encouragement.

Susan Shay, who loved Easy from the beginning and helped keep me inspired in the writing.

You guys are talented writers, great entertainment and the best road-trip companions Oklahoma has to offer. Here's to many more fabulous times.

Chapter 1

It was a hot Texas night. The Mesquite arena was filled with fans in the seats and cowboys behind the chutes. The competition had been stiff this Saturday night, but luck was with him. The time to beat was 8.6 seconds, and he could do that one-handed in his sleep.

He shifted in the saddle, adjusted his hat, tightened his right hand around the reins, then looked up to the stands. His gaze searched the center section on the left, skimming row over row until he saw her. She looked nervous, which eased his own nerves. There was no reason for him to worry when she worried enough for both of them. That was her job, and it allowed him to concentrate on his job—the horse, the calf, the rope.

He flexed his fingers, tensed his muscles and waited for the gate to open and release one frightened calf into the arena. He would leave tonight a winner. He knew it in his bones. The gate swung open, the calf darted out, and he—

Easy Rafferty started awake. His heart was pounding the

way it always did before a ride, but he wasn't in some rodeo arena on Gambler's back. He was behind the wheel of his parked pickup truck, and the engine was still running, the stereo still playing, the headlights still shining. Ignoring his body's protests, he straightened in the seat and looked around.

He was home.

For fourteen years, he'd been trying to find his way back here. Fourteen years—good and bad, best and worst. And now he was here.

The house he'd grown up in looked pretty much the same—square, with a porch stretching from end to end, one story, a weather vane stuck dead center in the roof.

Headlights and moonlight softened the effects of abandonment—the peeling paint, the screen door hanging crooked, the leaves and dirt that littered the porch. Nothing could lessen the effects of the memories.

The front door always open in warm weather so company could call a hello through the screen.

Sunday mornings in church clothes—white shirt, black trousers, black cowboy boots—waiting on the swing until it was time to go.

Catching lightnin' bugs on hot summer nights while his folks talked quietly in the rockers.

Sprawled on the steps with his best friend, Guthrie, while they planned their next adventure.

Gentling horses in the corral out back.

Riding fence, pulling foals, doctoring injuries—the horses' and his own.

Stealing a kiss from Mary Jane Phillips under the old maple.

Stealing his best friend's girl.

He shut off the headlights, then the engine, cutting off Garth Brooks in mid-lament. With his keys in one hand and a nylon duffel slung over his shoulder, he climbed out of the truck. His knees creaked and his hip throbbed, reminding him to grab the cane tucked between the seats before taking a step.

Though knee-high weeds hid the walkway, memory led him right to it. He stepped from stone to stone, bitterly comparing his slow progress to the hundreds of times he'd raced along the same path, his feet barely touching the ground. He'd been so young then.

He felt so old now.

It had been five months since the accident that had ended his career. It might as well have ended his life. He was a cowboy who couldn't cowboy any longer—a horseman who had crippled his best horse along with himself. He had no job, no other skills. No dignity, no pride, no woman. No family but the parents who'd smothered him. No future.

No damn future.

Hobbling up the five steps took more effort and resulted in more pain than he'd expected, and turning the key in the lock and walking inside took more courage than he'd known he had.

He'd always intended to come back here someday—to live in this house, to work this land, to raise the best damn horses and kids in the entire state of Oklahoma. But he'd never intended to come alone. He'd never intended to sneak into town in the middle of the night, and he'd certainly never intended to slink back even less a man than when he'd left.

He flipped the switch inside the door, and the overhead light came on. The frosted globe with its curly edges was missing, leaving the bare bulb to cast its bright light in all directions, creating harsh shadows. Joelle, a cousin so many times removed that most people didn't think of them as family, had taken care of the electricity and the water for him. She'd gotten a few pieces of furniture delivered—a sofa, a coffee table, a rocker and a television, a bed and a dresser. The refrigerator had come from her grandfather and was older than Easy. The stove and kitchen table had come from her uncle and were about as old. She'd offered to get the telephone hooked up, but he'd told her no. Who would he call?

Guthrie?

Shay?

Wincing—because his hip hurt, *not* because he'd let her name slip into his mind—he shut off the light again. Once his eyes had adjusted again to the dark, he limped to the sofa. The springs protested as he sank down. So did his joints. Tilting his head back, he closed his eyes.

Home. For years he'd thought that if he could just get back here, things would somehow be okay. The people he'd wronged would magically forgive him. The love he'd destroyed would spring back stronger than ever, and the woman he'd loved would want him again.

But no woman would want him like this. Women would pity him, maybe even fuss over him a bit, but then they would be glad to leave him. And why not? For years he'd been nothing but an empty shell, and now the shell was cracked and damaged. He had nothing left to offer anyone.

Especially Shay Stephens. She was probably married now, anyway—probably raising kids and being a good mother and a damn good wife. It would be some kind of perverted justice if she'd come back to Heartbreak and married Guthrie, the way she'd intended before *he* had interfered. It would serve him right, knowing that she lived just a half mile away, sleeping with another man, loving another man.

A strangled sound, part groan, part sob, echoed through the room. God help him, he'd made a mistake coming back here. First thing tomorrow, whether his body was up to it or not, he would climb back into his truck and he would drive until he'd outrun the pain, the hopelessness, the sorrow. He would drive until he found peace or forgiveness…or death.

That night in New Mexico, pinned in the wreckage of his truck, listening to his own labored breathing and the agonized screams of his injured horse, he'd prayed to die, but he'd already suspected that God had no time to hear his prayers. The fact that he was still alive proved it. The fact that he'd survived crippled and scarred proved one other thing—that God intended him to suffer his hell on earth.

All because he'd fallen in love with his best friend's girl.

He rubbed his eyes with one hand. He needed rest—had needed it so desperately for so long that the need had become a part of him. The only good thing about the accident was that in the early days they'd kept him sedated so he could sleep without pain, without dreams. He needed that sort of deep, restful sleep tonight, but he wouldn't find it. Not in this house. Not in this town. Not in this life.

In spite of his discomfort, he did doze off, but his sleep was neither deep nor restful. It was tormented by dreams, with memories he didn't allow himself to recall when he was awake, and it was filled with aches—real ones in his hip, his ribs, his hand, and intangible ones around his heart. He awakened in a cold sweat too many times to count, and he shifted often, seeking some relief. By the time he gave up the effort, the sun was up and he was even more fatigued than he'd been the day before.

He sat up and slowly swung his feet to the floor. Everything appeared to work, though he was for damn sure the worse for wear. Monday's long drive and the sofa's lumps and bumps had taken their toll on a body that was already taxed to its limits. The thought of climbing back into the truck was almost enough to defeat him, but another day or three of pure physical misery had to be easier than staying here.

He was reaching for his cane when abruptly he became aware of sounds—a horse's whicker, a hoof pawing at gravel, a voice. Gritting his teeth, he pushed himself to his feet. Pain, red-hot and throbbing, shot through him and made him curse as he awkwardly shuffled his way toward the open door. There he leaned heavily on the cane, close

enough to see out but not close enough, he thought, to be
seen in the shadows.

There were three horses out front—one gelding, two
ponies. The ponies were pintos and nearly identical, as were
the two girls on their backs. The woman astride the gelding
was clearly their mother, with the same fine, pale brown
hair, delicate lines and fragile air. She was a stranger. All
of them were, except the gelding.

Fourteen years ago he'd gotten the horse for free. He
was too wild, the owner had claimed, too unmanageable,
too dangerous. The man had wanted the animal put down,
but Easy had convinced him to give the horse to him. He'd
brought him here, had kept him in the corral out back, had
gentled him, calmed him, trained him, then given him to
Guthrie for his birthday. Was this woman connected to
Guthrie? Or had he come to hate Easy so much that he'd
give up a top-quality animal simply because it'd come from
him?

The woman's gaze locked on the screen door. He took
a slow step to the side, deeper into the shadows, but it was
too late. She urged Buck closer, then called, "Hello."

"Who're you talking to, Mom?" One of the girls guided
her pony closer, too, right up to the front steps, then
squinted. "Oh, hey, there's someone in there. D'ya see him,
Emmy? I see him."

Easy's left hand clenched around the handle of the cane.
"What do you want?" The words came out a growl, harsh
and unwelcoming, exactly the way he felt.

"I'm Elly Harris—"

The mother cut her off with a silent command before
looking back at him. "My daughters and I were riding by
and saw your truck. Can I ask what you're doing here?"

"What business is it of yours?"

She looked affronted by his rudeness, but the overall tone
of her voice remained pleasant. "Actually, I was wondering
what business you have here. This is private property."

"Yes, it is, and you're trespassing, so take your kids and your horses and get out of here."

She stared at him, but Easy knew she couldn't make out much. The screen was so rusty and dirty that he would hardly be able to see her if she wasn't standing in bright sunlight, and he had deep shadows on his side. She didn't follow his advice and leave, though. Instead, she dismounted and climbed the steps. He took a cautious step back.

"This house has been empty for fourteen years and it isn't likely the owner—" Abruptly she broke off. "You're— Are you—" She wet her lips. "Easy? Easy Rafferty?"

He scowled harder. "And who the hell are you?"

"Olivia Harris. Guthrie's wife."

Guthrie's wife. If she was Guthrie's wife, then Shay couldn't be. Relief swept through him, then died a sudden death. What did it matter if Shay hadn't married Guthrie? He wanted her married to *someone,* wanted her to be happy and in love and making a home and raising kids and living the life that he could never give her. He wanted to know that *his* was the only life he'd ruined. He wanted—hell, he *needed* to suffer.

She smiled the sort of full, womanly smile he'd been accustomed to before the accident but hadn't seen at all since. At least, not directed his way. "I can't believe you've come home. No one had a clue— We've wondered what you were doing since—"

He steeled himself against the friendliness in her molasses-thick, Southern-belle voice and instead concentrated on his own enormous bitterness to make his words colder, harder. "What I'm doing is no one's business but mine. Kindly take your daughters, Mrs. Harris, and get the hell off my property and don't come back."

For a moment he thought she might refuse, and then what would he do? He couldn't physically remove her. It took every bit of strength he possessed to simply stand there. He couldn't move two feet without the cane, which required his left hand. As for his right hand…it was useless. *He* was useless.

Fortunately, he didn't have to find an alternative action. She took a step back, then another, before spinning around and hurrying down the steps. She swung onto Buck's back with an ease he would never again manage and gathered the reins in both hands—another feat he would never achieve. He hated her for it, hated her kids for sitting their mounts so effortlessly. He hated everyone in the entire damn world.

Most especially himself.

The woman wheeled Buck around, then paused to look over her shoulder at him. "Welcome home, Mr. Rafferty. I hope you find what you're looking for here." Then she rode off with a daughter on either side.

The privacy to drown himself in self-pity, sorrow and booze. That was all he was looking for. That, and peace.

He watched until they were out of sight, then turned away from the door. In daylight the house looked worse than it had last night. The rugs his mother had spread everywhere were long gone, leaving scarred, scraped wooden planks uncovered. The wallpaper was peeling and still showed where all the pictures had hung. With no curtains or blinds to filter its light, the sun shone harshly, unforgivingly, across the room. It was an ugly, depressing place. Perfect for finishing out an ugly, depressing life.

His limp was worse than usual as he made his way to the couch. He'd left his duffel on the floor beside it. He couldn't kneel down to get it, didn't trust himself to bend over without losing his balance. Instead he braced his good leg against the sofa and used his cane to hook the rigid handle.

Inside the bag was a couple of changes of clothing, some papers, some money, a few old photos. He ignored all that and dug deeper, through towels and toiletries, to the pill bottle that had shifted to the bottom. Clutching it tightly between thumb and forefinger, he forced himself through the dining room and into the kitchen.

Joelle had seen to everything. There were groceries in the cabinets, along with mismatched dishes, pots and pans, and food in the refrigerator. He picked up the orange juice on the top shelf, then put it back and reached for a beer instead.

The bedroom was another difficult journey, but he made it, easing onto the bed, leaning his cane against the wall. It fell to the floor with a clatter, but he didn't care. Slumping back against the headboard, he uncapped the pill bottle, then the bottle of beer.

There'd been a time, not long after he'd left Heartbreak, when he'd drunk too much. Now, as he washed down pain pills with cold beer, he thought that maybe lately he hadn't drunk enough. Maybe he would get lucky and find his way out of the mess his life had become.

Not that he'd been lucky in a long time.

Not since he'd run off with his best friend's girl.

It was the middle of the breakfast rush in downtown Heartbreak when the phone beside the cash register rang. Juggling two plates of fried eggs with all the greasy side orders, Shay Stephens leaned across the counter to snag the receiver. "Heartbreak Café."

"Hey, Shay."

"Magnolia, hi. Hold on a minute." Letting the receiver dangle by its cord, she delivered the breakfasts, grabbed the coffeepot and refilled three cups, then swooped past the counter to grab the phone again. "Listen, I'm really busy here. Can I call you back in an hour or so?"

"Easy's back."

Shay stiffened, and the coffeepot slid from her hand to the floor, glass shattering, steaming coffee splattering across the tile. Everyone in the café was looking her way, and she knew at least a few were asking if she was all right, but she couldn't hear their voices over the roaring in her ears. She couldn't hear anything at all as she sank against the counter for support. She couldn't stand. Couldn't think. Couldn't breathe.

Olivia's voice cut through the roar—soft, Southern, concerned. "The girls talked me into a ride before school this morning, and we saw this truck at his house and went up to make sure everything was all right, and— He's back, Shay."

Her chest hurt, and for one awful moment she thought she was going to lose the breakfast she'd fixed herself three hours ago. Then her stomach settled, she managed to breathe, and the killing ache in her chest eased to a dull throb. She even managed to make her jaw work, to get words out in a coherent thought, though the voice sounded nothing like hers. "How is he?"

"He told us to get the hell off his property and never come back." Olivia hesitated. "He was very angry. Very…bitter."

"How did he look?"

"I couldn't tell. He was inside in the shadows and the screen door…" The rest trailed away.

Shay knew what the screen door was like. She'd been out to that house more times than she wanted to admit in the past six years, and Olivia knew it. She'd found her out there not too long ago, sobbing on the porch like some heartsick teenager. Though it'd been a long time since her teen years—half a lifetime—the first part of the description was sadly accurate. She'd been heartsick all of her adult life.

"What are you going to do, Shay?"

She combed her fingers through her hair, then suddenly realized that Amalia was on her knees, cleaning the mess she'd made. "I don't know," she said abruptly. "I'll have to think about that. Listen, I've got to go. We're awfully busy. Thanks for calling me."

Without waiting for a response from her friend, she hung

up, then pulled the young waitress to her feet. "My mess, Amalia. I'll clean it."

"But I don't mind—"

"Neither do I." She pulled the paper towels from Amalia's hand, then nudged her toward the kitchen. "You've got orders up. Go ahead and take care of them."

She knelt carefully on the wooden floor. The waitress had already disposed of the bits of broken glass and the plastic handle and mopped up most of the coffee. Now Shay finished that task, then dipped a towel in the bucket of soapy water and began scrubbing the wood.

So Easy was home and living in his folks' house. Bud and Betsey Rafferty had abandoned the place not long after the scandal. That was how they'd always referred to Guthrie's jilting—how they'd always referred to *her*. She was the scandal that had ruined their precious, innocent son's life. Everything that had gone wrong for Easy from that day forward—and probably retroactively, too—had been her fault in their eyes. No doubt, they'd probably found some way to blame his accident on her, too.

It seemed she was destined to get her news about Easy here in the café. She'd been working the day one of his old rodeo buddies had passed through town back in June, and he'd told her about the one-car wreck that had put Easy in a succession of hospitals and ended his career.

Some suspected he'd been drinking when he'd lost control of his truck and had driven into a ravine in the New Mexico mountains, and she could believe that. He'd become a heavy drinker—her fault, too. Some thought he'd just been tired, pushing too hard to get from one rodeo to the next, and she could believe that, too. From the moment he'd asked her to forget Guthrie and their wedding and leave Heartbreak with him, he'd been driven. She was probably to blame for those demons, too.

Everything in the whole damn world was her fault, and she'd paid. She'd paid so damn dearly.

But not as dearly as Easy.

"You keep scrubbing that floor, you're gonna take the varnish right off," a voice murmured near her ear.

Shay blinked, looked at the sparkling floor and the paper towel she'd scrubbed to shreds, then raised her gaze to Reese Barnett. The sheriff was watching her with a look that was partly amused and partly concerned. He offered her a hand and pulled her easily to her feet, then moved the bucket out of the way for good measure.

"I take it that phone call was bad news."

"Phone call?"

He guided her behind the counter to the cash register, then handed her his bill and five bucks to cover it. "Remember? The phone rang, you answered, turned white as a ghost, then dropped the coffee? Is there a problem?"

"N-no. Not at all." Just that her entire life was a mess and threatened to get even messier.

"Are we still on for tonight?"

"Tonight?"

"Dinner in Buffalo Plains?"

Right. Dinner. She and Reese were supposed to have dinner in the county seat, then go back to her house before *he* headed home and *she* started wallowing in regrets. It was what she did—how she'd passed the last six years, using other men, nice men, men she cared about. Men she pretended she might fall in love with, even though she knew before the first date that it wasn't going to happen. Still, she tried, and when she failed, she blamed herself and Easy and damned them both.

"Reese, I..."

He waited patiently, suspecting what she was about to say. She could see in his eyes that he expected the same sort of brush-off she'd given every man before him, and she gave it, but using different words than every time before.

"Easy's back."

For a moment he showed no reaction. Then he drew a deep breath. "I see. How is he?"

It was a polite question. He and Easy had never been friends. In school, she, Easy and Guthrie had needed no other friends. They'd been best buddies and so much more. Now she and Guthrie had managed a tentative friendship—more because of Olivia than anything else—and she and Easy were…

Unfinished business. That was all. She needed an end to their relationship that she could live with—something more final than waking up one morning in a dingy Montana motel to find him gone. Gone, with no note, no farewell, no *go to hell.* Just gone.

For six years she'd wondered why—wondered what she could have done to make him stay, whether anything she might have done could have made him stay. Six long, miserable years.

"Shay?" Reese prompted. "How is he?"

Offering an unsteady smile, she tried for a lightheartedness she couldn't imagine feeling. "With Easy, who the hell ever knows?" She didn't. She knew very few things about him except for an undeniable fact—that she'd loved him desperately. That she'd broken Guthrie's heart for him. That *he'd* broken *her* heart. That sometimes she hated him far more than she'd loved him.

"Well…" Reese combed his hand over his hair, then put on his Stetson. "If you need him run out of town or anything, give me a call. I'm always happy to accommodate you."

Her smile felt more natural this time. That last was true. He'd been most accommodating, right from the start. Of course, he had his own ghosts in the past—someone or maybe something he'd loved and lost. He'd understood. He understood now.

Remembering his ticket, she rang it up and started to make change. "Keep it," he said. "And let me know if you need anything."

Oh, the things she needed… She couldn't even begin to list them. But the first and most important was time alone.

Leaving the counter, she located Geraldine in the kitchen. The woman was the oldest of Shay's employees—could have been mother to *their* mothers, she liked to boast—and could work circles around any one of them. Right now she was giving the cook none-too-well-received pointers on his gravy, but the instant she saw Shay, the gravy was forgotten.

"What's going on?" she asked bluntly.

"Nothing's going on." Shay's cheeks warmed with the lie. "But I'm going home."

"Home? In the middle of breakfast?"

"Everything's under control. After all, *you're* here."

Geraldine subjected her to intense scrutiny. "You plannin' a rendezvous with the sheriff?"

Warmth turned to heat. "And would it be any of your business if I were?"

The waitress grimly shook her head. "Woman your age should be settled down."

"I *am* settled." She hadn't traveled more than a hundred miles from Heartbreak in six years.

"With a different man every time you turn around." Geraldine snorted.

"I don't pay you to worry about what I do every time I turn around. I pay you to help run the café. If you can't stay out of my business, you know, you *can* be replaced."

Geraldine didn't take offense but smiled broadly instead. "No, I can't. Some people are irreplaceable."

But *she* wasn't one of them, Shay thought bitterly as she let herself out the back door. Guthrie, who had wanted to marry her, loved his new wife in ways he'd never even thought of loving *her,* and Easy, who had sworn he would love her forever, had replaced her easily and often before abandoning her for good in Montana.

Her house was only a half dozen blocks from the café. It was a tiny place—a dollhouse, her mother called it— with a tiny porch and a tiny yard and a view of Pete Davis's horses out back. The siding needed replacing, the kitchen updating, the bathroom remodeling, but it was home. There were flower beds out front, soft colors inside and no memories to haunt her.

She let herself into the living room, walked through to the kitchen, then into the bedroom. Geraldine was right. A woman her age should be settled. If her life had gone according to plan, she and Guthrie would have been married for more than fourteen years. She'd be living with him out at the ranch, working alongside him, passing Sunday mornings in a church pew between him and their children. She would be the mother of teenagers, going to soccer games, setting curfews, worrying about all the temptations that faced kids today.

That had been her plan, Guthrie's—even their mothers'. No one had counted on Easy, least of all her.

From the depths of the closet, she dug out an old photograph, then sank into the chair tucked into the corner near the window. The picture had been taken on her twentieth birthday, the day Guthrie had proposed. The day she'd realized that something was not quite right—no, entirely *too* right—between her and Easy.

He'd driven all night from a month's worth of rodeos in the Dakotas and Wyoming to make it to her afternoon party around her folks' pool. He'd been late, and he'd found her alone in the kitchen, refilling the punch bowl. He'd given her a gift—she couldn't remember what now—and he'd kissed her and—

She touched her fingertips lightly to her lips. She'd known. That little nothing kiss, and she'd *known,* damn it, that she'd just accepted a marriage proposal from the wrong man.

Easy had known, too. He'd kissed her again, and she'd damn near burst into flames. They both had.

He hadn't come home so often after that, and on every visit he'd kept his distance, but it had been hard. The times they couldn't avoid touching, they had practically sizzled.

Even when they could avoid it, the connection was still there—so dangerous, so potent.

When he'd come home for the wedding, they had *really* connected. The sex had been raw, desperate and incredible, and afterward, when he'd pleaded with her to run away with him, she had gone. She'd had no choice.

Eight years later he'd still been running, but with a difference—he'd been running away *from* her, not with her. Finally he'd succeeded. But now he was back again.

And what in God's name was she going to do about it?

With his eyes still closed, Easy shifted, taking stock. Apparently he'd slept, because the sun was now low in the western sky. He had a bad taste in his mouth, a jackhammer pounding in his head, ungodly aches elsewhere, and he smelled like sour beer.

At least the last was easily explained when he lifted a beer bottle from where it had rolled against his ribs. He'd fallen asleep with an open bottle of beer. What he hadn't managed to drink now dampened his shirt, the covers and the mattress.

What had awakened him? It wasn't that he'd had enough rest. He could have slept another ninety-six hours and still not taken the edge off his weariness.

Then the sound came again—a knock at the front door. His muscles tensed as he slowly sat up. Who would be visiting him this evening? Guthrie? He imagined his old friend might have a few things to say to him, all starting with "You bastard" or some variation thereof. Shay's mother? According to his own mother, Mary Stephens had had more than a few things to say about him after the wedding had been called off. Maybe she wanted to unload, face to damaged face.

Shay?

Not if there was a God in heaven.

He reached for the cane, but it wasn't there. Vaguely remembering a clatter, he bent forward to look down and saw it, half under the bed, completely out of his reach. Well, hell.

From the front of the house came a creak as the screen door was opened, then the scrape of metal against metal.

The tension knotting his muscles eased slightly. Only one person besides him had a key to the house—Joelle. Though he'd rather not see her, if he had to deal with anyone, better her than the other choices.

Slow, measured steps tracked her movement through the house. Slow Jo, they'd called her when they were kids. She was quiet, smart and totally unflappable. He'd never seen her excited, angry, giddy or sad. She was the calmest, coolest person he'd ever known.

The steps stopped at the open bedroom door. Knowing how he looked, how he smelled, how damn pitiful he must be, he didn't look at her but stared instead at the empty wall across from him.

"Your mother called and asked me to check on you. She said you promised to call her last night when you got into Heartbreak. She said she knew you wouldn't." Joelle came into the room, picked up the cane and offered it to him.

She'd changed little in the sixteen years since he'd last seen her, he thought as he instinctively slid his right hand behind his back and took the cane with his left. Neither tall nor thin, she'd always been described by her father as sturdy. Her black hair was worn in a braid that fell to her waist, and her dark eyes showed the same patient, calm expression they always had. She wasn't pretty, not in the way most people defined the word, but there was something appealing about her. She'd never lacked for attention. Everyone liked Jo.

"I'll call her and tell her you're alive. Barely." She moved to the window, opened it, then circled the bed and opened the other one. When she came back, she picked up the beer bottle where he'd left it. "It's customary to drink it, not soak in it. But if you're going to pickle yourself in this stuff, I guess it's best to do it from the outside in."

She went into the kitchen, tossed the bottle in the trash with a clang, then came back. "Rough trip?"

"Rough life." From the corner of his eye, he glimpsed her nod. She understood about rough lives.

"I brought dinner. Feel like sitting at the table?" Without waiting for an answer, she returned to the kitchen.

He pulled off his damp shirt and left it on the bed, then eased to his feet. By the time he made it to the kitchen, she'd already set two places and was dishing up a Mexican casserole of some sort. He sat down, waited for her to fill two glasses with milk, to get sour cream from the refrigerator and take her own seat, then he laid his hands on the table. "Well?"

Joelle's gaze moved over him, from the scar that slashed across his temple and down along his cheek, over the thicker scar that sliced the length of his neck and the neat, thin surgical ones that crossed his chest, to his mangled right hand. She didn't flinch, didn't show any revulsion, didn't, he'd swear, even blink. "You're not such a pretty boy anymore, are you?" she asked before turning her attention to her dinner.

For the first time in five months he felt the urge to smile, but it was gone in a heartbeat. "Oh, the scars are hardly noticeable," he said, his sarcasm barely controlled, the anger strong and hot beneath it. "Before long they'll fade altogether and no one will ever know to look at me that anything had happened."

"Sounds like Betsey," Joelle said with that unshakable quiet. "She must have been appalled."

Appalled. Yes. By the sight of her own son. If he closed his eyes, he could recall her expression exactly.

He didn't.

"You may be too busy feeling sorry for yourself to want to hear this, but even with all that, you're still better looking than most men could ever hope to be. And if the people you meet care that much about the way you look, then you're meeting the wrong people."

Nice sentiments…and worth about as much as the air it had taken to give voice to them. People cared about looks—maybe not Joelle, but damn near everybody else. He'd known that before the accident, because he'd traded on them. It was all he'd had to offer anyone—no friendship, no trust, no commitment, no loyalty, no affection. Just his physical self, and because that had been a better-than-decent package, it had been enough. The lesson had been reinforced after the accident, by every person who'd looked at him with revulsion, who'd avoided a second look or had taken a second and third to be sure they'd seen it all.

"Why'd you come back here, Easy? To hide out? Just to be home? To make things right?"

If she thought there was any way he could make things right, then she clearly didn't understand all he'd done wrong. Betraying his best friend. Stealing his fiancée only three days before the wedding. Letting down his parents, disappointing Shay's folks and Guthrie's mother. Running off like a coward. Hurting Shay over and over again. Betraying her over and over again. Damn near everything he'd done in fourteen years had been wrong. There was nothing he could do to make it right.

So why had he come back?

He didn't know.

Rather than admit that, he picked up his fork with his left hand and started eating. He was less than adept, but he managed…barely. She let him eat in silence, and he let her clean up afterward in silence. When that was done, though, she sat down across from him again.

"Are you sure you don't want a telephone?"

"There's no one to call."

"Your mother."

He shook his head.

"What if something happens? If you get sick or hurt or you fall?"

Then maybe he'd get lucky and die. The last thing he'd want to do, though, was call for help. Wouldn't that do wonders for his pride to call a stranger and say, Help, I've fallen and I can't get up? Like a helpless baby or a useless old man.

He was so damned *useless.*

He gave another stubborn shake of his head, and Joelle dropped the subject. "I'll let your folks know that you're all right. Do you need anything the next time I come out?"

One more headshake.

"I'll remake the bed and take the covers home to wash."

He started to protest, but she was already on her way out of the room. Besides, what argument could he offer? That he would do it himself? He could make the bed—though it would take him a good while—but he couldn't do laundry here, and he didn't care enough about clean sheets to make a trip into town.

He couldn't do a lot of things and wasn't good at a lot of others. He hadn't stayed in the rehab hospital long enough to learn, and once he'd moved to his parents' home, there'd been no reason to do anything. They would have fed him, bathed him and dressed him if he'd let them. He hadn't—a man had to have *some* dignity—but he'd relied on them for too much.

He wouldn't rely on Joelle so much. He would never rely on anyone again—not even himself.

While Joelle worked in the bedroom, he stood up and hobbled to the sink. He rinsed his glass, then filled it from the tap and took a deep swig. The water came from a well and tasted of iron, and it brought back memories. Drawing a grim breath, he shut them out.

"I'll be going now. Think of anything you need?"

"No."

"All right. Good night."

He continued to stare out the window. The muscles in his neck and shoulders were knotted, and his good hand clenched the bull-nosed edge of the countertop as he listened to Joelle's leaving. The screen door closed behind her with a bump. A moment later a car door closed, followed by an engine that revved, then faded into the distance.

Slowly he blew out his breath, let his shoulders round. He was alone again, free to do whatever he wanted. He could go back to bed or head outside for a look around the dilapidated buildings. He could wander off across the pasture and into the timber and never come back. He could even spend the rest of the evening standing there, holding on to the counter for support and doing nothing. He could do whatever he damn well pleased. He was alone. And free.

And miserable.

Chapter 2

The news of Easy's return spread through Heartbreak like a hot summer wind. Because of it, business had never been better at the café—though Shay wished her customers would show more interest in their food and less in her private business. For two days she'd been asked the same questions—for two days had given the same answer.

"Why'd he come back? Is he planning to stay? How is he doing?"

"I don't know. I don't know. I don't know."

And everyone's favorite: "Are you going to see him?" Olivia had asked. So had her mother. Her father. Geraldine. Reese. Every damn customer to walk through the door.

"So what's the answer, Shay?" she muttered as she wiped the counter after closing Thursday evening. "*Are* you going to see him?"

"Well, *are* you?"

Startled, she knocked a saltshaker off the counter. It sprinkled salt across the floor she'd just swept, before rolling to a stop between Guthrie's feet. He returned it to the counter, then slid onto a stool across from her.

"I didn't hear you come in," she said crossly.

"Because you were talking to yourself."

"What are you doing in town so late?" It wasn't really late, only a little past eight, but for a rancher whose day started before sunrise, it was late enough. For that matter, for a café owner whose day started at 5:00 a.m., it was late.

"Teacher-parent conferences."

"Don't those take place at school and require the presence of the parent?"

"We're finished. Liv's buying the kids a treat for having good reports, more or less."

For the first time since Olivia's Tuesday morning phone call, Shay felt like smiling. "Good, more or less?" she repeated. "Let me guess. Emma's the more, Elly's the less."

Guthrie grinned. "Elly doesn't quite grasp why the teacher gets to talk whenever she wants while *she* has to wait for permission."

"I seem to recall having a little trouble with that concept myself. Tell Olivia to volunteer one day a week. It buys the teacher's tolerance—at least, it did for me."

Slowly the lighter moment faded. Guthrie neatly arranged the salt and pepper shakers next to the napkin dispenser, then rearranged them before finally asking again, "*Are* you going to see Easy?"

She crumpled the damp cloth, then tossed it through the pass-through into the kitchen with enough force to make it splat on the floor. "What's the point? He's made it clear how he feels about me." Every birthday he'd missed, every holiday he'd stayed away—hell, every single day, special or not, that he'd spent someplace besides with her—proved how little he cared.

"How he feels isn't important. How *you* feel is."

And how *did* she feel?

Sick. Sad. Sorry.

And angry. Angry that after she'd waited so long, after she'd given up hope, he'd finally come back. That he hadn't come back for *her*. That he'd disrupted the life she'd made for herself. That he'd stirred up old emotions, old hurts best left unstirred. That he hadn't been able to resist snubbing her one more time.

Coming by the café or her house—that would have been the adult thing to do. Saying, *I don't want to see you, I don't want you to be part of my life, but I'm back and I'm staying.* Acknowledging her existence and her right to know that he'd returned.

But, no, not Easy. He'd had to put her in a position where everyone would know that he hadn't cared enough to even let her know he was in town.

"Are *you* going to see him?" she asked with a scowl.

Guthrie's answer came swiftly, certainly. "Nope."

"Then why should I?"

"Because you've been in love with him half your life."

His words touched her more than she wanted to admit. For so long he'd hated her for choosing Easy over him. He'd never understood that she'd *had* no choice. Easy had been such an integral part of her that she couldn't have *not* run away with him. Now he understood, because now he felt the same sort of destined-for-each-other love for Olivia.

"You loved him, too," she pointed out gently. "He was your best friend."

"*Was* being the operative word."

"How can you forgive me but still blame him?"

Guthrie sat silent for so long that she thought he had no answer. Finally, though, he sighed and gave her a sidelong look. "Maybe because I loved him more."

She was surprised, even stunned, by the admission—and amused, too. "So you could forgive me because I wasn't as important to you. Gee, thanks."

"Hey, fiancées are easy to find. Best friends are harder to come by." He grew serious again and asked the hated question one more time. "So…are you going to see him?"

Torn between a definite, for-her-own-good no and a wistful true-love-of-her-life maybe, she gave him the only answer she had, then quickly changed the subject. "I don't know. But right now I see two critters outside my windows making faces at us. I think they belong to you."

The smile that spread across Guthrie's face when he saw the twins was painful to watch. She'd always dreamed of a family of her own—just her and Easy and however many babies they could afford. She'd waited patiently for him to make enough money, to retire from the rodeo, to come back here and settle down, and while she waited, she'd watched their relationship deteriorate until they had no future—not even a present, and certainly no babies.

Now she would probably never have a child of her own. One more failure to add to her long list.

Olivia stuck her head inside the door. "Hey, Shay. How are you?"

Shay put on her best phony smile. "I'm pretty damn good, Magnolia."

"Have you—"

"Don't ask."

"Sorry. Guthrie, we need to get the kids home. It's past their bedtime. Shay, if you need to talk—"

"I won't." She softened the bluntness of her response. "But thanks for offering. See you guys." She made a face at the twins, sending them into giggles, then watched them leave. Guthrie wrapped his arm around Olivia and held tightly to Emma's hand while Elly claimed her mother's free hand. They looked so damn...*familial,* as they crossed the street to their truck, that it raised a lump in her throat.

She could never begrudge Guthrie and Olivia their happiness. God knows, they'd both been through a lot. They deserved to be happy.

But didn't she deserve it, too? Had she really committed such sins that she deserved to be punished forever? All she'd ever done was fall in love. With the wrong guy. Live with him. Lose him. Try to get over him. And fail. Again.

Heaving a forlorn sigh, she switched off most of the lights, locked up and stood for a moment on the sidewalk. It was a beautiful September night, with a breeze stirring out of the west, the temperatures short-sleeve comfortable. Maybe when she got home, she would fix herself a drink, lie on the chaise longue in the backyard and search the sky for shooting stars.

Or maybe she wouldn't go home at all. Maybe she would go to the bar on the edge of town or, better yet, drive over to Buffalo Plains and hit her favorite club. Maybe she'd get lucky and meet a gorgeous man and spend the night with him at a shabby motel, where she would wake up alone, well-used and paid for her services—

Been there. Done that. Got a broken heart and would never do it again.

Shoving her hands into her pockets, she started walking toward her car, a block away in the feed store parking lot. There was little traffic on the street, and the few cars that did pass were driven by people she'd known all her life. Knowing everybody was one of the benefits of small-town living—and one of the disadvantages, too. She had no secrets. Everyone knew her good times and bad, and they felt they had a right to stay up to date on both. There was no such thing as *personal business* in Heartbreak. Whether she caved in and drove the nine and a half miles to see Easy was very definitely *personal,* but every soul in town would make it *their* business.

So was she going to cave?

There was a part of her that didn't want to see him ever again as long as she lived—the part that had been betrayed, lied to, hurt and abandoned. The other part—the part that had loved him—did want to see him. The choice was obvious—a dozen reasons to stay away versus only one to drive the nine and a half miles.

And the one was going to win. She had no doubts. She was going to get in her car—tonight, tomorrow, maybe the next day or next week—and drive to the Rafferty ranch, and she was going to see him. She might not talk to him, certainly wouldn't resolve anything, but she would see him. Look at him. Show herself that he was all right. *Please, God, let him be all right.*

So why delay the inevitable? Why subject herself to more questions, more prying, more stupid "I don't know" answers?

She climbed into her car, told herself to head for home and merely grimaced when she turned onto Cody Street. She followed the road she'd driven thousands of times in her thirty-four years, drove at a reasonable speed as if this were the most reasonable of trips. She passed the Rocking S, her folks' place, and the Harrises' ranch, and she came to the broken-down board fence that marked the beginning of the Rafferty ranch.

At the entrance, she slowed, her car bumping over the cattle guard. Her headlights shone straight down the overgrown lane that ran between two pastures, bounced off the barn and the corrals as she turned right, then illuminated the darkened house as she pulled to a stop out front. There was a pickup parked there—brand-new under a light coat of dust, with Texas tags. It was black, of course. Easy had always liked black—had worn black shirts and a black Resistol, had even trained himself a black gelding, and when he'd strayed, it had usually been with a black-haired woman.

There wasn't a single piece of black clothing anywhere in her closet.

She shut off the headlights, then the engine, then simply sat there. This was a mistake. If he'd wanted to see her, he would have come to her. She had nothing to say to him. He had no use for her. It was only going to hurt.

But it was going to hurt whether she did it today or next week. The sooner she suffered the hurt, the sooner the healing could begin.

The sound of the car door closing reverberated around her. She'd grown up on a ranch, had spent most of her free time until adulthood on other people's ranches, but she'd never known one that was cloaked in such eerie silence. There was no stock, no activity. No life.

Negotiating the weed-choked yard took more attention than it should, but it still went faster than climbing the steps. She forced herself to place one foot ahead of the other, to cross the rough boards to the screen door.

The door was open, and the sounds of a television show drifted through the screen. The TV provided the only light in the living room, but she could see through the dining room and into the kitchen, where the overhead light gleamed. A muted sound came from that direction—the refrigerator closing, she thought—and then he stepped into view.

His back was to her, but she recognized him as easily as if she'd seen his face. She knew from the trembling spreading from the inside out, knew from the ache that swept over her, from the fear, the rush of anger.

He wore jeans and a T-shirt. His black hair curled over the collar—he was always forgetting to get it trimmed—and his feet were bare. When he finished whatever he was doing, he reached out of sight, then slowly turned and started toward her with a bottle of beer in his right hand, a cane in his left.

His progress was slow, his limp significant. She stared in horrified fascination at the cane, at the obscene evidence of the injuries he'd suffered. She should have been prepared for this. Troy had told her that his hip had been shattered, that the doctors hadn't known if he would ever be able to walk again, but the prospect had seemed impossible. The Easy she knew had been too vital, too powerful, too graceful. She couldn't have prepared herself for this sight—this reality—not even if she'd been with him from the first day on.

He reached the living room doorway before he realized she was there. The cane she was watching came to a sudden stop. The jeans-clad legs stopped, too, and stiffened.

Slowly she forced her gaze up—over the T-shirt that looked as if it had been slept in, across broad shoulders that she had clung to and cried on and, in the end, cried for—and finally reached his face. He stood in shadow, backlit by the kitchen light, touched in front only with flickers from the TV screen.

But she didn't need to see. She knew his face as well as her own. It had haunted her dreams since the day she'd turned twenty.

For a long, still time, they both stared, then abruptly he moved. He circled the end of the sofa, dropped down on the cushions, dropped the cane to the bare floor with a clatter. He switched the beer to his left hand, used the remote to change channels, then pretended to watch the new show.

She thought about leaving without a word. Hadn't he done it to her first? The difference was, while his leaving had broken her heart, hers would only make him happy. Besides, she wanted to hear his voice. Just one last time, she wanted to hear the voice that had made such sweet promises to her.

The screen door wasn't latched. She opened it and stepped inside on unsteady legs. There she tucked her hands behind her to hide their trembling and pressed back against the doorjamb for support, and she waited for him to speak.

Second after second ticked by. His gaze remained locked on the television screen with an intensity that meant he was concentrating hard on ignoring her. Good. She wanted to be hard to ignore. Hell, she wanted to be *impossible* to ignore.

After a long swig that drained half the bottle, he finally looked in her general direction. ''What the hell do you want?'' His voice was raspy, his hostility sharp. There had been a time when merely looking at her had made him smile, when being with her had made him happy. What had happened? How had they traveled from that place to this? When had he learned to hate her, and why, and how?

She took her sweet time in answering. "Everyone in town has been anxious for me to see you and give them all the juicy details. I decided I shouldn't keep them waiting any longer."

"So you've seen me. Now get out."

"Oh, they won't be satisfied with that. They've got a lot of questions. They want to know how you are, why you came back, what your plans are." She wanted to know, too. She wanted to hear him say that he was only here for a few days, maybe a few weeks, and then he would be gone again. She wanted to hear him promise that when he left this time, she would never, ever see him again as long as she lived—even if the promise would hurt as much as his being here was going to hurt.

"I've seen how you are," she went on in a forced casual voice. "So why are you back, and what are your plans?"

He finished the beer, then fixed a scowl on her. "I came back to be left alone, and my plans are none of your damned business. So go tell your tales and leave me the hell alone."

She should do as he demanded—walk out, never come back and forget he ever existed. But if forgetting were that easy, she would have done so fourteen years ago, and ten and eight and six. She would have gladly traded the joy of their early years together to escape the sorrow of the last years.

But she couldn't take his advice—couldn't even take her own. Instead, she sighed melodramatically. "You shouldn't have come back. Everyone was perfectly happy watching this place fall in on itself. Nobody wants you here."

A commercial came on, casting bright light on his face. Annoyed, he hit the off button, turning the screen dark, leaving him in shadow. "Do you think I give a damn?"

"No. Not as long as you've got what you want."

"That's right." His voice was low, his words razor sharp and cold. "And what I want is to be left alone. So get out and don't come back."

Perversely she baited him. "That would be a turnabout, wouldn't it—me doing the leaving. What if I refuse? In the time it takes you to get to your feet, I can be on my third lap around the house. You can't *make* me go. You can't *make* me do anything."

She felt the tension in him increase until it all but crackled in the air between them. His fingers tightened around the bottle until she thought it might shatter, then they slowly relaxed. The tenor of the tension changed, turned as ugly as his smile as he softly agreed, "No, I can't make you go. No matter how badly I treated you, you kept coming back for more. You always were pathetic that way. It's good to know some things never change."

A chill crept through her as softly, as insidiously as his words. It dulled the raw ache deep around her heart and gave her the ability to match his smile. "And you always were a bastard. You're right. Some things never change."

From somewhere she found the strength to push away from the jamb, to move with her normal, easy gait, to open the screen door with a steady hand before looking back at him. "Welcome back to Heartbreak," she said quietly. "And go to hell."

With that, she left. She followed the path she'd followed hundreds of times as a kid, but instead of skipping, she walked. Instead of jumping onto her mare's back, she climbed into her car. Her movements were automatic, instinctive—close and lock the door, start the engine, fasten the seat belt, turn on the headlights. She backed around the shiny new truck, drove down the narrow drive and headed back to town. If she held the steering wheel tighter than usual, well, that was understandable. If she drove faster than was safe, hey, she knew the road. It ran straight as an arrow until close in to town, and it was seldom traveled at night.

She reached her house in record time, squealed to a stop in the driveway and simply sat there. Her hands were shaking, her stomach hurting, and her cheeks were damp. With

her headlight beams breaking up the shadows all the way
back to the pasture, with the engine running and George
Strait singing, she sat there in her car, alone in the night—
alone in the world.

And she cried.

It was three in the morning, and Easy couldn't sleep. His
body hurt. His head hurt. Hell, if he had a heart, he'd say
it hurt, too.

But if he had a heart, he never would have talked to
Shay the way he had. He never would have hurt her again.
He never would have caused her a moment's pain all for
the sake of the tattered remains of his ego.

God help him, for just one instant when he'd seen her
there on the porch, when he'd recognized her, he had been
so damn happy. For that one moment, he'd wanted to touch
her, hold her, kiss her, lose himself in her—but then he'd
remembered. She wasn't his anymore—would never be his.
He'd had nothing to give her six years ago when he left
her, and he had even less now. No future, no kids, no home,
no love. Nothing but anger, resentment, bitterness and sorrow.

He wished she hadn't come—and wished she'd come
because she couldn't stay away, because she had missed
him, because she still felt something for him. Instead, she'd
wanted only to report to the gossips back in town—to people who didn't care enough to drive out here and see his
misfortune for themselves, people who would gloat or
shake their heads as if they'd known he would come to
this. Hadn't they always said he was wild, reckless, a no-
good Indian cowboy?

So let her go back and talk. He didn't care. He didn't
give a damn what anyone said. Besides, what could she tell
them? That he limped and used a cane. She hadn't seen
anything else, couldn't possibly guess at anything else.

Oh, she could guess. She could tell them that the Easy
they knew was gone. He had no desire to be brash, had too

much fear to be bold and was left with nothing to be cocky about. She could tell them that his rodeo career was over, that his dream of raising horses was dead, and that he might as well be dead, too. She could tell them that he was a sorry reflection of the man he used to be.

He *was* sorry. He was so damn sorry.

Leaving the bed, he shuffled through the dark house, making one stop in the kitchen before going out onto the porch. The night air was chilly on his bare skin, but he didn't bother returning for a jacket or a blanket. In the past few years he'd become an expert at ignoring discomfort. He could do it now as he settled on the swing and unscrewed the top on the beer.

The night sky was dark, with just a sliver of cloud-shrouded moon, but he didn't need light. He could go anywhere on these few acres by memory. That was how much a part of him this place was. God, he'd missed it when he was gone!

When he'd started rodeoing, he hadn't meant to make a career of it. Nope, he'd had his future all planned. His folks were already planning their move to Houston, and he would take over the ranch. He would become partners with Guthrie, raising cattle on the Harris acreage and horses—paints—on his own land. Guthrie and Shay would get married, and eventually he would marry, too, and they would work hard and make their partnership the biggest success Heartbreak had ever seen.

But they'd needed some cash, and the easiest way to come by it, they'd determined, was the rodeo. He'd earned enough to cover his expenses and show a healthy profit his first season. He'd also earned the attention of practically every pretty girl along the circuit. A championship belt buckle or even just a winning time was enough to get him all the female attention he wanted. He'd had the time of his life.

Until he'd kissed Shay.

That afternoon had changed his life. In the end it had

cost him more than he could afford to lose—his best friend, his home, his self-respect, his pride, his honor, his future, Shay herself. He'd lost everything, and even as he was destroying it, he'd wanted it back, but he could never have it. That was his punishment.

She had looked so beautiful tonight. From the time he'd become aware of her as a woman—not his buddy, not Guthrie's girl, but a woman, full grown and desirable—he'd thought she was gorgeous. In their first few years together, simply watching her had been one of his greatest pleasures. She was so beautiful, so incredible, and she wanted *him.* That fact had never failed to fill him with wonder.

But it hadn't stopped him from hurting her.

Six years hadn't changed her. Her hair was shorter and sleeker than the heavy, thick mass he remembered, and her brown eyes would probably seem a little deeper brown. They always had after they'd been apart awhile. She was still tall, still slender, still golden tanned and golden haired and guaranteed to haunt a man's dreams.

She'd haunted his for years.

If he ever slept again, that wounded little smile she'd given him tonight would surely haunt him.

Pathetic. What kind of bastard begged a woman to run away with him—*begged* her to give up everything for him—then told her she was pathetic for putting up with him?

The kind he was. The kind that knew she pitied him for his limp and hated her for it. The kind that knew she would never want him again once she saw the extent of his injuries. The hopeless, useless, less-of-a-man kind.

Better to be hated for his character deficiencies, he thought bitterly, than for the physical deficiencies he could do nothing about.

Better to be hated than pitied, especially by the woman he'd always loved and had finally, for the last time, lost.

If anyone around here was pathetic, it was *him*. Pathetic, pitiful, pitiable.

He drank the beer slowly, though he had no taste for it, and he stared into the distance, working at keeping his mind as blank as the darkness out there. As the minutes slipped into hours, fatigue crept over him. His eyes grew heavy, but every time he started to drift off, the dreams started, jerking him awake.

The last time he awoke, he could tell with his eyes closed that the sky was light, and it was no dream that had awakened him. It was the whicker of a horse. His back hurt, and he had a crick in his neck from the awkward way his head hung. He was on the porch swing—he remembered coming out here clearly enough—but he wasn't so cold anymore, because the quilt from the sofa was spread over him. Could he have gotten up in the night, gotten the quilt and come back without remembering it?

Yeah, right. And while he was wandering around, he'd brought back a horse, too.

He wondered who his visitor was. Probably Olivia Harris. Shay had given up horseback riding when she turned fourteen and got interested in makeup and clothes, and after last night it would be a cold day in hell before he'd see her again. Despite living on a ranch for nearly forty years, Mary Stephens was afraid of horses, and Guthrie wouldn't come over here to save his soul. Olivia, with that accent too soft and Southern for Oklahoma, won by default.

How had Guthrie found himself a Southern belle? He'd probably never set foot outside the state unless he was on a cattle-buying trip. Such a trip would be handled as quickly as possible, since someone back here would be shouldering Guthrie's responsibilities as well as his own. There'd be no time for romancing a wife.

Though how long could it take to fall in love? An evening? An hour? How long had it taken him with Shay? Twenty years? Or the span of a kiss?

Footsteps approached the swing, then a shadow fell over

him. "I seen your eyes movin' under your eyelids. You're no better at playin' possum than me an' Emma are."

With dread tightening his chest, he opened his eyes and found the worst possible answer to the question of who had come visiting. I'm Elly Harris, she'd announced the other morning before her mother had cut her off with a look.

Guthrie's little girl. Come a half mile by herself—no doubt sneaked off by herself—on her pony to visit her father's worst enemy.

She was looking at him with a load of curiosity but nothing else. Her light brown hair was tucked under a dress-up cowboy hat, snugged under her chin with a red strap, and she wore mismatched colors and patterns bright enough to hurt his eyes.

"I'm Elly Harris—well, I will be soon's the adoption's done. Are you hunged over?"

He eased his head into an upright position slowly, wincing at the pain that stabbed through cramped muscles in his neck, then slowly rotated it a time or two before focusing on her. "Hunged—?"

She pointed to the beer bottle lying on its side next to her turquoise cowboy boots. "My daddy doesn't drink. Well, my other dad did, but he's dead, and now Mr. Guthrie's my dad, and he don't drink."

So Guthrie hadn't helped produce the twins—not that that fact would lessen his anger at finding out one of them had wandered over here. They were his now, and Easy was still his enemy.

He rubbed his eyes, hoping to ease the ache behind them, but it didn't work. "Do your parents know where you are?"

"Of course not. I sneaked out. Mama'll think I'm with the horses, at least till she sends Emma out to get me. I'll be back by then." She whirled around and retreated to the steps, then came back. "Look. I bringed you breakfast."

The napkin she gave him contained a cinnamon roll with caramel frosting that drizzled between the layers. It was one of Mary Stephens's specialties that had won her a blue ribbon at every fair she'd ever entered, including the Tulsa State Fair. It smelled sweet and rich and made his stomach roil.

"Go ahead, eat." She plopped down on the floor a few feet in front of him. "*Are* you hunged over?"

"No. I had trouble sleeping last night so I came out here." Hell, why was he explaining himself to Guthrie's little girl? He was a grown man, living on his own property. He didn't owe anyone any explanations, least of all some color-blind little squirt whom he didn't know and had no desire to know.

"You was sleepin' real good when I got here, 'cept you was cold. That's why I got the quilt." Abruptly she pointed at his face. "I bet that hurt, didn't it?"

He felt his face grow warm, and he would have sworn the scar actually tingled. "Yeah," he said grimly, though truth was he didn't remember his face hurting at all in those minutes after the crash and before help arrived. He'd had bigger problems than a six-inch laceration—like Gambler, screaming in the twisted wreckage of the trailer. Like his han—

"You got a great big owie on your hand, didn't you?" she asked matter-of-factly. "I seen it while I was covering you up. Does it hurt?"

"Sometimes."

"I bet all the kisses in the world couldn't make that feel better, huh?" She didn't wait for him to respond but launched into another change of subject. "See my pony there? My daddy gave him to me. His name is Cherokee. That's an Indian tribe here in Oklahoma. Are you an Indian?"

He stared at her. So that was all she had to say about his hand—an owie that kisses couldn't help. After five months his mother refused to look at it. Hell, he avoided it himself. And the little squirt couldn't care less.

"Is 'at rude? Askin' if you're an Indian?"

"No," he said at last. "It's not rude. I am. I'm Cherokee, too."

"That's neat." She sprang to her feet, dusted her purple-and-pink-striped pants. "Hey, I gotta go, else Emma'll catch me gone and tattle to Mom. Emma *always* tattles to Mom."

"Wait a minute." He threw back the quilt and slowly swung his feet to the floor. "I'll walk out to the road with you." From there he could see Guthrie's driveway—could make sure she made it there safely.

"You don't got to," she said in a long-suffering voice that said she knew he would, anyway.

He was so stiff that it took him longer than usual to get his shoes on, to find a flannel shirt and get it properly buttoned. She was waiting at the bottom of the steps when he returned, the saddleless pony's reins in hand. He looked at the pinto, swallowed hard and reluctantly asked, "You need a boost?"

"Not till we get to the road. Cherokee an' me'll walk faster'n you do, so I'll walk with you."

Except for the week or so he'd spent in a rehab hospital in Texas, he hadn't walked as far as the road in more than five months. The distance seemed endless, though, in reality it was less than a quarter mile.

"Are you gonna have horses here?" Elly asked, patiently matching her pace to his.

"No."

"Why not? You gots plenty of room."

"Because—" His throat tightened. He hadn't said the words out loud, though they'd been in his mind every day since he'd awakened from the first of numerous surgeries. Like thoughts of Shay, they'd taunted him, tormented him, left him feeling hopeless and helpless and so damn useless.

Swallowing hard, he forced them out, strained, hateful, sorry. "I can't work with horses anymore."

"Oh, 'cause of you can't walk right and your hand?" She tilted her head back to look at him. "I'm real sorry.

Daddy says you trained Buck. He says you could sweet-talk any horse in the world into doing what you want. I'd'a liked to seen that.''

Easy was surprised her daddy even allowed his name spoken in his house. He was even more surprised that Guthrie had anything at all good to say about him. Of course, he would watch what he said in front of his kids. He would save his true sentiments for when they weren't around.

Finally, after what seemed—and felt—like an eternity, they reached the gravel road. Once again he offered to lift Elly onto the pony, but she led him to the fence and climbed on that way. Appreciative of her resourcefulness, he backed off a few feet to give a little advice as politely as he could manage. ''You shouldn't have come here without your mother's permission.''

''She wouldn't give it. I'm not allowed to ride nowhere by myself, in case I fall off and Cherokee gets scared and runs away.'' She snorted. ''Like I'm gonna fall off. I'm a *good* rider. Daddy says I'm a natural.''

''But you can't come back without asking.''

Her sigh was loud and forceful for such a little kid, then she grinned. ''All right. I'll ask next time. See ya.''

He hoped not. He hoped there was never a *next time*.

The road ran straight from his house to Guthrie's. By the time she reached the driveway, she and the pony were little more than an indistinguishable blur that turned off the road, then disappeared.

Slowly he turned back toward his own house. The distance looked impossible. Gritting his teeth, he took it the way he'd taken the last five months—one step at a time. He had to stop a time or two to catch his breath, and by the time he reached the front door, he was sweating with the strain. He didn't stop, though. He went inside, into the bathroom and stripped down for a shower.

The hot spray helped. So would the pills he took after he dried off. Once he got some food in his stomach, he just might feel more or less normal.

Even, he thought as he looked at himself, if he didn't look it.

Normally he avoided mirrors. He only had to see the way others looked at him to know what they saw—other adults, not kids who didn't know better. This morning, though, he looked—looked hard.

The scar that marked his face wasn't hideous. The plastic surgeon who'd stitched him up had been pretty damn proud of his results. The one that started on his jaw and ended below his collarbone wasn't awful, either. The surgical scars were too neat to care about, though the heavier scarring on his hip was ugly—just not as ugly as the limp. As for his hand, hell, if that were his only problem, he could keep it hidden. That, he had discovered, was what pockets were for.

None of the souvenirs of the accident, taken individually, were a big deal. But all of them together… Together they were more than he wanted to deal with. They generated more pity, more shock, than he could handle. Even Shay who had loved him—*him,* not his body, not his face—hadn't been able to hide her revulsion when she'd seen the way he walked. He'd glimpsed the look on her face before she'd realized he was watching her. And she hadn't even seen his hand.

He raised it now, looking at the reflection for a long time before focusing on the real thing. The scarring was extensive, the rounded bumps where fingers should have been obscene. The doctors had told him how fortunate they were to have saved his thumb and forefinger, how lucky he was.

Lucky. They'd chopped off parts of his body and told him he was lucky. They'd left him—a right-handed man, a roper, a horse trainer—two mutilated, barely functional fingers where once he'd had five strong, flexible, capable ones, and told him he should be grateful.

What did he have to be grateful for? Living?

There were times when he thought he'd be better off dead.

There were times when he thought everyone else would be better off if he were dead.

And there were times when he *knew* it.

Chapter 3

On Saturday morning, the temperature had already topped eighty degrees by nine o'clock. Shay lay in bed, watching the curtains flutter in the breeze and considered what to do with her day off. She could go shopping, if she could think of anything she needed. A drive into Tulsa to catch a movie at one of their deluxe, ultracomfy theaters would blow four hours or so. If she didn't mind being asked to help out with the gardening, she could visit her folks. If she didn't mind answering questions about Easy, she could visit the Harrises.

Or she could stay here in bed all day and be extraordinarily lazy. She hadn't done that...heavens, in more years than she could count, and she'd *never* done it alone.

Frowning, she backed away from the thought. It could only lead to dangerous territory, to old memories best left tucked away—but never forgotten. She feared if she lived to be eighty, she would never forget.

She sat up, brushed her hair back and was faintly surprised to feel bare skin across her shoulders. She'd worn her hair the same way her entire life—long and heavy and styled just so—until six weeks ago. After hearing about Easy's accident in June, she'd spent weeks trying to locate him, to find out how he was, to find out, she admitted with painful honesty, if he might need or want her. She'd made countless calls—to the trooper who'd investigated the accident, the Albuquerque hospital that had treated him initially, the Houston hospital and the rehabilitation facility he'd been transferred to, to every Rafferty within two hundred miles of Houston and every old rodeo buddy she could locate, pleading for information. Told by the last hospital that they would forward a letter, she'd written note after note, but never found the courage to send them.

And finally she'd given up. She'd stopped talking about him, stopped looking for him, stopped acknowledging—outside the privacy of her own sorrow-filled thoughts—that he existed. She'd renewed her acquaintance with Reese Barnett, cut off the long hair Easy had always liked and started living her life for herself. But even after six weeks, it still surprised her that the hair was gone. And that Easy was back. And that she'd ever thought she might have a chance in hell of living her life for herself.

After showering, she finger combed her hair to give it that seductive, tousled, just-crawled-out-of-bed look and dressed in her shortest denim skirt and her snuggest white tank top. She did her makeup carefully, spritzed her cologne liberally, added earrings, a necklace and an armful of bracelets. She told herself as she locked the front door behind her that she would simply go wherever the spirit led her—and that the spirit most definitely would not lead her nine and a half miles west of Heartbreak.

Her first stop was the café, where Geraldine gave her a head-to-toe disapproving look. "Child, you could use about six inches on that skirt."

Shay was used to the criticism and paid it no mind. "And then it would look like every other skirt in town," she

remarked as she sniffed the turkey roasting in the oven.
"What would be the fun of that?"

"You know, when cooler weather gets here, you're
gonna have to give up those outfits for real clothes. Then
we'll have to get you a lime-green sign with rotating lights
and a loudspeaker that hollers, 'Hey, look at me!' It would
serve the same purpose."

"When cooler weather gets here, maybe I'll just buy a
long fur coat and wear nothing at all," Shay retorted on
her way to the dining room.

Only a couple of guests remained from breakfast, and
Amalia was chatting with one of them. Shay picked up the
coffeepot and sashayed across the room to chat with the
other.

Reese looked up from his newspaper and gave her the
same sort of all-encompassing look that Geraldine had subjected her to, but with a whole different appreciation in his
dark eyes. "Ah, Shay, you're a cruel woman. You tell me
you can't see me anymore, then you show up looking like
this."

She refilled his cup, then slid onto the bench opposite
him. "Refresh my memory. Why can't I see you anymore?"

"Because Rafferty's back."

"Uh-huh. And—?"

"And you don't feel right leading me on, making me
think you might feel something for me when you aren't
going to get over him in a million years."

Her good mood flattened. "Gee, thanks for the encouraging words."

"Sweetheart, if I could make you forget him, I would."

"And who are *you* trying to forget?"

For a moment he looked startled, then his expression
went totally blank. "No one," he said, and she knew he
lied. "Nobody at all."

"Right." She smiled tightly. "We're a fine pair, Reese.

Two capable, intelligent, quite attractive people who can't get free of our pasts long enough to find our futures.''

"What are you going to do?"

"I don't know. Keep trying."

"You've already broken most of the available hearts in the county."

"Well, there are seventy-six more counties out there." She punctuated the words with another brittle smile. "If that doesn't do it, hell, there's always Texas."

He stirred a packet of sugar into his coffee, then paid great attention to stirring it as he said, "Call me crazy, but rather than ruin all the single men in the state for any other woman, why don't you try with Rafferty?"

The smile froze, then slipped away, and her voice became harsh. "Easy doesn't want me."

"Has he told you that?"

No matter how badly I treated you, you kept coming back for more. You always were pathetic that way.

Her fingers began to tremble, and she pressed them hard against the tabletop to stop them. "Many times." In many ways.

"So change his mind. You're certainly dressed for it."

"You're suggesting that I seduce him." The idea was ludicrous, impossible—and too damn appealing. Whatever other problems they'd had, the sex had always been incredible. From the first time to the last, she had been enthralled— No, she'd been in love. Losing him had almost killed her. Living without him had been a daily struggle— was still a struggle. And Reese was proposing that she deliberately put herself through it all again.

"I'm suggesting that you remind him of what he lost. That you turn your considerable charms on the man you really want instead of some poor sap who doesn't realize he's nothing more than a temporary substitute until it's too late."

"I can't do that," she said flatly, ignoring the devilish little voice in her head that was asking, Why not? It wasn't as easy to ignore Reese's deep, quiet voice asking the same question.

"Why not? Because you might get hurt again?" He shook his head. "Honey, you've been hurting so long that you've forgotten what it's like to *not* hurt."

"If this is such a great idea, why don't you use it? Why don't you go after this woman *you* want?"

"Because she belongs to someone else."

He looked so bleak when he answered that she directed her gaze away to the street outside. Saturdays were errand days around Heartbreak. Everywhere she looked, she saw people she knew—and all of them had somebody. All of them but her and Reese. At least her *somebody* wasn't married to another woman.

But he didn't want her. He'd made that clear.

Finally she swung her gaze back to Reese. "I'd better go before they put me to work."

"Try not to walk down the street dressed like that. You'll surely cause a couple of car crashes and put *me* to work."

"Don't worry. I'm parked in the alley out back. I'll slither out that way. See you."

She reached her car without seeing anyone, not even Geraldine, buckled up and pulled out of the alley before she scoffed. Seduce Easy. Right. She would have to be crazy to even consider it. Masochistic. A damn fool. Only an idiot man, thinking with some part of his anatomy other than his brain, could ever come up with an idea so outrageous.

"Frankly," Olivia said a half hour later when Shay repeated the suggestion to her, "I think it's a good idea."

Shay stared at her. "A good idea?" she echoed, her voice little more than a horrified squeak.

"Why not? You were in love with him. He was in love with you. You obviously still have very strong feelings for him, and I suspect he still has feelings for you. Why else would he come back here?"

"Because he wanted to be left alone."

"Left alone?" Olivia repeated skeptically. "After a horrific accident that destroys his future, he comes back to live within a few miles of his best friend and his best girl, and you really believe he wants to be left alone?"

"Yes! I *saw* him. I talked to him. I saw—" She broke off abruptly and stared across the yard to where the twins were playing with their puppy.

"You saw what, Shay?"

The gentle tone of her friend's voice made her feel vulnerable. Shaky. Conversely, the gaze she fixed on Olivia was hard and steady. "I saw the way he looked at me. As if he couldn't bear the sight of me."

"Or maybe he couldn't bear to look at what he'd lost."

What he'd lost. Reese had used the same phrase, and she'd let it slide. This time she didn't. "He didn't *lose* me, Magnolia. He left me in a dirty little motel in Montana with nothing but my clothes and a wad of cash on the nightstand, like some whore he was paying for her services. Before he'd even gotten out of the parking lot, he'd replaced me with a pretty little black-haired barrel racer named Clarissa. She wasn't his first affair, and I'm sure she wasn't the last."

For a long time the words seemed to hang in the air between them, ugly and angry and thick with tears that she would be damned if she would cry. Then a stiff wind blew the length of the porch, literally clearing the air. She took a tentative breath, then a deeper one, and willed the moisture in her eyes to dry up—willed her heart to dry up. It would be better to feel nothing at all than to live with this constant ache.

"I'm sorry," Olivia said quietly.

Shay leaned forward, picked an apple from the basket at her friend's feet and examined it before taking a bite. "It's not your fault, Magnolia. You didn't make him a bastard, and you didn't make me a fool."

"Can I ask you something?"

Shay's response was a shrug.

"Do you regret running away with him? Do you ever regret not staying here and marrying Guthrie?"

For a long time she avoided answering, as if she needed to think it over. She didn't. If she found herself in the same situation today, she would take the same action. Even knowing how it would turn out. Even knowing how dearly it would cost her.

Finally she looked at Olivia and shook her head. "No. I regret a lot, but not that. Never that."

And that made her the biggest fool of all.

After lunch Saturday afternoon, Easy ventured outside for only the second time since he'd arrived. The rock-strewn, uneven ground between the house and the outbuildings required more of his attention than a simple stroll ever should, but he made his way without incident through weeds and clover to the corral out back.

When he reached the fence, he rested his arms on the top board and listened to his ragged breathing. He'd leaned in this exact spot hundreds of times, watching one horse or another, but this afternoon he wasn't merely leaning. He needed the support.

He'd never seen the place so quiet. His father had always kept horses—at least two dozen, usually more—and there'd been dogs, barn cats, a small herd of Herefords. But the animals were long gone. Fence was down, and the equipment shed that had housed the tractor wouldn't survive the next strong wind. The barn was suffering, too, like the rest of the place.

His father had bought the property at the age of twenty-one, and he'd brought his pregnant bride here the next year. They'd turned it into a ranch any man would have been proud of, but they hadn't loved it, not the way Easy did. After every hard winter and every miserable, dry summer, Bud and Betsey had talked about heading south to Texas, where they both had family. She had thought the convenience of city living had Heartbreak beat by a country mile.

He had liked the idea of milder winters and a regular job with a regular paycheck, where a few months without rain couldn't wipe you out, where health insurance, vacations and paid holidays were a fact of every worker's life.

They'd left a few weeks after Easy had taken off with Shay. They'd sold all but thirty acres to the Rocking S. They'd unloaded the cattle on Guthrie at below-market prices—trying to make up for their son stealing his fian-cée?—and had sold the horses to buyers all over the coun-try. The thirty acres and the buildings they'd deeded to *him,* so he could come back someday and raise those horses he'd always dreamed of.

That would never happen now.

He should sell the place—turn it over to someone who could appreciate it, who could fix the fence and replace the buildings and bring it back to life. Someone with hope for his future, and not just sorrow in his past. But he knew he would never sell. This was his land. It was all that was left of his dream.

The sound of an engine out of tune disturbed the after-noon quiet. Though he turned to look toward the driveway, he didn't panic, didn't consider taking refuge in the barn. Though he'd heard the engine only once before, on Tues-day evening, he recognized it as belonging to Joelle.

She parked near his truck and climbed out with a laundry basket that she left on the hood of the car. After giving him a wave, she ducked back inside, then straightened this time with her arms full of grocery bags.

He didn't head toward the house to help her. By the time he hobbled all the way there, she would have already put the groceries away and would be on her way out again. Instead, he leaned once more on the corral railing, closed his eyes and recalled a few of the horses he'd trained there. The accompanying pang hurt way down deep inside.

"I never imagined you the meditating type," Joelle said when she joined him a few minutes later.

He glanced at her. "Nope, not me. Don't you have better

things to do on a Saturday afternoon than delivering my groceries and laundry?''

"Nope, not me.''

"What *do* you do?''

"When I'm not looking after wayward relatives? I teach school. First grade." She gave him a sidelong look. "I have Emma Miles in my class. She's—''

"I know who she is.'' Emma, who was no good at playing possum, who *always* tattled and looked damn near identical to her braver, bolder sister Elly. Emma, one of Guthrie's daughters.

"You did him a favor,'' Joelle said quietly. "If he and Shay had married, it never would have lasted. But he and Olivia... You should see them, Easy. They were meant for each other.''

You should see them. He would like to. He'd missed Guthrie more than his folks, his other friends, the ranch— sometimes even more than Shay. They'd been like brothers from the time they were in diapers. The summer they were seven, they'd made it official, using Easy's pocketknife to pierce the pads of their thumbs, mixing their blood. They'd thought they were so tough and macho—one skinny white boy, one scrawny Cherokee boy—when in truth, they'd both been scared spitless. The swaggering hadn't come until after the deed was done and the sting had faded. Shay had gone home mad because they wouldn't let her do it, too, but who wanted to be blood brothers with a *girl?* Not them.

They'd never had a clue that thirteen years later that girl would end their friendship forever.

God, they'd been so young, and he'd grown into such a fool. But he honestly didn't know what he could have done differently. He hadn't *planned* to fall in love with Guthrie's fiancée. He sure as hell hadn't planned to run off with her a couple of days before their wedding.

He had come back to Heartbreak that April determined to stand up as Guthrie's best man, to never let him or anyone else know what he felt for Shay. Even though he'd thought it might kill him, he'd intended to do the right thing.

It *had* almost killed him. He'd never suspected that seeing Shay—talking to her but not touching her, holding her or kissing her—could actually hurt, but it had torn him up inside. He'd wanted her so badly that he was sick with it.

And then he'd gotten the chance to take her.

It had been the Wednesday before the wedding, and he'd run into her coming out of McCaffrey's Five-and-Dime. He could close his eyes and still see the dress she'd worn, the sparkly gold band that had secured her ponytail, the hopeless, wistful look in her eyes. After a moment's awkward mumbling, she'd laid her hand on his arm and very quietly said, "I'm driving out to the lake."

He'd followed her and made love to her there on the newly greening grass on the shore of Buffalo Lake, and afterward he'd begged her—*begged* her, with no pride, no honor—to leave Guthrie and run away with him, and she had.

Best man? More like *sorry excuse for a man.*

He knew Joelle was waiting for him to say something. He had to clear his throat to make his voice work. "I imagine I'm the last person in the world Guthrie wants to see."

"No, that's probably Ethan."

Ethan the pest, they'd called Guthrie's six-years-younger half brother. Apparently, he hadn't improved with age. "What's Ethan up to these days?"

"Scamming every honest soul he meets, I imagine. Same thing he's been doing since he was sixteen. That's how Guthrie and Olivia met."

"Ethan scammed her?"

"Her husband—the twins' father. Sold him a ranch, phonied a deed and disappeared with his money. When the husband died a year later, Olivia discovered that he'd left her flat broke. The only thing he hadn't gambled away was the ranch, and so she came here to claim it. Unfortu-

nately—or fortunately, I guess, considering how things
turned out—the ranch wasn't Ethan's to sell. It belonged
to Guthrie.'' She turned to lean with the fence at her back.
''Ethan did have a change of heart. He came to the wedding
and gave Olivia whatever money he hadn't blown. He spent
one night partying over in Buffalo Plains, then disappeared
again. As far as Guthrie's concerned, he can stay gone this
time.''

A backstabbing best friend, an unfaithful fiancée and a
thieving brother, Easy thought bitterly. Guthrie must be
wondering what in the hell he'd ever done to deserve such
losers in his life. But he'd gotten his reward. He'd won the
grand prize—Olivia, Elly and Emma.

And Ethan, Shay and Easy had gotten exactly what they
deserved.

Deliberately he changed the subject. ''So why aren't you
married and having your own kids instead of taking care
of wayward relatives and teaching other people's kids?''

Joelle shrugged. ''Some women are destined to go the
wife-mother route. Some are meant to be schoolmarm spin-
sters.''

The image made him smile wryly. ''And maybe some
women are just too picky for their own good.''

''Oh, yeah, that's me. Picky, picky.'' She pushed away
from the fence and took a few steps. ''Come on, walk back
to the house with me so I can leave.''

''I can watch you leave from here.''

''Humor me. Prove that you can stand on your own two
feet and don't really need that fence you've been clinging
to since I got here.''

Like Elly, she let him set the pace, giving no indication
of impatience at how slowly he moved. She didn't fill the
silence with chatter, either, the way his mother always did,
as if meaningless conversation could disguise the fact that
he was no longer agile or quick on his feet.

When they reached the cars, Joelle moved the laundry
basket from the hood to the top porch step, then came back,

keys in hand. "I picked up your dirty laundry. I'll have it back in a few days."

"You don't have to do that, Jo."

"What are you going to do? Drive into town to the Laundromat and do it yourself?" She saw his flinch and smiled sympathetically. "It wouldn't be too hard after the first or second time. People would talk in the beginning because they're curious. But once they got used to seeing you around—"

What she really meant was once they got used to *seeing* him. Once they became accustomed to the fact that Heartbreak's hotshot rodeo star was a scarred, deformed cripple who wouldn't be breaking any more hearts.

He didn't intend to give *anyone* the opportunity to get used to seeing him. He was going to stay here. Alone. Lonely.

"Let me get you some money—"

She brushed him off. "Don't worry about it. I know you're good for it." Distracted, she glanced over her shoulder to the road. "Looks like your day for company."

He followed her gaze and watched the small silver sports car slow down for the turn into his driveway. He'd never seen it before, but he knew who it belonged to. It was sleek, beautiful, dangerous—just like its owner. His fingers tightened around the cane, and the muscles in his stomach knotted. "I don't suppose you'd send her away while I go inside."

"No. I wouldn't."

They both watched the car ease around the last turn, then come to a stop beside Joelle's beat-up wagon. He tried to look away but found it impossible to *not* watch as the door opened. As tall and leggy as she was, Shay exited the small car gracefully, so damn tantalizingly and with such confidence. She didn't check to make sure her hair was in place, didn't straighten the scrap of fabric that passed for a skirt, didn't tug at the skin-tight top. She just sort of *emerged,* perfectly presentable, perfectly poised. Just plain perfect.

And *he* was this decade's poster boy for *im*perfect.

As she strolled toward them, he slid his hand into his pocket, but there was nothing he could do to hide the rest of his flaws. He wished he'd gone inside and locked the doors, wished he could hide in the shadows and gloom of the house instead of having to face her here under the bright afternoon sun.

"Hi, Joelle," she said in her everyday, unconsciously sultry voice. No matter how innocent the words, he'd always found the voice too feminine, too husky, too incredibly seductive for his own good. It made his skin far warmer than the hot sun could account for, made his heart beat faster than his physical exertion could be blamed for. "How are you?"

"I'm fine," Joelle replied. "How about you? They keeping you busy at the café?"

"All the time. I'm lucky to get Saturdays off. How's Vince?"

The mention of Vince, whoever he was, softened Joelle's voice. "He's all right. Unfortunately he doesn't get many Saturdays off. How about Reese?"

Easy knew who Reese was—Reese Barnett, star quarterback on the football team their senior year, star center on the basketball team, star pitcher on the baseball team. He'd gone away to Oklahoma State on a baseball scholarship, and Easy had gone off on the rodeo circuit and had never heard of him since.

He didn't like hearing of him now connected to Shay.

"He's fine, too. I saw him this morning at the café. I'll tell him he needs to give Vince more weekends off." Finally she turned her attention to *him*. He would have felt her gaze if he hadn't been looking, would have heard the coolness enter her voice if he hadn't been listening. "Hello, Easy."

When he didn't respond, Joelle touched his arm. "Behave. I'll see you in a few days. Shay, take care."

They stood there, he and Shay, six feet and fourteen

years between them, while Joelle climbed into her car, then drove away. When she turned into the driveway, Easy turned, too, heading slowly for the house.

Shay followed. "So Joelle's taking care of things for you." Her tone was cautious, empty of emotion. What emotion, he wondered, was she keeping out of it? Simple curiosity? Minor disapproval?

Maybe a little jealousy?

When he didn't answer, she asked, "Are you interested in her? I only ask because she's been seeing Vince Haskell for a couple of years and I think he's pretty much got his heart set on marrying her, if he can convince her that it would work."

The steps came a little more easily than the other times, he realized once he'd reached the top. There he turned and looked down at her. "Jo's my cousin."

She looked surprised. "I didn't know— How?"

"Her mother and my father are second or third cousins— something like that."

"Which would make you…fourth cousins? Fifth? Not close enough to matter."

"To the Raffertys and the Barefoots, it matters." This would be a good time to tell her to go, he thought, before she'd climbed even the first step. All he had to say was, I don't want to see you, you're not welcome here, go away and leave me alone, and make it sound as if he meant it. But he *did* want to see her and he was damned tired of being alone. "What's wrong with Vince Haskell that Jo needs convincing marriage to him would work?"

"Nothing's wrong with him. He's a deputy—a nice guy. Came here from Topeka. He's just a little younger than Joelle."

"How much younger?"

Shay shrugged, and her second-skin clothes seemed to hug her even tighter. "A few years. Like…oh, eleven."

He thought of serious, capable Jo, who'd been old when she was born, married to a man on the kid side of twenty-five, and was tempted to smile. Haskell should give it up now, or come back when he was fifty, when eleven years didn't seem like a lifetime.

But who was he to give advice? He'd been only six years without Shay, and that seemed like two lifetimes—and neither worth living.

The thought made it easier to scowl at her. "Why did you come here? You need more gossip? Did your pals hear about the scars and ask for more details?"

Her gaze shifted fractionally, and damned if the scar didn't start tingling, sending a shiver of pain through that side of his face. "What happened?" she asked somberly.

"Who wants to know? You? Or everyone in town?"

"Everyone's curious. How could they not be? They've known you since you were a baby. They followed your career. They were proud of every championship you ever won. Of course they want to know. But it's *me* who's asking." She moistened her lips as she climbed the first step. "Some people say you were drunk. Some say you fell asleep. Some say you just lost control."

She climbed another step, and he backed away a corresponding step. "You were with me eight years. Did you ever once know me to hit the road while I was drunk?"

"No." Her advance continued, one slow step at a time. "So what happened?"

He took one last step and felt the wall against his back. Grateful for the support, he leaned against it. *What happened?* He'd answered that question a dozen of times the first week after the accident. He'd given the same answer to the trooper, the doctors, his folks, the few friends who took the time on their way elsewhere to check on him. *I don't know.*

Had he fallen asleep at the wheel? Maybe. He'd always had so much to forget—how miserable he was, how lonely he was, what a lousy son of a bitch he was—and so he'd pushed himself hard. He'd taken too many chances, both in the arena and out. He'd surely been tired that night—

had always been emotionally exhausted. Maybe he *had* fallen asleep. Maybe the fatigue, the night and the monotony of the long trip alone had been a combination his body couldn't resist.

Or maybe he hadn't drifted off but had simply lost control of the truck. Maybe he'd taken his eyes off the road at the wrong instant. Maybe his mind had wandered. Maybe he'd gotten lost, as he often had, in thoughts of Shay.

He shrugged. "I don't know. One minute I was driving through the mountains. Next thing I knew, the truck had rolled down the side of a ravine, and Gambler was hurt, and I couldn't get to him. I couldn't move at all."

Barely breathing, Shay listened to the dispassionate sound of his voice. He could have been talking about the weather for all the emotion he showed, rather than the accident that had almost killed him.

It wasn't surprising that his first thought had been Gambler. He'd loved that horse, had felt a respect and admiration for him that he'd rarely felt for any humans—and the feelings had been mutual. She'd been with Easy when he'd seen Gambler for the first time. It had been as if, with that first, long look, they had each taken the other's measure and formed a bond that could endure anything. If ever forced to choose, it would have been easier, she'd always thought, for Easy to give up *her* than the horse. When he *had* given her up, when he'd left her behind and taken off with Gambler and Clarissa, she'd envied them both. One had had his attention, the other his love. She would have given anything for one of those two things.

She would have given everything for both.

"How bad was he hurt?"

Tension tightened his jaw, made his black scowl reappear. "Bad," he said and abruptly turned toward the door. He moved too quickly, though, and threw himself off balance. Without thinking, she reached out to steady him, but the instant before she made contact with his arm, he caught himself and gave her a savagely angry look. "I don't need your help!"

Her own jaw tightened, and she folded her arms over her chest, her knotted fists tucked between upper arm and ribs so he wouldn't see. "Fine. Next time you start to fall, I'll just step back and watch you hit the floor."

For a moment he stood there, breathing heavily. After a time, though, his breathing evened out. He squeezed his eyes shut for a moment, then, with a shake of his head, opened them again. "What do you want, Shay?" His voice was dark and shadowed. He sounded weary, as if he'd traveled too many miles, roped too many calves and run from too many ghosts without rest. It was a sound—a condition—she remembered well from their years together.

She thought of the answers she could give, all of them true. *I want you. I want to forget you. I want to be with you. I want to remember every moment we spent together, to spend every moment we have left together. I want to erase you completely from my memories. I want to love you. I want to hate you.*

I want to love you.

"I don't know if I want to punish you or get you out of my system or get back in your life." She shrugged ineloquently. "I don't know."

For a moment he stared at her, his face still beautiful in spite of the scar. It was startling—masculine perfection marred by thickened tissue that pulled the corner of his right eye into a slight distortion—but it didn't make him ugly. Any woman who looked would still find him incredibly appealing.

"I don't *have* a life," he said, his voice low and intense.

That didn't surprise her, either. It had been a conscious choice on his part to limit his life to three pursuits—women, rodeo and horses. He was vain enough to be self-conscious of his imperfections, and those imperfections made the other two impossible. If this was the best he could walk after five months, he would never rodeo again, and he would probably never ride again. If he couldn't have it all, he wouldn't want any of it.

"You have a life," she softly disagreed. "It's just not the one you thought you'd be living."

His gaze moved past her to sweep across the overgrown pasture, the weeds and broken fence, the empty fields. "Some life," he said scornfully, then carefully limped inside.

Shay stood there a moment, listening to the irregular shuffle as he crossed the living room. Then, with a surge of impatience, she snatched up the laundry basket he'd forgotten and went after him, catching up with him in the kitchen. "Grow up, Easy," she said sharply, emphasizing the command with the slap of the plastic basket hitting the tabletop. "You think you're the only one who's had to face disappointments? The only one who's had to make adjustments? Do you think Guthrie wanted to live fourteen years by himself, trying to make a go of the ranch and figure out what the hell went wrong? Do you think I wanted to be thirty-four, single, childless and running a nothing little café in downtown Heartbreak?"

He faced her from the other side of the kitchen table. "Then why are you? You don't want to be single, get married. You don't want to be childless, have a baby. Hell, you've got Reese Barnett on the hook. Reel him in. That ought to make your parents real happy—you married to a hotshot ex-jock white boy, turning out little blue-eyed, blond-haired grandkids by the dozen. Problem solved. You've got your perfect little future."

"My parents never cared that you were Indian," she said, her voice cold enough to make his cheeks turn bronze, because he knew it was true. "As for Reese, he was never a part of my perfect future."

She knew he recognized the truth in that, too, because her idea of *perfect* had always included *him*.

He didn't acknowledge it, though. "The point is, if you're not happy with the future you're facing, you can change it. *I* can't. Nothing I can do will take these scars away. I can't heal my hip. I can't make myself walk normally. I sure as hell can't do anything about this.''

Without warning, he pulled his right hand from his pocket, slapping it down on the curved rim of the laundry basket between them. She looked down, swallowed a horrified gasp and swiftly looked away. After only an instant, though, she forced her stunned gaze back to his hand, staring at scars, at misshapen fingers and empty space where three other fingers should have been. The scars were thick, discolored and covered the entire back of his hand. They were ugly, brutal, and they made her feel sick for the pain he must have suffered, the loss he'd been forced to endure.

''Oh, Easy,'' she whispered and reached out. He didn't let her touch him, though, didn't let her brush even the tips of her fingers against his skin. Instead, he jerked back, hiding his hand in his pocket once more, turning away to stare out the window at the empty corral.

''Ropers are always at risk of getting hung up in their ropes and losing a finger or two.'' His voice was flat, totally without emotion. ''I roped professionally for more than sixteen years and never had a problem, and now... Funny, isn't it?''

Now he would never rope a calf again. He would never train horses again, would never do a lot of things. It was so far from *funny* that it made her want to sink to the floor and cry.

But she didn't. She breathed deeply a couple of times, made an effort to get her emotions under control, then softly asked, ''Why didn't you call me?''

''When?''

''After the accident.''

Swinging around, he fixed his dark scowl on her. ''After the accident,'' he repeated. His words grew harsher, his tone disbelieving as he went on. ''And what was I supposed to say? 'I know I've been a bastard to you and I broke your heart, but I'm so screwed up now that no other woman would ever want me, so, hey, would you come back?'''

"It probably would have worked," she acknowledged. "Though I would have preferred if you'd just said, 'Shay, I need you.'''

He stared at her so long that edgy discomfort began to tingle down her spine. When he finally spoke, discomfort was joined by hurt. "You're a fool."

"Maybe," she acknowledged, then somewhere deep inside she found a sorry smile. "Probably. For fourteen years my mother's called you 'a good-for-nothing rodeo cowboy,' and I've been her 'empty-headed, fool-minded daughter.'''

After a moment he turned back to the window over the sink. The silence between them was uneasy, thick with sorrow, regret, unhealed wounds. The sounds of the refrigerator motor cycling on and off, a fan whirring nearby or a quail calling in the weeds outside weren't loud enough to break the stillness. But the sound of her heartbeat was, and the slow, tautly controlled sound of his breathing.

Finally he sighed. It shuddered through him, made his shoulders shake, before whispering into the room. "How is your mother?"

Shay breathed and realized for the first time that she'd stopped. Her lungs were tight, her stomach muscles clenched, her fingers knotted. She breathed again and consciously relaxed her fingers, eased her muscles, filled her lungs. "She's fine. She keeps busy running the house and the town and everyone's lives."

"And Jim?"

"Dad's fine, too. He devotes his attention to the ranch and lets Mom handle everything and everyone else."

Two civil questions, two civil answers. That was enough to qualify for polite conversation, she thought with a cynical smile. If they could master that, who knew what they might manage next? Someday they might even reach the point where they could discuss important questions like,

Why did you leave me? and, Why did you do it that way? and, Don't you feel anything besides guilt for me?

But he didn't ask another question, and she couldn't think of any of her own that weren't important. After a moment's fruitless search for one, she picked up the laundry basket and went into the hall that led to the bedrooms.

He was sleeping in his old room at the back of the house. It was sparely furnished, with wallpaper so faded the pattern was barely distinguishable. She remembered it, though—small dots interspersed with geometric shapes on an ivory background. Once, when they'd been sent off to play while the adults talked around the dinner table, they'd started a game of wallpaper dot-to-dot with crayons. By the time they'd gotten caught, she'd filled two dozen squares with her initial. As punishment, the next week she'd been farmed out to Betsey for spring cleaning, working harder than she'd ever worked before.

The only furniture in the room was a bed and a dresser, mismatched in style, material and finish. There was no mirror on the dresser, no curtains on the windows, no bedside table with a lamp. Not surprisingly, the bed was unmade—he'd spent the better part of sixteen years living in motels with maid service—but the room was clean, no doubt thanks to Joelle.

She didn't put the laundry away, but simply set the basket on the dresser. She was turning back to the door when she saw him leaning there. His mere presence in the doorway changed the whole feel of the room. It was no longer an austere bedroom—plain, a little shabby, serviceable but nothing more. It was a room with tremendous potential— a room that promised passion and pleasure, disappointment and pain, heartbreak and healing. Some of their best times had been spent in similar rooms, in similar beds—some of the hottest, sweetest, most tender moments she'd ever experienced.

And some of her worst times had been spent in those same beds—alone, while Easy partied without her. Crying because he'd ignored her in favor of another woman. Hating him for going home with someone else. Hating herself for knowing she would welcome him back without an apology, without pride, without self-respect.

He had always come back, and she had always welcomed him, except that last time. She'd waited, ready to swallow her dignity—waited day after day for seven days before finally accepting that he wasn't coming back. That time he'd done more than take up with another woman for a night or two. That time he'd really left her.

God, how she'd missed him!

And, God help her, how she'd suffered. She'd paid dearly for having him, and she'd paid even more dearly for not having him. And here she was, putting herself back in his life again.

Suddenly she wanted out of the bedroom. She didn't want to remember, didn't want to hurt, didn't want to want. She'd been through enough with Easy—way more than too much. She wanted desperately to be free.

But she would never be free.

Her throat tight, her nerves on edge, she slipped past him and walked away. She didn't go far, though, just to the front porch, where she could stand in the sunlight, breathe the hot, dry air, warm the chills that had rushed through her, cool the panic that had followed.

It was a simple fact of life, one that she'd accepted when she'd run off with him fourteen years ago. One she'd faced again every time things got bad, every time they fell apart, every time they put themselves back together. Whether he was here or gone, a part of her life or just bittersweet memories, she would never be free of him.

That was a promise.

Or was it a threat?

Chapter 4

Easy stood where she'd left him, eyes closed. She'd passed so close that with no more than a deep breath, he could have touched her. He could have let his cane fall to the floor, could have laid his hand on her arm, brushed his fingers over her skin, held her round the waist and pulled her tight and hard against him, and then he could have—

What? he thought bitterly. What the hell could he have done next? Seduced her? Maybe, if she was feeling generous. Undressed her? Probably, after a time, after working and fumbling and failing.

Made love to her? Possibly. After a fashion. In one way or another.

And what would it earn him, besides the incredible pleasure of her body? Besides some semblance of the affection she'd once given him freely? Besides a tenuous connection, however brief, to the man he'd once been?

It would gain him her pity. Quite possibly her disappointment. It could earn him her farewell. No matter how insufferable he'd been before, at least the sex had always been fantastic. Now, at best, it would be tolerable. His body didn't look the way it once did, didn't work the way it once did. With his hip as badly damaged as it was, he didn't know whether he was even capable of making love to a woman.

Until he'd come back here, he hadn't cared.

Now that she'd come here, he did.

Slowly he followed in the direction she'd gone, pausing when he reached the screen door. She was standing near the swing, facing west, hugging herself.

Sometimes he wished—for her sake, for his own—that they'd never met. Sometimes he thought she'd been a test of his character, a temptation he was supposed to resist, a way to prove that he had honor, strength, loyalty, will-power. His punishment for failing—for going with her to Buffalo Lake that April day, for running away with her that afternoon—was *this*. Having her, but not having her. Looking at her and seeing not just the woman he'd loved, but every person they'd had to hurt to be together. Lacking the honor to stay away from her, but possessing too much loyalty to his friend—too much shame and guilt were more to the truth—to allow himself to be happy with her.

He had always wanted desperately to be happy with her.

He pushed the screen door open with a creak, cleared the threshold and closed the door quietly so it didn't bang. Though she didn't turn, didn't flinch, didn't react at all, he knew she knew he was there.

Moving to the swing, he sat down and stretched out his left leg in an effort to ease the cramping, the pain in his hip. He braced the cane against the wall, fixed his gaze on a stunted mimosa just east of the house and wondered just how normal he could make himself sound. "You said something about a café."

Her deep breath sounded stressed. After a moment she turned, lowered her arms and went to lean against the porch railing at the top of the steps. "Yeah. Heartbreak Café, operated by me, owned by the bank, my folks and me."

"So you learned to cook." Most of their meals had been taken on the road, in cafés and diners across the country, but for a few months each year when there were no rodeos to compete in, they'd settled into a temporary home somewhere. During those months, her ineptitude in the kitchen had been a constant source of bad jokes, heartburn and worse.

She almost smiled. The corners of her mouth lifted fractionally, and the shadows in her eyes—browner than ever, just as he'd expected—lightened. "No, 'fraid not. But I learned to hire good cooks. I'm only allowed into the kitchen to inventory supplies so I can place orders, and to wash dishes."

"If you didn't want a café, why'd you buy one?"

"I came back here with no money, no job skills, no ambition—nothing but the desire to not live off my parents, who were still very unhappy with me. The café had closed just a month or two before, and Dad thought helping me buy it might be his only chance to get me off his hands and out of Mom's house."

"You could have gone back to Guthrie." Their old friend had loved her dearly. He would have forgiven her, would have taken her back.

"I didn't *want* Guthrie," she said flatly.

The no-room-for-doubt certainty of her statement pleased him somewhere inside, because *he* was the reason she hadn't wanted Guthrie. And since he was also the reason she'd come back with no money and no job skills to a family who was angry with her, the pleasure just confirmed that he was a first-class bastard.

"So other than run the café, what have you done for six years?"

She tossed her head—a much more effective action when she'd had heavy blond hair reaching halfway down her back—and looked hard, unflinchingly, at him. "I took a cue from you. I dated a lot of men. Used them, then dumped them."

In spite of the sun's heat on his back, a chill crept over him—cold, ugly, angry. It took all his willpower to control it, to remind himself that when he'd left her, he'd lost his place in her life. He had no right to be jealous, no right to expect her to remain loyal to him. He for damn sure had no right to expect her to stay faithful to him when he'd betrayed her in every way but that.

"If I were in the habit of carving notches in my bedposts, I imagine my lifetime total might rival yours," she said, her voice unsteady, her tone taunting.

"I doubt it," he replied quietly.

Taunting turned reckless. "You don't think I could find that many willing men?"

"I think any man you meet would be willing. But I *know* I haven't been with that many women. In fact, I could count them on one hand." He glanced down at his right hand and smiled bitterly. "Well, I could count them on my left hand."

For one long moment she stared at him, disbelief and distrust heavy in her expression. Then she muttered an oath that was vicious, scornful. "You had that many in any one year we were together."

He shook his head. In spite of the fact that he'd spent eight years fostering her disbelief and distrust, it stung that she'd learned it so well, that all these years later she was as ready to believe the worst of him as she'd been then.

"What about Clarissa? Tracy? Loreena? That redhead from Texas, the rodeo queen in Arizona, the reporter in Wyoming?"

He shook his head again.

"All those women, all those dances and drinks, all those nights you never came home, and you're telling me you never made love to any of them?"

"I never made love to anyone but you."

Making an impatient gesture, she damn near stamped her foot. "You never *had sex* with any of them?"

"Only before you, and after." Long after. Two, maybe

three years, when he'd gotten particularly morose and unbearably lonely. It'd been a futile exercise, though, like
drinking vinegar to satisfy a thirst for water. It wasn't mere
intimacy he'd craved, but intimacy with Shay, to the ex-
clusion of all other women in the world.

She stared at him with such derision, and such hurt.
"You bastard," she murmured, then her voice grew
stronger, colder. "You arrogant, manipulative, self-
centered bastard! You *hurt* me! Every time you went off
with another woman, every time you didn't come back to
our room to sleep, every time you came back smelling of
another woman... You let me believe—you *made* me believe you were sleeping with them, and it hurt so bad I
could hardly stand it, and it was *lies?* You made up lies to
hurt me?"

He rubbed his forehead to ease the ache forming there,
then let his fingers slide the length of the scar before falling
away. "That was the point," he said at last. "I wanted you
to leave. I thought if I hurt you enough times you would
get angry enough to go."

"If you were so damn anxious to be free of me, why
didn't *you* leave?" she demanded.

"I couldn't. It took eight years to find the strength to
walk away." Eight years of loving her. Eight years of hating them both.

She didn't have a problem finding the strength. After
staring at him for one long, hostile moment, she did exactly
that. She turned away, walked down the steps and across
the yard to her car.

His jaw clenching, he watched her go, torn between the
desire to call her back and the certainty that her leaving
was best. She'd wasted too many years, too many tears, on
him. He'd had nothing to offer her before and even less
now.

But it hurt too damn bad to see her drive away, to know
that this time she probably wouldn't return. This time he
had probably lost her forever, and while he had no doubt

that would be best for her, he also had no doubt it would be one of the saddest things in his whole sorry life.

Sunday mornings were slow in the café, but five minutes after the first church service ended, the dinner customers would start arriving and they wouldn't stop until Shay was tired and had made a nice chunk of the week's profit. Calculating she still had about twenty minutes to spare, she poured herself a glass of cold milk, stirred in a generous spoon of chocolate syrup and went to sit in an empty booth.

She hadn't slept well last night and had downed a pot or two of high-test coffee to make up for it. It hadn't helped, though. She'd already been on edge, and now she felt about ready to explode. The first whiny kid or difficult customer, and she was going to drop everything and stand in the middle of the dining room screaming until she'd run them all off. Then she would send her staff home, put the Closed sign on the door and go hide somewhere. The utility closet in back sounded appealing—small, dark, the last place anyone would look.

The bell over the door rang, but she didn't look up. Instead, she twisted her glass around in circles and wondered if she could justify a vacation. Better yet, maybe she could revert to old habits and simply run away. In her travels with Easy, she'd seen the entire country west of the Mississippi, with the exception of Alaska. She was familiar with most big cities and countless little towns. She could find a new place to live.

But it wasn't the place that was getting her down. It was the life. Where could she get a new one of those?

"Mind if I join you?"

Her mother's soft question startled her. She looked up, saw Mary watching her and smiled wanly. "Have a seat. You can have sixteen whole minutes of my time, give or take a few. What are you doing out of church early?"

"Your father was up most of the night with his cows. I

told him I'd come home early and bring him a hot meal.''
Mary slid onto the bench. "You don't look good.''

"Gee, thanks,'' Shay said dryly, but she didn't mind the
comment. For too many years she'd been like Easy—too
vain about her appearance. For a long time she'd been trying to hold on to him. Later, she'd been trying to prove to
herself that his not wanting her hadn't meant that other men
wouldn't. Today, this one day, she didn't care how she
looked. She'd been miserable and it was only fair that it
showed.

"So tell me what's going on.''

"Nothing's going on, Mom.''

"I know Easy's back—not that you bothered to tell me.
I also know you went to see him twice. It's a sad thing
when a mother has to pick up information about her own
daughter through the grapevine.''

Letting go of the glass, Shay dried the condensation on
a napkin, then wadded it tightly in her fist. "I wasn't sure
you'd want to listen to me talk about him.''

"I listened when you found out about the accident.''

"But that was different.'' That had been two people la-
menting the misfortune befallen a third person they'd both
known and loved—though in vastly different ways. This
time would have been a jilted daughter speaking with great
sorrow—and, yes, just a little hope—about the man with
whom she had broken hearts, scandalized their town and
jeopardized their mother-daughter relationship.

"I take it things didn't go well.''

Shay glanced at her faint reflection in the plate-glass window. "Is it that obvious?''

Mary tapped the tumbler between them. "Ever since you
were tiny, chocolate milk has been your answer to all of
life's hurts. Do you want to talk?''

"Do you want to listen?''

For a time Mary sat silent, then she brushed back a strand
of gray hair before laying her palms flat on the table. Shay
couldn't help but notice all ten of her fingers, and all ten

of her own. She couldn't help but recall Easy's disfigured hand with a shudder.

"Sometimes I wonder," Mary began, her voice low and distant, "if Nadine and I hadn't pushed you, whether you and Guthrie ever would have gotten engaged. She was my best friend in all the world—closer, even, than Betsey. We couldn't imagine anything more perfect than the two of you married, having babies, giving them the same kind of up-bringing that we'd given you. When it looked like it was going to happen, we were ecstatic. When you ran off with Easy instead…"

She didn't need to finish. Shay knew. They'd been angry, hurt and disappointed—*so* disappointed. It'd taken fourteen years and Guthrie's falling in love with Olivia Miles to earn her mother's forgiveness. Nadine Harris had died without granting hers.

"No one wanted to consider that maybe you'd done the right thing—even if the way you did it left something to be desired," Mary said dryly. "You'd been dating Guthrie for five years, but it took only a few days for Easy to persuade you to run off with him. Obviously your feelings for Guthrie weren't quite what we all thought."

"I loved Guthrie," Shay murmured. "I'll always love him. But Easy…" Lacking the words to finish, she broke off and smiled instead.

"See? That's what I mean. I never saw you smile like that over Guthrie, but after all these years, after all this heartache, you still have that smile for Easy. That same smile Guthrie has for Olivia."

Shay knew exactly what Mary was referring to. Every time she saw Guthrie smile at Olivia, she thought her friend must be the luckiest woman in the world to be loved like that. Had Easy ever thought he might be the luckiest man in the world to have *her?*

Or did he wish he'd never known her?

"I have to admit," Mary went on, "that Easy isn't the man I would have picked for a son-in-law. Obviously—

he's not the man I did pick. He enjoyed his fun too much, took too many chances, put too much effort into charming his wild horses and his wilder women. But I'm not the one who would have had to live with him. I'm not the one who would have had to worry about him.''

According to him, Shay had had nothing to worry about—at least, when it came to other women—and she was half convinced that he'd told the truth. She wasn't at all convinced, though, that she believed him because she trusted him or because she needed to believe he hadn't chosen those women over her or because she was a fool.

But believing him didn't make it hurt any less. It was just a different kind of hurt, a different kind of betrayal.

''So, yes,'' Mary went on. ''I want to listen. Do you want to talk?''

''Yes, I do.'' The tension that made her body ache eased a bit, and her unsettled stomach began to settle. She felt a great relief at the prospect of being able to say anything she wanted to her mother without worrying about stirring up old grudges. But now that she had the freedom to talk, she couldn't think of anything to say.

''How is he?'' Mary asked.

Shay described his injuries in order of importance—scars, limp, hand—and saw sympathy soften her mother's face. She talked about the shape the old house was in, the mostly empty rooms, and the shape the whole ranch was in, and then she fell silent.

''Was he glad to see you?''

What wouldn't she give, Shay wondered, to truthfully answer a wholehearted, emphatic *yes* to that question? But she couldn't lie about it. ''No. He was…not friendly.'' *Hostile* was more like it. Antagonistic. Downright mean.

''Didn't want you seeing him that way, did he?'' Mary shook her head. ''Men and their egos. You'd think the boy would be too smart to believe that a few minor imperfections would change the way a woman feels about him.''

''These are more than minor imperfections, Mom.''

"Did they change the way you feel? Would you be ashamed to walk in here with him and his cane in front of a roomful of customers? Would it sicken you to sit down to eat with him and have to look at that hand?"

"Of course not!"

Mary shrugged. "Then my point is made."

The bell above the door rang as a family of four came in. Shay watched Amalia seat them before turning her attention back to her mother. "I wouldn't be ashamed. But I do feel this incredible..." Not pity. She could never pity him for his handicaps. Doing so would only infuriate him and would diminish her.

"Sadness," Mary suggested. "Sorrow. Horror. Those are perfectly normal feelings. For heaven's sake, Shay, the man you loved went through a horrific experience that left him with injuries he can never recover from. If you weren't horrified by it, if it didn't sadden you and fill you with sorrow, then there would be something wrong with *you*."

Injuries he can never recover from. The finality of those words sent a chill of despair down Shay's spine. It wasn't fair. He deserved better than to lose everything in one awful night. If he had to suffer such a terrible accident, to endure such horrendous pain, he deserved to come out of it whole and healthy.

But life wasn't fair. He deserved to not be maimed in a way that made his dreams for the future impossible. She deserved to find a little happiness as she grew older. Her mother deserved to have a daughter who didn't disappoint her and rob her of the chance to fulfill her own dreams of becoming a grandmother. Everyone in this town—hell, in the whole world—deserved something they didn't have and couldn't get.

But somehow Easy was more deserving than the rest.

The last thought brought her a bittersweet little smile. "I've got to get to work, Mom. Want me to put in an order for two specials-to-go for you?"

"Don't bother. I'll go back and say hello to Geraldine and put in the order myself."

Shay stood up as two more families came through the door. "Thanks for listening."

Mary stood up, too, and patted her shoulder reassuringly. "Thanks for talking. I've enjoyed it."

After disposing of her milk, Shay pasted on a phony smile and went about the business of waiting tables and ringing up bills. She was as friendly as always, but she refused to be drawn into any conversations about Easy. That cut her chat time by about half and left her with more energy than usual once the rush was over. By three-fifteen, things were so quiet that she sent everyone else home. When the old clock on the wall read four o'clock, she had already cleaned up and closed out the cash register.

She was in back, packing a foam container with leftovers for her own dinner when the bell announced a late arrival. "Sorry, we're clo—" She broke off as she came through the swinging door and stopped so abruptly that the door banged against her on its return swing.

Easy stood a few feet inside the door, looking about as *un*easy as a man could look. He kept his back to the street, his hand in his pocket and his gaze on the wooden floor. Dangling against his cane was a plastic bag of the sort the cook put takeout orders in.

Taking a few awkward steps, she laid the foam carton on the counter before it could slip from her shaky hands, then slid her hands into her hip pockets. Out of deference to the church folks, she left her short skirts, tight dresses and shorts at home on Sundays and dressed modestly in jeans and a T-shirt. Right this moment, feeling more than a little vulnerable, she was glad she did.

"Hi."

"Your mother told me to bring this back." He crossed the short distance to the counter, the bag banging with a ceramic ping against his cane with each step.

Shay looked inside. The heavy white plate, saucer and

utensils matched the dishes in the kitchen that she spent a good part of her days washing. What was he doing with them? He certainly hadn't been in the café before now, and they never sent takeout on real dishes or they'd be serving on paper plates in no time.

But he'd mentioned her mother, who had gone into the kitchen to give her takeout order directly to Geraldine. Her mother, whose job was running the house, whose hobby was running everyone's lives. No doubt she'd suggested to Geraldine that they skip the throwaway plastic and foam on this particular order—for Shay's sake, of course.

She sighed heavily. "You didn't have to do that."

"Mary seemed to think I did. It's not easy telling her no."

"No, it isn't." But if he truly hadn't wanted to come, he could have successfully refused. He was the only person she knew who was more stubborn than her mother.

Not that she was reading anything into his being here.

She placed the dishes, bag and all, on the pass-through, then turned back, her manner as nearly normal as she could force. "What do you think of the place? It's about as classy as all those places where we used to eat, isn't it?"

He gave it only the briefest of glances. "It's fine."

She took the long look around that he didn't. The benches in the booths were turquoise vinyl repaired with black duct tape. The tables didn't match, and more than a few owed their stability to matchbooks under one or more legs. The chairs matched neither the tables nor each other, the walls were in dire need of a coat of paint, and the torn stained menus needed replacing altogether.

"Fine," she echoed. "It's a dive."

"Some of the best meals we ever had were in some of the sorriest-looking places."

That was true, and it was true here. No matter how worn the surroundings, the food was the best in town. She had that much to be proud of. "Would you like something to drink? Maybe a piece of apple cobbler?"

"Sure," he said in a very no-way sort of voice.

"Iced tea? Pop?" Her smile was wobbly, as if it might disappear at any second. "I don't have anything stronger, and I'm not allowed to touch the coffee maker."

"Pop's fine."

She fixed two glasses and set them on the counter, then went into the kitchen to warm two servings of apple cobbler and top them with vanilla ice cream. When she came out again, he was gone from the counter. For one heartstopping instant, she thought he'd left, then she realized the glasses were gone, too. He'd simply moved to a booth—the one back in the farthest corner that couldn't be seen from the street.

Balancing cobbler, spoons and napkins, she slid onto the bench opposite him. There was something so incredibly familiar about sitting there—because they'd done it so many thousands of times before, she supposed. It just seemed *right*. Even if neither of them knew what to say to the other. Even if there was this tremendous discomfort between them. Even if neither of them seemed to even know where to look.

"So…" She spooned melted ice cream back over the cobbler and watched it drizzle down. "What do you think of Heartbreak?"

"Hasn't changed much."

"No. We lost a few old businesses, gained a few new ones. Jerry Danvers took over his father's law practice, only he has to practice in two other counties, too, to make a living. The post office burned down a few years ago, and they gave us a trailer in the old post office lot. They say they're going to rebuild, but you know how slow the government works. It took them months to get the debris from the old building hauled off. The high school girls' basketball team won the state championship last year, and they're predicting the football team will do the same."

Easy fought the urge to smile as he listened to her. He knew from many years' experience that she babbled only when she was nervous. She hadn't done it the first time they'd made love, but the second time, that night in a motel outside Salina, Kansas, she'd babbled away until he'd kissed her. She'd been grateful for a reason to stop talking. He'd been grateful for the right to kiss her. After that, whenever she'd gotten edgy and started prattling, he'd slid his tongue into her mouth and calmed her down in one way while getting her all stirred up in others.

What would she do if he tried it now?

Probably grab hold and take him for a ride. They'd always been like gas and fire, ever since that first innocent kiss in her mother's kitchen. Even when sex was the last thing in the world they'd needed between them, all it had taken was a touch, a kiss, sometimes nothing more than a look, and the need consumed them.

Right now was one of those times when sex was the last thing they needed.

There would never be a time when *he* wasn't the last thing *she* needed.

"—have the Founders' Day celebration and fireworks at City Park for the Fourth and—" Abruptly she stopped, took a great, noisy breath, then said, "I should be quiet now, shouldn't I?"

"No. Go ahead and talk." He'd listened to her voice for so many years in his head. It was one of his fonder dreams to hear it for real.

She gestured toward his plate. "Your cobbler's getting cold and your ice cream's getting warm."

He looked down at the spoon. It rested in the bowl, its handle extending on the right—the normal position for someone who was right-handed. He clumsily reached across with his left hand, scooped up a bit of ice cream, then watched it slide back into the bowl. They'd tried to teach him to learn everything with his left hand in the rehab hospital, but he'd refused. He'd been too bitter, too damn miserable to care if he never did anything but lie unmoving in bed until he died. Instead, he'd taken his meals alone and used his right hand. But expecting someone else to eat and look at that mess…

Grimly, he laid the spoon in the dish and pushed it away. He hadn't wanted the damn cobbler in the first place. He'd only wanted an excuse to sit with her for a minute.

"You can use your right hand," she said quietly.

"No."

"Why not? You're right-handed. People who are right-handed tend to use that hand when they eat."

"Not when they have less than half a hand." His voice was sharper than he'd intended it to be. It made her flinch and lower her gaze to her own dish.

Though it seemed a contradiction in terms, silence really could be deafening. It reverberated in his head, pulsing, smothering, until finally he broke it. "I didn't know how much damage I'd done until nearly a week after the accident. My entire hand and part of my arm were wrapped in bandages so huge that I couldn't see that anything was missing. They told me I'd broken a lot of bones, and I believed it. I could feel the pain in all five fingers. Finally, when they were pretty sure I wasn't going to die, they told me the truth. I didn't believe them until they took off the bandages and showed me. Even then, I still felt pain in those fingers."

At first he'd been too shocked to understand all the implications. He'd needed first to deal with the plain and simple horror that his fingers were gone. It hadn't been until the middle of that night that he'd realized the full impact. No more rodeo. No more working with horses. No more life. He'd cried, and his father, sitting beside the bed, had cried, too. It had been a first for them both—and hopefully a last.

"I know it sounds too Pollyannaish," Shay said quietly, "but at least you were lucky enough to keep the thumb and a finger. You can do a lot with a thumb and a finger."

"You'll have to pardon me for not feeling lucky when they've cut off parts of my body," he said dryly. "I was extraordinarily fond of every part I was born with. I had hoped to die with them.''

She smiled faintly but said nothing. The silence went on so long that he began thinking he should leave so she could get on with whatever she had planned for the evening. Of course, what he *should* do and what he did do were often complete opposites. When Mary came to his house this afternoon, he should have sent her away. When she told him to return the dishes to Shay at the café, he should have refused. When she left without taking them, he should have set them aside for Joelle the next time she visited.

After making Shay leave angry and hurt yesterday, he should have kept his distance and prayed that she did the same.

But it was damned hard to keep his distance from the one thing he'd wanted most since he was twenty. He'd managed for six years by staying on the road, staying busy, never spending any more time in Oklahoma than was necessary to pass through to the next state. Even then, with hundreds of hard miles between them, it hadn't been easy to stay away. Now, with only nine and a half miles separating them, it was proving impossible. Hell, here he was. He'd actually driven into town, had walked down the sidewalk, had gone into a place where he might see other people—all so he could see her. Because he *couldn't* stay away.

''How are your folks?''

It took him a moment to realize that she'd spoken, that his desire for more conversation to prolong the visit hadn't conjured the words in his mind. ''They're fine. Dad's working in a factory that makes custom cabinets. He works regular hours, says all that wood smells so much sweeter than the cattle he was used to, and those cabinets haven't kicked or stepped on him once.''

''And, of course, sawdust is much more appealing than the droppings that cattle leave behind. What about your mother?''

"She's...okay. She's having a hard time dealing with me. She can hardly bear to look at me." As soon as he said the last words, he wished he hadn't. He wasn't looking for sympathy, and he sure as hell didn't mean to remind Shay that other people found him hard on the eyes so it was understandable if she did, too.

But she didn't have any problem looking straight at him. "I imagine it's tough to be a mother and see your child going through something that you can't make better."

And thanks to him, *imagine* was all she could do. If he had stayed out of her life, she would have had three or four kids by now, if not with Guthrie, then someone else. If he'd managed to get his own life straightened out, maybe with him. That had been her dream—and his, too. Marrying Shay, the ranch, the kids, the horses, happily ever after.

All his dreams, summed up in one lousy sentence.

All his sorrows.

She was about to speak again when a knock sounded at the door. His first impulse was to turn and look. He acted on the second—sitting utterly still, hoping they were too deep in the shadows to be seen.

"It's Reese," Shay said. "I'll see what he wants."

He listened to her footsteps cross the wooden floor, heard the key turn in the lock and the bell ring as the opening door tripped it. "Hi, Reese."

"Shay. I noticed your car was still in the feed store lot and saw this pickup parked out front. Thought I'd make sure everything's all right."

She was smiling when she answered. Easy could hear it in her voice, and it made the ugly, irrational jealousy twist in his gut. "Everything's fine. Easy and I were having a Coke and a piece of Manuel's cobbler."

"I didn't think he got out much," Barnett said.

Only when he got so damned needy that he couldn't bear it, Easy thought.

"He doesn't. Listen, thanks for stopping by. I appreciate it. I'll see you around." She closed the door and locked it, then returned to the booth. She didn't sit down again, but gathered their dishes, stacking bowls together, one glass inside the other. "Since we've wasted two pieces of perfectly good cobbler, why don't you give me a ride to my car, then come over to the house and we can not-eat dinner together."

He should refuse and go home. He'd satisfied the need to see her, to spend a little time with her, but it had merely intensified other needs—needs he couldn't even think about satisfying. It wouldn't take much to make them as unbearable as they were impossible. Spending more time alone with her, going to her house with her—that would probably do it, and he'd wind up in a world of hurt.

But he didn't want to return to the ranch just yet. Didn't want to spend one more evening alone. Didn't want to keep his own company when he could share hers. Even if it meant paying for it later.

"All right," he agreed, and she turned away with a nod, leaving him to slide out of the booth and get to his feet in private. He waited by the counter while she puttered in the kitchen, and he wished it were already dark outside. He'd parked only ten feet from the door. Even as slow as he was, it'd taken him only a moment to get inside. Still, he felt more comfortable in the dark. He could hide more easily there.

She came out of the kitchen with a plastic bag, shut off the lights except those over the counter, then held the door open. He hesitated a few feet away. "Tell me something."

She didn't make him ask. She stepped outside, looked in both directions, then said, "There's no one around—no cars, no people."

His face burning with embarrassment, he moved past her, went to the truck and climbed inside. In the time it took him to get settled, stow his cane and fasten his seat belt, she'd locked up, covered the same distance, climbed in and fastened her own seat belt. He admired her agility at the same time he envied it. Once he'd been able to move like that—even faster, smoother—and he had the championship titles to prove it.

Now… He took a couple of steady breaths. Now he had to adjust. He had to quit regretting what he'd lost and learn to live with what he'd been left.

But he'd lost so damned much, and he'd been left so damned little.

He drove her the block to the feed store lot, waited while she moved from his truck to her car, then followed her to her house. It was on the west side of town, with a six-foot-tall hedge of forsythia separating her yard from one neighbor and only a driveway between it and the other neighbor. There were no cars at home next door, though. Hopefully that meant nobody at home.

"Welcome to my humble abode," she said with a wry smile as she opened the door.

He followed her inside and felt an immediate sense of… Not welcome. Belonging. Homecoming. Compared to this strange place where he'd never set foot before, his house where he'd lived the better part of twenty years felt as impersonal as all those motels where he'd spent thousands of nights. It was a place to spend as little time as necessary. A place to sleep, then leave.

This was a place to live.

Shay closed the door behind him, left her purse and the food on the coffee table, then gathered an armful of pillows from the sofa and divided them among the chairs in the room. "It's not much besides small, but for a reasonable rent that doesn't stretch my budget, it's mine."

"I like it."

She gave him a sidelong look before retrieving the food. "Right. If this impresses you, then you've spent too many nights on the road. Have a seat while I put this up."

Ignoring the sofa and easy chairs, he followed her into the next room. The kitchen filled two-thirds of the space, with the rest taken up by a round table and four chairs. It was a bright room, with white cabinets and yellow walls, with a bouquet of scarlet, orange and hot-pink flowers in the center of the table. It would be a pleasant place to have breakfast, a pleasant place to eat dinner—hell, to do damn near anything that included Shay.

She glanced at him as she put their dinner cartons in the refrigerator but didn't say anything. She didn't ask him to not go through the door that connected dining room to hall, to not look into the hall bath, done in eye-popping electrifying blue, or to not go into her bedroom.

He stopped inside the door and took a deep breath. It was enough to tell him, even if he hadn't already known, that this was *her* room. The air smelled of her—of those sweet fragrances that combined to become her. Perfume, powder, shampoo, laundry detergent, fabric softener, makeup, lotion. For a time after he'd left her, the fragrances had stayed with him—had permeated his clothing, the interior of his truck, even his own skin. They'd threatened to drive him insane, but once they were gone, he'd wanted them back. Like he'd wanted her back. Desperately.

This room was painted a soft shade of rose. The trim was white, the bed iron and flaking white paint. The dresser and chest had come from her parents' house and were topped with doilies of the sort he'd watched his grandmother crochet when he was a kid. There were fresh flowers on the chest, delicate lamps on the night tables, fussy curtains over the windows that matched the bedcovers. The bed was a double and looked inviting as hell, and not just because Shay slept there. The comforter—flowers that matched the walls on a deep-green background that matched the rugs—was thick and puffy, and the pillows—dozens of pillows—promised a soft place to rest his head.

He could sleep in this room. He could overlook the doilies and frills and be more than comfortable there.

If it didn't make him feel like a selfish bastard.

Abruptly he turned away and came face-to-face with her. She looked around the room, then at him, at his scowl. "You don't like my room?"

"This is what you wanted—what you always wanted. It's not a lot. Just a stupid room with pillows and lacy curtains and furniture that isn't bolted to the walls—but I couldn't give it to you." His voice sounded harsh, out of place in the cozy, serene space.

Her gaze remained level, her expression steady. "You could have. It just didn't fit into our plans."

"*Our* plans?" he echoed. "*We* didn't have any plans. Your plans included settling down, having a house, a family, friends. My only plan was to keep running for as long as I could."

She smiled as her gaze moved slowly again around the room. "*My* only plan was to be with you. Settling down, having a house and a family would have been nice, just like having that ranch and raising horses and kids would have been nice for you. It would have been the icing on the cake. But all I really wanted, Easy, was the cake." Her gaze settled on him, and so did her smile, for a moment before she walked away.

He remained where he was, surrounded by her fragrance, and listened to her last words echo. *But all I really wanted was the cake.* And *he* had been the cake. And all he had really wanted was her—more than the ranch, the horses, the kids—so how in the hell had they wound up like this?

Because he'd never been able to forgive himself for betraying Guthrie and, though it made no sense, he'd never been able to forgive Shay for doing the same. He had hated that she'd found it so easy to leave Guthrie at the same time he'd been on his knees thanking God that she'd done it. Guthrie had deserved a better best friend, a better fiancée, and Easy had despised both himself and Shay for not being better.

As he stood there, his gaze settled on a photograph on the night table. He didn't need to go closer to recognize it, but he did. He circled the bed, picked it up and tilted it to the light. It had been taken by the pool in the Stephenses' backyard. He, Shay and Guthrie stood in the middle, surrounded by all their friends, celebrating her birthday and her engagement to Guthrie. But it wasn't her fiancé she was looking at. It was *him*. She was looking at him as if she didn't quite know what to do, and he wore exactly the same expression.

In fourteen years they'd never managed to figure it out. He wondered if they ever would.

Chapter 5

Shay felt as nervous as a girl on her first date. *More* than she actually had, in fact, on her first date. She'd been best buds with Guthrie all her life, so when he'd invited her to the spring dance at school, it'd been more like hanging out with her brother than a date. As for Easy, they'd skipped the dating routine altogether and gone straight to sex, then living together.

And this wasn't a date, either, she reminded herself. He'd come over for dinner, nothing more. Though if he wanted something more...

She sighed and plumped the pillow she'd pulled into her lap. If she didn't get her hopes up, she couldn't be disappointed, right?

Oh, yeah, right, the little devil inside her whispered as Easy returned from the bedroom. *You bet.*

She hoped he would sit at the other end of the couch. He chose an armchair instead, laying the cane aside, propping his left foot on the edge of the coffee table, looking troubled and tired and too damn handsome for her own good.

"Are you okay?" she asked as he rubbed his forehead, his fingertips bumping over the scar with each stroke. She'd seen him do it before and wondered whether he was easing a headache or reminding himself of his flaws.

"Yeah." He let his hand drop to the chair arm. His right hand was tucked out of sight.

"Have you given any thought to what you're going to do?"

"About what?"

"Life. Living."

A puzzled look came into his dark eyes. "I'm going to stay at the house."

"But what are you going to do?"

"Nothing."

Grimacing, she moved to the end of the couch nearest him. "What about money?"

"I had some good years, and I invested everything I could. I've got money."

"What about something to fill your time? You can't just sit on the sofa and watch TV for the rest of your life."

The stubborn look she knew too well came across his face, darkening his eyes, setting his jaw in a never-gonna-back-down jut. "I can if I want."

"You'll get bored. You'll get lonely."

"I've been bored before, and I survived."

A beat passed, then another, before she softly asked, "What about lonely?"

His fingertips took on a purplish hue from pressing so hard against the chair arm. "I've been lonely," he admitted, his voice husky, "and I survived that, too."

There was no denying that. He was surviving, but just barely. She knew that because she was just barely surviving, too. They were living day to day, finding no joy, no peace and damned little satisfaction, and that was a sorry way to be.

"Have you considered getting a horse?" The question popped out of her mouth without warning, without thought, but once it was out, she wouldn't have called it back if she could. He'd loved horses since he was a baby, had had one since he was three. Just because he couldn't ride right now was no reason why he shouldn't have one now. It might do him good, might give him some badly needed incentive—to say nothing of acceptance by someone who cared nothing about his handicaps.

"Have you considered minding your own damn business?" he growled.

"You *are* my business."

He shook his head but didn't voice his denial on that topic. "I can't handle a horse."

"You don't have to handle him. You put him in the corral, feed him, see that he's got water, then sit back and admire him." She gestured toward the rear of the house. "Pete Davis's pasture ends at my backyard. His horses are out there all the time. When I'm tired or down—" *or missing you* "—I like to go out to the fence and just look at them. They're so beautiful, so…" At a loss for words, she simply shrugged. "Just looking at them makes me feel better."

"So looking at something I used to have but can't have anymore, something that I've lost forever—*that's* supposed to make me feel better," he said sarcastically, then followed it with an obscenity.

"I don't know," she disagreed, giving him a long, thorough look. "It works for me." Looking at him—even if she couldn't have him—made her feel less empty, less sorrowful, more hopeful. Looking at him reminded her of the wonderful times that had often gotten lost in the bad. It reminded her that once in her life, she had loved someone wholly, completely, with a great, soul-stealing passion, and he had loved her the same way. A lot of people never knew what it was like to love like that, to be loved like that, and that was sad.

Of course, a lot of people also never knew what it was like to lose a love like that. She could tell them. Boy, could she tell them.

She deliberately changed the subject. He looked relieved. "Does this trip into town mean that you're not going to hole up out there forever? That maybe you'll start buying your own groceries, doing your own laundry? Maybe you'll even get a haircut?"

"No. It means—" He thought better of his answer and looked away without finishing it.

What? That after only a week, he'd gotten tired of his own company? That he was entirely too accustomed to following her mother's orders? That he hadn't wanted her to come out to his house to reclaim the dishes herself? That—maybe, possibly, please—he'd wanted to see her?

"Maybe," she said evenly, "it means that your next visit will be to Guthrie."

His gaze jerked back to hers. He looked guilty, as if he should never even consider the idea, and startled, as if he had already considered it, and, underneath all that, just a little wistful. But there was no wistfulness in his voice. Just harsh, cold insistence. "No. That's *not* going to happen."

"Why not? Because you still feel bad for running off with me?" She didn't wait for an answer. "Guthrie's a forgiving man. He's no good at holding grudges." At least, not after fourteen years or so—or, more truthfully, not since Olivia came into his life.

"The hell he's not. According to Joelle, he's holding quite a grudge against Ethan."

"Did she tell you what Ethan did? He *stole* Guthrie's ranch and sold it to some businessman in Georgia. Jeez, you think that's not worth holding a grudge over?"

"And I stole *you.* You think that's not worth holding a bigger grudge over?"

Her smile came quickly, unexpectedly, and it felt so good. "No, but I'm flattered that you do."

He struggled to keep his harsh expression in place, but

the corners of his mouth twitched with a hint of a smile. "As I recall, you're easily flattered."

"Hmm. Tell me I'm pretty and I'll follow you anywhere." She stood up to go into the kitchen, then stopped in the doorway and looked back. "Do you also recall that it didn't work with anyone else? It was just you, Easy. You were the one I would have followed anywhere."

She left him to think about that while she fixed dinner. She'd brought home leftover turkey and roast, along with Geraldine's homemade bread and a half dozen of Manuel's oatmeal cookies. She was a chocolate chip fan herself, but Easy liked oatmeal. Once, while they were staying with friends in Utah, she'd baked a batch for him, but they'd never found out whether they were any good. He'd lured her off to bed to make love while their friends were out shopping, and the cookies forgotten in the oven had burned to a crisp. While they'd been busy airing smoke out of the kitchen, their hosts' dog had been busy polishing off the rest of the dough, which he had immediately thrown up.

They had cleaned up, gone back to bed to make love again and innocently denied when their friends came home that they smelled anything at all funny in the kitchen.

They really *had* had some good times. If only they'd learned to get through the bad....

But it wasn't too late. As long as they lived, it could never be too late.

She fixed sandwiches and pop, added chips from the cabinet, then carried it all into the living room in two trips. She pulled a small table to the left of his chair so he could set his drink there, then left hers there, too, for good measure, before she settled on the sofa again. "So...what were we talking about?"

"I don't remember," he said.

He lied, and she let him. Instead, she turned the conversation to people they'd gone to school with—the shy dweeb who'd become a renowned heart surgeon, the flamboyant cheerleader working some glamorous job in Hollywood, the brainy bookworm who was writing her own books now. Of course, those few—plus the brash cowboy who'd become a rodeo star—were the exception. Most of their classmates were living ordinary lives—working for a paycheck that was too often too small, raising families, trying to make marriages work or still looking for Mr. or Ms. Right.

When she'd recited the abbreviated life stories of virtually everyone they'd known, she fell silent. It was a good silence, though, not angry, not tense. Just two people with enough history between them to not require constant chatter.

After a time she unfolded from the couch where she'd curled up, and collected their dishes. "Want some coffee?"

"No, thanks."

"Another pop?"

He shook his head and lowered his foot to the floor as he reached for the cane. "I'd better head home."

She left the dishes in the kitchen, then returned with the remaining cookies in a plastic bag. At the door she turned on the porch light. He turned it off again before he stepped outside onto the tiny porch.

Even though she was barefoot and it had gotten chilly after the sun went down, she walked to the truck with him. While she hugged herself, he opened the door and eased inside with great care, sparking a distant memory. "Remember Custer?" she asked out of the blue.

He glanced at her as he settled in. "The general, the town or the—" the same memory flashed into his mind and made his mouth quirk in another near smile "—the bull."

They'd been at a small rodeo somewhere in Oregon, and a bull rider friend had bet that he could do better in Easy's event than Easy could in *his*. For whatever reason—too much testosterone, booze or just plain conceit—Easy had accepted the bet. He'd won, too, but it hadn't been a pretty sight.

"You were moving like this then, too."

"Yeah, but *then* it went away. Now it won't."

Her smile faded at that reality as he closed the door and started the engine. An instant later he rolled down the window. "As I recall, Custer paid off pretty well."

"A few hundred bucks," she scoffed, "plus the hundred from the bet."

"Actually, I was talking about that night."

Her cheeks grew warm under his gaze. That night…oh, yeah. Once she'd gotten him, bruised and battered, back to the motel, she had put him to bed, raging all the while. He wasn't a bull rider, he could have been killed, how could he be so reckless. And he had grabbed her by the shirt, tumbled her into bed and told her between greedy kisses exactly how she could make him feel better. In spite of his limitations—or perhaps because of them, because *she* had been totally in control—they'd had an incredible night.

But most of their nights had been incredible.

"Thanks for dinner."

Reminded, she gave him the cookies.

"And the cookies."

"Come back sometime." *Like tomorrow. And the next night. Every night.* "If I'm not at work, I'm usually here."

His only response was a faint smile as he shifted into gear.

"Easy?"

He looked at her.

"What did it mean?"

Does this trip into town mean that you're not going to hole up out there forever? she'd asked, and he'd replied, *No. It means—*

Second after second ticked by before he finally answered. "I wanted to see you." Then, before she could respond, he backed out and drove away.

Pleasure bubbled up inside her as she watched his taillights disappear around the corner—pleasure and pure, sweet need. Maybe she was a fool for falling for him all over again. Maybe their history should have proven to her that theirs was one of those grand passions that weren't destined to last. Maybe she was going to get her heart broken all over again.

But she couldn't turn away—not from him or her feelings for him. She couldn't *not* give them another chance. She couldn't stop hoping, and Easy was her best hope.

Always had been. Always would be.

Tuesday dawned a gloomy day. Before he even opened his eyes, Easy knew it was going to rain. He could smell it in the air that came through the open windows, could feel the humidity on the sheets, on his skin. He could feel it in his bones literally, he thought with a grunt as he sat up. His joints protested every move with more than the usual early-morning stiffness. Rodeo was hard on a body, to say nothing of the endless traveling and the excessive partying that were part of the whole life. Add in a near-fatal car crash, and he was fast approaching decrepitude.

As he turned to sit on the side of the bed, his gaze swept across old varnish and older wallpaper. For as long as he could remember, the room had looked like this, and that was a *long* time. It needed new paper, or, better, paint in some color that was soothing and easy on the eyes. The floor needed to be stripped, refinished and sealed and could use a couple of rugs to ward off the coming winter chill. Curtains or blinds would be nice, too. Even though he lived in the country, that didn't guarantee privacy. Hadn't he already had six unexpected visitors in only a week?

But what did he know about paint and curtains—about making a house a home? Less than nothing. But he knew someone who'd done just that with a tiny little place with far less potential than this house had.

''Ah, Jeez, Rafferty,'' he muttered as he dragged his fingers through his hair. Redoing his whole damn house, just so he'd have an excuse to spend time with Shay? That was pathetic. Why couldn't he just admit that he wanted to see her? Why did he even need an excuse?

Damned if he knew. He could just drive into town tonight after the café closed. Hell, he could go this morning, instead of overcooking his own eggs here. At worst, he could have an appetizing breakfast. At best, he could have it with Shay. If she wasn't too busy, if he could persuade her to join him. He was pretty sure he could.

He was also pretty sure it wasn't going to happen. He wasn't going to become Heartbreak's resident freak. He wasn't going out where people might recognize him, where they would look and whisper even if they didn't recognize him. He was safer here.

And if he was going to hole up here, then he needed Shay's advice. He couldn't spend twenty-four hours a day in a place that rivaled the dingiest of motels for bleak, drab and depressing. There were too many things about his life he couldn't change. This was one he could.

After getting dressed, he went into the kitchen to pour a glass of juice. He was heading for the front porch with it when a knock sounded at the door.

Elly Harris, wearing a bright yellow slicker over a red, orange and green outfit, greeted him with a broad grin. Tied to the railing eight feet behind her was Cherokee, munching contentedly on the tall grass there.

"Mornin'," she said, then thrust out a paper napkin. "Mama made doughnuts—*made* 'em. She never did that back in Atlanta. Back there if we wanted doughnuts, we went to the Krispy Kreme and bought 'em." She gave an admiring shake of her head. "I *love* Oklahoma."

He accepted the napkin and found two warm, if slightly squished, doughnuts inside. They were glazed—his favorite. When they were kids, Shay's mother had made a big batch every Saturday morning, using the recipe handed down from her mother-in-law. He, Shay and Guthrie had always managed to be there, waiting for samples fresh off the cooling rack. He would bet this was Mary Stephens's recipe, passed down not to a daughter who couldn't cook but to an almost-daughter-in-law who could.

Elly pulled another napkin from a pocket inside her

slicker. "I thought we could have breakfast together, so I'd bringed extra." Eyeing his juice, she smiled sweetly. "I like orange juice, and it's good for you. It helps build strong teeth and bones."

"I think that's milk," he said dryly. "Come on into the kitchen and I'll get you some." As he began retracing his steps, he asked, "Do you remember what I told you last time?"

"That you was Cherokee, just like my horse. And you can't work with horses no more."

"And?"

She climbed into a chair at the kitchen table and shrugged out of her slicker. In the drab, forty-years-unpainted room, her mismatched outfit provided a welcome—startling—splash of color. Like the flowers on Shay's kitchen table. Like Shay herself. "And that I had to ask my mom before I came here again."

"Did you?"

"Yup."

"And did she say yes?"

She unfolded both napkins, smoothing them away from the doughnuts, then, with the same gestures, smoothed her hair away from her face. "She said, 'You're too young to go riding by yourself, Elly. You know that.'"

He set a glass of juice in front of her. "So she didn't say yes."

"No-o-o-o." Then her blue eyes brightened. "But she didn't say no, neither."

"But she *meant* no."

She waited until he sat down, then slid two doughnuts over. "You should always say what you mean and mean what you say. That's in one of the books Daddy reads to us at bedtime."

Daddy. Easy gave a bemused shake of his head at hearing Guthrie called *Daddy.* It had always been a part of their plans—the ranches, the cattle and horses, marriage and kids. But it was hard to imagine Guthrie, frozen in Easy's mind at the age of twenty, father to twin girls, reading them bedtime stories, answering to *Daddy*.

Under better circumstances, Easy would have been close to Guthrie's kids—probably would have been their uncle Easy, named their guardian in case tragedy struck. Now he didn't have the right to even know them.

"Can I ask you somethin'?" Elly asked. When he nodded, she went on. "How come your name is Easy? Didn't your mama like you?"

Better at one time than she did now. Now she liked him. She just couldn't bear to be around him. "Easy's my nickname. My name is Ezekiel, but no one ever called me that."

"That's an old man name, with a gray beard and a funny walk and a cane." Her gaze shifted to his cane and suddenly she became earnest. "It's okay that you got the cane, 'cause you don't got the gray beard and you're not old. At least, not very."

He gave her a wry smile. "Do you always say exactly what you think?"

"Uh-huh. Sometimes," she added matter-of-factly, "it gets me in big trouble. Don't you always say what *you* think?"

"No."

"Why not?"

He thought of Shay—of all the times he'd hurt her, of all the apologies he owed her—and grimly replied, "Because sometimes it's easier not to."

"Like when?"

Like when you had a fourteen-year history with someone, of love and hate but never indifference. When you needed her desperately, even though she didn't need you at all. When you'd done too many wrongs to ever make them right again.

He finished his doughnuts and juice and changed the subject. "Are you in Miss Barefoot's class?"

"Nope. I got Miss Gardner. Emma's got Miss Barefoot.

The principal, he wouldn't put us in the same class and Emmy cried the first four days of school. Mama says Emma is timid. Our other dad, the dead one, he said she was a big dumb coward.''

Wondering what kind of father made such a comment to a child, Easy asked, ''And what does your new dad say?''

''He says she's his best girl. And so am I. And so is Mama. And he loves us all best.'' She answered with the complete faith of a child. It made him envy Guthrie—and her.

''Miss Barefoot's an Indian, too,'' Elly said. ''Is she your girlfriend?''

''No. Just a friend.''

''She's a nice lady. Emma likes her a bunch—and she don't like a lot of people, on account of her bein' timid and a coward and—''

Out front a car door slammed, interrupting her and making her eyes double in size. ''Uh-oh. I think I'm caught.''

He started for the front door, with Elly following a cautious half dozen paces behind. Through the screen he saw Olivia Harris, looking perturbed and short-tempered. She didn't knock, but kept her hands in her jacket pockets until they were only a few paces away. Then she freed one hand and snatched the door open. ''Eleanor Marie Miles Harris, get on that horse.''

''Oh, boy, now she's got *four* names to yell at me with,'' Elly muttered. ''Thank you for the juice.''

''Thank you for the doughnuts.''

She slipped past him and onto the porch. ''Mom—''

''*On the horse.* Go home with your father.''

Her words made Easy look past the porch. An older pickup was parked near his, with Elly's timid twin inside. Between the two trucks stood Buck, with Guthrie on his back.

It sounded stupid, but he'd hardly changed. Easy would have known him anywhere. There were more years on his face, he'd put on some muscle, and he had an older-wiser-experienced-more look, but he was still the same man Easy remembered.

The same man who'd long hated him.

Ignoring Olivia, Easy walked to the top step, where he could lean against the post for some badly needed support. "Hello, Guthrie."

For a moment it was as if his words had gone unheard. Then Guthrie shifted, tilted his Stetson back a bit and fixed his cold, dark gaze on him. "She won't be back again." His voice was hard, unforgiving.

"She wasn't bother—"

Guthrie wheeled Buck around. "Let's go, Elly. *Now.*"

As she nudged Cherokee forward, Elly flashed him a sad smile and waved goodbye.

Once they'd turned onto the main drive, Olivia came to stand at the opposite side of the steps. "We were worried when we realized she'd gone off alone on her pony. She's so little—"

"She was just curious. She brought me breakfast." His throat was tight, and he wasn't sure why. Because Guthrie had looked at him as if he'd always despised him? Because he hadn't wanted to hear one word Easy might say? Or because he'd lost one of the only two visitors who truly didn't care that he was crippled?

Regretting the loss of a five-year-old girl's company. Hell, he really was pathetic.

"It's not you," Olivia went on in that soft Southern voice. "She's just a child. She can't think it's all right to go wherever she wants."

"Of course not." Especially when where she wanted to go was the home of her father's most hated enemy. He glanced at Olivia. "I would have made sure she got home okay."

She didn't ask how, but simply nodded. After a moment, it was her turn to glance at him. "Guthrie will come around…eventually."

"Shay said he wasn't holding a grudge."

"Shay has a sick sense of humor," she said, her dryness underlaid with affection.

And was he a part of it? he wondered bleakly. Was that why someone so beautiful, someone who could have any damn man she wanted, wanted to spend time with *him?*

Because the possibility, however remote, was too hurtful to contemplate, he forced his attention back to the subject. "I never meant—" To hurt Guthrie. To make him so unhappy. To destroy their friendship.

"I know. And in his heart, Guthrie knows, too. But his pride and his ego…" She shrugged, then repeated, "He'll come around. He just needs time, and a subtle little push in the right direction."

"Is that your job—subtle pushes?"

Her smile this time was more normal, more genuine. "I like to think of it as putting things in perspective for him. After a while, holding grudges becomes habit. He's had fourteen years of being angry with you and Shay. It's routine, like taking care of the cattle and doing the books. But the truth is, what you did has no importance in his life today except what he chooses to give it. If he's going to choose, it's easier to choose to invest in a good relationship than a bad one."

"You make it sound simple."

"Forgiving someone you love can be the easiest—and the hardest—thing you'll ever do."

To a man who needed a lot of forgiveness, that wasn't particularly encouraging.

"Are you planning to stay?" she asked.

"Yeah."

"When you're ready to start fixing up the place, let me know. We'll help."

Maybe *she* would, and Elly, and maybe even Emma, but not Guthrie. The only help he would give would be to move Easy out of here.

"Fix it up for what?" he asked.

"You can't bring horses in here with the fence like that. And the barn needs some work and the corral—"

"I'm not bringing horses in. I'm not doing anything."

She studied him for a long moment before slowly smiling. "Maybe not. I've got to get Emma back home. The bus will be by any minute for them. I'm sorry Guthrie's being so stubborn."

"He was born that way," Easy remarked as she descended the steps.

"From what I've heard, so were you. You two must have been quite a pair."

She was halfway to the truck when he spoke. "Hey. Olivia." Her name in his voice sounded odd—friendlier than her husband would want them to be. "Could you—" Breaking off, he gave himself a moment to think better of his request, a moment to come to his senses, for Shay's sake if not his own. It didn't work. "Could you call Shay for me?"

"Sure. And tell her what?"

Right. Tell her what? That he was lonely? He wanted to see her? He wanted her advice on his house? He needed her presence in his life? Was there one single thing he could tell her that wouldn't be better left unsaid?

Nothing he could think of.

"Forget it. Never mind."

She watched him for another long moment before nodding. "I'll see you," she called, then climbed into the truck and backed away.

Not likely, he thought morosely. No doubt Guthrie had given Elly a stern lecture all the way home. She would never sneak over here again. He would probably repeat the lecture to Olivia if she tried giving one of those subtle pushes. He was comfortable holding his grudge, and he wasn't going to give it up.

Frankly, Easy couldn't think of one damn reason why he should.

* * *

Rainy days weren't good days for the diner. They had their regulars—mostly people who worked in town, plus a handful of retired folks who sat around all morning drinking a dozen cups of coffee for the price of one—but there was little new business. Most days Shay didn't mind. Today she could have used a few more customers—say, oh, fifty or so—to occupy her time.

Instead, she was sitting in a booth that looked out on the drizzly, gray day, with the Tulsa newspaper open in front of her, alternating her time between reading and watching the water run along the curb. If the temperature would drop fifteen degrees, it would be the perfect day for curling up at home with a good book and a pot of beef stew simmering on the stove.

Not that she could make beef stew. Or could concentrate on a book. Or cared to curl up at home alone.

She gave a melancholy sigh and turned back to the newspaper. She'd had the pages opened to the movie schedule for twenty minutes now and hadn't yet gotten around to reading what was playing. Of course, she didn't want to drive to Tulsa today, either, not in this steady soaker rain that wasn't about to quit. And she didn't want to sit alone in a darkened theater and watch some superhero save the world or some superbeauty fall in love.

When the door opened, she automatically looked up. A royal blue slicker came in, the hood pulled far forward to protect from the downpour. From under it emerged Olivia, her brown hair mussed, her face damp. She hung the slicker on the coatrack just inside the door, looked around, then started toward Shay. "Amalia, could I get a cup of coffee, please?" she asked as she passed the waitress.

"Shay's got her own pot. I'll bring you a cup," the waitress replied.

Olivia slid onto the empty bench, combed her hair back, then smiled. "Good morning."

Shay made a production of looking outside at wet and

dreary, then at her friend. "That's debatable. What are you doing in town?"

"The girls missed the bus, so I had to take them to school. I figured I might as well get groceries, too, and stop by McCaffrey's."

No one who lived in the country missed an opportunity to make the most of a trip into town. For some of them, they came too rarely. For one in particular.

They both watched as Amalia brought a cup, then filled it from the pot Shay had set on the table. It was strong stuff, and after a grimacing taste, Olivia doctored it heavily with sugar and cream. "We've had quite a morning," she said when they were alone again. "Elly went out to see Cherokee this morning, like she always does, and when I sent Emma out to get her, she was gone. So was Cherokee. I had to get Guthrie, who was already out on Buck, and we went looking for her. We found her at our nearest neighbor's house."

Shay's interest in the story doubled immediately. "Guthrie went to Easy's house?"

Olivia gave her a wry smile. "Thank you for your concern for my five-year-old daughter who wandered off alone."

Shay's gesture was impatient. "Elly's like I was at her age. She gets into trouble, and she always comes out unscathed."

"Well, I think she's a little *scathed* today, after the talk Guthrie had with her."

"Did he talk to Easy?"

Her smile dimming with regret, Olivia shook her head. "Other than to say, 'She won't be back again,' in his most hostile voice. He greeted Ethan after the wedding with more warmth."

Shay was disappointed by the report. "Hell, Magnolia, can't you work some of your Southern charm on him? It's so stupid of them to not be friends just because of me."

"It's not just you, Shay. In Guthrie's eyes, the person

he loved most, the person he trusted most, betrayed him. That's not an easy thing to forgive.'' Olivia smiled. ''But I'm working on it. I'll do what I can.''

A black-and-white Blazer belonging to the sheriff's department drove past out front, and Shay allowed it to distract her for a moment. But a moment's distraction was all Olivia allowed before she prodded, ''Well? Aren't you going to ask about Easy?''

''Ask what?''

''How he looked, how he acted.'' Olivia's smile turned sly. ''If he asked about you.''

Shay would have given a lot to play it cool, to airily say she knew how he looked and acted and didn't really care if he'd asked about her. But Olivia wouldn't be fooled. She did care, damn it. Still, she deliberately downplayed her interest, running the questions together as if their answers were insignificant. ''Okay, Magnolia. How did he look, how did he act, did he ask about me?''

''He asked me to call you.'' Olivia beamed, then her smile turned bittersweet. ''But when I asked what I should tell you, he got an odd look on his face and said forget it. Like he didn't know what to say or if he should even say anything.''

It wasn't necessarily bad news, Shay thought. At least he was thinking about her. Though he'd stayed away yesterday, she was on his mind. He wanted *some* contact with her. He just wasn't sure about letting himself have it.

''Why don't you go see him?''

''Great idea. It's only eleven hours until closing.''

''It's raining. You won't have as many customers today as usual. Geraldine and Amalia can take care of them.''

That was true. Her employees were as efficient as they came. Just as she'd taken off last Tuesday, when it wasn't raining, she could take off today and no one would miss her. And didn't she deserve an extra day off now and again? Hadn't she worked steadily for six years—fourteen-hour days, often seven days a week?

And didn't she want, more than anything, to see Easy again?

"You're trying to be a bad influence on me, Olivia."

"Ooh, O-li-vi-a. I don't know that I've ever heard *that* come out of your mouth. I think you might be trying to influence *me*." Teasing passed, she turned serious again. "Go see him. Maybe you'll catch him in a weak moment."

"And what would I do with him then?"

As she stood up, Olivia gave her a wide-eyed, innocent look. "You're the one who can steam up a room by simply walking in—the one who makes men's heart rates soar and sends their libidos into overdrive. If you don't know what to do with one incredibly handsome cowboy, I'm going to be incredibly disappointed."

"And, of course, the last thing I'd want to do is disappoint you."

"Why, thank you."

Shay walked to the door with her, helped her pull the wayward hood over her hair. "See you, Magnolia."

"Give my best to Easy. Better yet, give him *your* best."

Standing in the open door, Shay watched her run to the truck, then glanced up at the sky. It was dark all the way to the horizon. There was a front stalled in the area, according to the old farmers guzzling her coffee, so the rain would be around awhile.

She didn't want to be around awhile. Not around here, at least.

Abruptly she let the door close, told Amalia she was leaving, repeated the message to the others in the kitchen, then grabbed her umbrella and handbag. By the time she got to her car, her clothes were damp, her shoes soaked. She stopped by her house to change, then drove to Easy's house.

He was sitting on the porch swing, wearing jeans and nothing else. Wet sneakers had been kicked off near the door, and a wet chambray shirt hung over the swing's arm.

His hair was wet, too, slicked back from his face, giving him an appealingly wicked look.

As she climbed the steps, he laid an apple and a knife aside, picked up the shirt and pushed his arms through the sleeves. He didn't try to button it, simply pulled the two edges together—but not before she caught a glimpse of the scars across his chest. They sparked her sympathy and made her swallow hard, but she made damned sure nothing showed in her expression.

"Are you so low on groceries that you've resorted to picking apples in the rain?"

"Nope. I saw them from the window and wanted one. I'm surprised that old tree's still standing, much less bearing fruit." He picked up an apple from the bowl on the floor in front of him and tossed it.

She caught it easily as he resumed peeling his. Holding it in one hand, she wriggled out of her jacket, then strolled to his end of the porch. While he watched intently, she spread the jacket over the damp slats of the swing, seated herself beside him and took a slow, deliberate bite from the apple.

She knew from his stillness that she was sitting closer than he wanted, though not as close as *she* wanted. But if he wanted to protest, she could play innocent. After all, it was the only place on the porch to sit. Surely he didn't expect her to sit on the floor. Taking a modest seat on the floor in her very short, very tight red dress would be nearly impossible, and who knew what those rough boards would do to the fabric? Why, she might wind up with snags and possibly even splinters in places where she wanted neither.

"Isn't the café open on Tuesdays?" His voice sounded a bit strangled as he turned his attention back to the apple.

"It's open seven days a week, except holidays—7:00 a.m. to 8:00 p.m. Monday through Saturday, 8:00 a.m. to 4:00 p.m. on Sunday."

"And you're there every day but Saturday? When do you find time for a life?"

"The café *is* my life," she said with a laugh that she knew sounded regretful, because the statement was more true than not. "I can do a lot on Saturdays, and I have a good staff who can run things without me from time to time."

"You put in a lot of hours."

"That's easy to do when something's important to you." She surreptitiously watched him with the fruit. When they were kids, they'd all snatched apples off the trees that grew in each other's yards. She and Guthrie had eaten them as they were, but Easy, from the time he was old enough to have a pocketknife, had peeled his. He'd gotten good at it, finishing up with one long, paper-thin strip of skin and a smooth, unblemished apple.

The skin falling into the bowl this morning was in short strips, unevenly cut, taking more flesh in places than it left. It looked like the apples he'd peeled when he was six or seven. But he had learned then. He would learn again now.

"What brings you out here?" he asked as he removed the last bit of skin, then cut a wedge of fruit. His tone was cautious. So was his glance. Was he wondering whether Olivia had disregarded his *forget it* and called her, anyway? Probably. But she didn't intend to volunteer the information. She wanted to see if he brought it up first, if he confided that he'd seen Guthrie.

"Business is always slow on rainy days. They didn't need me, and I—" She looked at him. "I wanted to see you."

He took another quick glance as a flush gave his cheeks a deep coppery hue. Did her admission please him as much as his had pleased her Sunday night? Or was it embarrassment that she was being so obvious?

"I had thought you might come by last night." She'd cleaned up early, closed at exactly eight and gone straight home, just in case. She'd been prompt for nothing.

"You could have come out here."

"I didn't have an invitation."

He gave her a chastising look. "When did you ever wait for an invitation?"

"When I showed up without one last week, you got a little testy."

"Me? Testy?" His tone was dry, mocking. "Gee, what do I have to be testy about? Ending my career? Damn near killing my best horse? Spending the rest of my life as a cripple?"

"So your horse didn't die. That's a good thing. You're living back home on the ranch you love. You have the money to support yourself. You're in pretty damn good shape, considering." She smiled as she tossed the apple core over her shoulder and heard it splash in a puddle. "Olivia thinks you're incredibly handsome."

Scowling, he leaned forward, elbows on his knees, and snagged another apple to peel. The position pulled his shirt taut across his back. "So she called you, anyway."

"No. She had to take the kids to school, so she came to see me."

"And you're here to find out what I wanted her to tell you."

"I told you why I'm here. I wanted to see you."

"Why?"

"Well, let's see... We were best friends all our lives. I fell in love with you when we were twenty. I jilted my fiancé to be with you. I lived with you for eight years. I traveled hundreds of thousands of miles with you. You broke my heart when I was twenty-eight. You disappeared from my life for six years. Now you're back again. You tell me—why would I want to see you?"

He turned his head to look at her. The too-long black hair combed straight back and the scar that slashed down the side of his face added to the hardness of his gaze. "Olivia says you have a sick sense of humor."

She wondered how in the world *that* had come up in what she'd assumed was a brief, polite conversation. "I suppose you could say that—though I would prefer dry, sarcastic or cynical. What do you think, Easy? My being here is some sort of joke and you're the punch line?''

"No," he said grudgingly.

What would he say if she told him the truth? That she was here because Reese and Olivia had persuaded her that seducing him was in her best interests? Because she'd long known that *he* was in her best interests? Because she'd never been able to get over him, no matter how many ways she'd tried. Because she'd sworn to love him forever when she was twenty, and forever was still a long way from over.

"What makes Olivia think I'm sick?" she asked conversationally.

"You said Guthrie wasn't holding a grudge."

"Maybe I exaggerated a bit—"

"I saw him this morning. You exaggerated a lot. He wouldn't talk to me—wouldn't even listen to me."

And that hurt. Easy wouldn't say so, but she knew. She'd lived with him too long, had seen how melancholy he'd gotten on holidays and birthdays. Even seeing a road sign for the central Oklahoma town Guthrie was named for had been enough to make him fall silent for hours. The anniversary of the first time they'd made love had become cause for sorrow, because for him it had marked the day he'd betrayed his best friend.

If only it had been Easy who had asked her to the spring dance, Easy who had proposed on her birthday... It would have been like a fairy tale. *And they lived happily ever after.*

They could have, if Guthrie hadn't been such an intimate player in their romance.

"He wouldn't talk to me, either, when I first came back," she said with a sigh. "It only took—oh, six years before he could speak civilly to me."

"And you suggested that I go see him?" he asked cynically.

"He's different now. So are you."

''Oh, so you think he'll pity me enough to be friends with me again?''

''*No.* I mean, he's not alone anymore. He's not lonely and feeling betrayed. He couldn't be happier. He's got Olivia and the kids, and he's got to set a good example for them. He's got to consider what's best for them. And you're not running anymore. You came back here to stay.'' She smiled triumphantly. ''And like it or not, Easy, that means you came back to resolve the past. With Guthrie and with me.''

Chapter 6

Losing his appetite for both apples and conversation at the same time, Easy tossed the apple away, wiped the knife blade clean on his shirttail, closed it and stood up. He stepped over the bowl on the floor, then walked to the door, where he turned back to her. "You're full of—"

Shay wagged one long, slender finger. "Watch what you say. It'll save you from having to apologize when you prove me right."

"My reasons for coming back had nothing to do with resolving my past," he insisted. "I came because my parents were suffocating me with their pity. Because I had no place else to go. Because I wanted to be left alone. Because I thought both you and Guthrie would give me that much."

"I don't believe you." She uncrossed her long, long legs and stood up gracefully.

He wanted to move like that so badly he could taste it— or was that bad taste the lies he'd just told? He wanted to make things right with Guthrie almost as much as he wanted to fix them with Shay. But when the best friend he'd ever had could look at him with nothing but contempt, when he'd snap at his beloved stepdaughter rather than hear a word Easy had to say... It was easier to lie, to pretend he didn't care, than to add one more thing to his list of things he wanted but couldn't have.

"You believe what you want, Shay," he said quietly. "I'll believe the truth."

The truth. If he told many more lies, he wouldn't know the truth if it bit him.

He went inside and to the bedroom, where he removed his wet shirt. He'd taken a dry T-shirt from the dresser and was about to yank it over his head when she spoke softly behind him. "Why did you ask Olivia to call me?"

He stiffened, the soft fabric knotted around his hands, the dresser providing support. "Go away."

"It bothers you for me to see you without a shirt?" Her voice was still soft, but strong in spite of it. "I've seen you naked thousands of times. I know your body as well as my own."

"Not anymore, you don't."

The silence in the room was heavy, tense. He stood motionless, willing her to leave but to not go far. No farther than the living room or the porch.

Finally, when he was about to accept that she wasn't going, she sighed. "You know, Easy, if I'd just wanted a pretty face and a nice body, I would have stayed with Guthrie or taken up with Reese or any of a dozen other guys. I admit, you were handsome and you had a great body, but that wasn't what I wanted. It wasn't what I fell in love with. It was *you*. The package didn't change the fact that you were a good, decent, honorable man. It still doesn't."

"Oh, yeah," he said savagely, turning instinctively to face her. "I showed a lot of honor in seducing my best friend's fiancée. I had tons of honor when I begged you to run away with me. Hell, I had so damn much honor in treating you the way I did while keeping you away from

Guthrie and your family that I'm surprised someone didn't pin a damn medal on my chest.''

Her brown-eyed gaze was steady on his face as she quietly pointed out, ''A dishonorable man doesn't grieve over the dishonor he commits.''

And he *had* grieved. Not every day. No, there'd been plenty of days when he'd thanked God for having her, days when he'd thought there was no price on earth too dear to pay for her. And there'd been days when he'd been sickened by what he'd done, when he'd known all the love in the world couldn't justify the way they'd betrayed Guthrie.

''Guthrie is happy now,'' she went on.

''And he hates me.''

''So what? Regret it. Be sorry for it. But don't let it ruin your entire life. He's *happy*.'' Her voice took on a fierce tone. ''There's no reason why we can't be happy, too.''

He wanted to believe her more than he could admit, but it was too simple. Guthrie no longer suffered and so they were off the hook? Life didn't work that way. Life demanded punishment, penance.

He'd been doing penance for fourteen years. He figured he'd be doing it for forty more.

After a moment he turned his back. ''Go away. Let me get dressed,'' he said softly—he pleaded softly.

She left. He listened to determine where she went, but her footsteps faded before she left the hall. His movements jerky, he pulled on the shirt, stripped off his damp jeans and put on a pair of sweatpants. Then he went to see if he'd driven her away—again.

He hadn't. She was sitting at one end of the sofa, the quilt tucked over her feet and legs. It was a bright, colorful sight in the drab room—blond hair, red dress, quilt in yellow, blue and green. It was a sight he could easily become accustomed to brightening his entire house—his entire life.

He considered sitting in the rocker, but the hard wood seat combined with the damp chill wouldn't be kind to his bones, especially after the time he'd spent on the porch swing. Besides, he wanted to sit close to her, close enough to smell her fragrances. Close enough to reach out and touch her if he thought he might. If he thought he could.

"Why did you ask Olivia to call me?" she asked as he lowered himself to the cushions, then turned toward her to ease the weight on his hip.

"Gee, where have I heard that question before?"

"I'll keep asking until I get an answer. I'm stubborn that way." A smug smile touched her lips. "I took lessons from the most obstinate man alive."

He gazed out the west window for a moment before focusing on her. "I wanted to ask a favor of you."

"Ooh, Easy Rafferty asking favors. Mark this day on the calendar," she teased. "What do you need?"

You. A new hip. A new hand. A new life.

Or maybe just a chance at a different life.

"It occurred to me that this place is..."

"A little drab? A wee bit gloomy? A tad depressing?"

"A dump," he replied less generously. "If I'm going to stay here—"

"If?"

"I've got to do something."

Her gaze swept around the room before coming back to him. "By 'do something,' I assume you mean to the house. Paint, paper, buy furniture?"

He nodded.

"And the favor?"

That was the hard part. Though she'd teased, it was true that he didn't often ask for favors. If he couldn't do something for himself, he'd just as soon not do it. "I'd like your help. I've never painted, papered or bought furniture."

He'd expected an immediate agreement, because Shay was a generous person. Because, for whatever reason, she wanted to spend time with him. Because she knew how rarely he asked for help.

A quick yes wasn't forthcoming, though. Instead, she studied him—and for the life of him, he couldn't read anything in her expression. Finally she asked, "Do you want me to do this *for* you? Or do you want me to help?"

"What does it matter?"

"If you want me to it *for* you, so that you can avoid going to the paint stores, furniture stores and so on, then the answer is no. If you want me to help—to go shopping with you, to help you make your choices, to actually help do the work—then I would be glad to."

He thought about it, about going into not one store but a half dozen, dealing with sales people and clerks in store after store, facing all the other shoppers.... "Then forget it."

"Easy—"

"Forget I asked." He didn't need her help. Joelle would pick up a few cans of paint for him, and everything else he needed he could get from mail-order catalogs. One phone call to his mother would get him more catalogs than even he had time to look through. For that matter, one phone call would bring Betsey here. She would be more than happy to do the shopping for him and would never suggest he should do it himself. It was hard enough for her to be around him. She would never think that he should inflict himself on strangers.

"Easy, damn it—"

"I said forget it. I'll take care of it."

She muttered a curse that would have gotten her mouth washed out with soap when she was a kid. Even now, he thought, it would earn her a stern warning from her mother. "Have you been out at all since you got out of the rehab hospital?"

He shifted so that he wasn't facing her, propped his feet on the coffee table, picked up the remote and switched on the television. The annoying sounds of a game show filled the air before the picture filled the screen. He *hated* game shows and flipped to the next channel to a talk show. He hated those more. He found kids' TV, religious programming and two more talk shows before she reached across and hit the off button. Stubbornly he turned it on again. More stubbornly, she got up and unplugged the damn television.

She stood between him and the blank screen, hands on her hips, and demanded, "Answer me."

"What constitutes 'out'?"

"Have you eaten in a restaurant?"

"Yes."

"Besides mine?"

He didn't answer.

"Have you gone shopping for clothes? Have you gone out for a beer? Have you been to a movie? Have you gone anywhere at all?" She gestured toward the screen door. "Did you even pick out the truck yourself?"

"No," he replied angrily. "My dad did. My mom bought my clothes. He brought my beer to the house. She picked up movies at the video store. Between them, they pretty much took care of everything."

She stepped over his left leg and sat on the coffee table. It was an intimate position. If he pulled her closer, if she reached out...

Swallowing hard, he closed off that line of thought.

"Where have you gone since you got out of the last hospital?" Her voice was steely quiet. He knew her well enough to know that she wouldn't let it rest until he answered, and so he did.

"I've had doctors' appointments. Physical therapy. Coming here, I had to get gas three times, and I stopped at drive-throughs twice. I went to the café and to your house." And that was it. He'd left the house maybe ten times in three months, plus the trip from Houston to Heartbreak.

"Jeez, Easy." That was all she said. It was enough.

Though he told himself he owed her no explanation, he offered one, anyway. "The doctors' appointments and physical therapy—those were at the hospital, where they're used to seeing people like me, and I still got stared at. People still looked at me with pity and whispered behind their hands. What do you think they're going to do if I walk into a paint store or a furniture store where they *don't* see freaks every day?''

"Did you *hear* the whispers?"

"Of course not," he grudgingly admitted.

"Then how do you know they weren't saying, 'Look, there's Easy Rafferty. He won the National Finals championship in calf roping last year'? Or maybe it was 'Look at that incredibly handsome cowboy—' Olivia's words, not mine '—I wouldn't mind playing rodeo queen with him for a while.'''

Wearily he dragged his fingers through his hair. "Because I *know*. You spend enough time with people who can't look at you, who talk to your chest because that way they can avoid the scars, the hand and the cane, or with people who can't *stop* looking at you, you know."

Wry, dry humor softened her voice. "Men have talked to my chest for twenty years. I didn't realize it was because they were avoiding my face."

He didn't try to stop the smile that tugged at his mouth, because he knew it was true. He'd watched too many cowboys over the years all but drool over her—but their dazed, lusty expressions hadn't turned to revulsion once their gazes finally made it to her face. "Any man with eyes in his head would love looking at your face. You're so damned beautiful."

"And you're too damned handsome. You've been told so by too many women to doubt it. One nice, neat scar doesn't change that."

"It's not just the scar. I could live with the scar. It's all of it together. The package, as you called it, is damaged and deformed in ways people can't bear."

"Then you're seeing the wrong people."

Joelle had said the same thing the night they had dinner together. It meant no more now coming from Shay. "You're right. And the only way I can control the people

I see is to stay here. That way no one comes around who isn't prepared for what they're going to see.''

Looking weary herself, she didn't argue the point with him for one simple reason—there was no argument to make. The only way to preserve even a shred of his dignity was to stay here in this house. No matter how dependent it left him on others. No matter how lonely it made him.

After a long, still moment, she stood up, and he lowered his foot to the floor to let her pass. ''All right,'' she said in a defeated sort of voice as she turned in a slow circle. ''What do you want to do with this room?''

On Wednesday afternoon Shay took a break to walk down the street to Heartbreak's only hardware store, located in a block of empty buildings. Over the years every other business had gone under, but Prescott's had managed to survive. It was probably more a testament to Jed Prescott's tightfistedness than his business sense. It was said around town that he could squeeze blood from a turnip. He'd certainly managed to squeeze a living from the hardware store—and the life from his wife and daughter. His wife had had the good sense to run off years ago. His daughter hadn't been so lucky.

Grace sat at a desk behind the counter, her head bent over the books. She was eight or ten years younger than Shay, so their paths had never crossed in school. Unless Shay had reason to come in here—which she rarely did—she never saw the girl. She came to work with her father in the morning, went home with him at night and had no life of her own. She was a sad child, Mary always said when she came up in conversation, and Shay had to agree.

''Hi, Grace.'' Shay leaned on the counter that could give her own counter back in the café a run for its money on cleanliness.

Grace looked up so quickly that her glasses slipped down her nose. She was really a pretty young woman, but she wore no makeup, her auburn hair was pulled straight back into a tight ponytail, and her glasses gave her an owlish look—a baby owlish look. "Miss Stephens."

"Please, Grace, call me Shay." It wasn't the first time she'd made the request. It wouldn't be the first time it went ignored. The next words out of Grace's mouth proved her right.

"What can I do for you, Miss Stephens?" she asked, glancing nervously over her shoulder, no doubt looking for her father. Prescott was a hard man, who lived by rigid rules and expected everyone else to do the same. He commanded instead of asked, ordered instead of requested, shouted instead of talked. Frankly, he scared Shay. She could easily see him resorting to physical violence against anyone who crossed him—including his timid little daughter.

"I need some paint samples, and I was wondering if you had any wallpaper samples I could borrow to show a friend."

"The paint samples are over here," Grace said, coming out from behind the counter to lead the way to the farthest corner. "The wallpaper samples are right next to them, but I'm afraid I can't—I'm not allowed—" She drew a deep breath and blurted out, "They can't be taken from the store."

"That's all right. I can get some ideas to talk over with Easy." Shay pulled out a stool and slid onto it. Grace hadn't even blinked at the mention of Easy's name. There were probably only two people in the entire county who wouldn't have *some* reaction to Easy, his misfortune or his return. Grace was one. Her father was the other.

The girl hovered nearby, so tense that she damn near hummed with it. After flipping past a couple of samples, Shay glanced at her. "Are you all right, Grace? You look—"

"I—I think I'm coming down with—with a cold or some—something. I—I'd better get back to the books. If you need anything…'' With an awkward shrug, she rushed away.

Shay stared after her. The girl was extraordinarily pale, with shadows under her eyes. She looked thinner than usual, too, and nervous enough to quake. On top of that, she'd interrupted a customer—something she'd probably never done in her entire life. That must be one hell of a cold.

Dismissing Grace and her problems, Shay turned her attention with some reluctance to the samples before her. Some part of her was convinced that doing Easy's shopping for him was wrong. He couldn't live the rest of his life cooped up in that house, all for the sake of avoiding insensitive fools, and she was doing him no favors by making it possible.

On the other hand, if he was determined to stay there, then he deserved someplace that wouldn't depress the hell out of him. Maybe coming to grips with other people's reactions to him was something he had to do on his own terms—on his own timetable. Maybe, if he wasn't surrounded by shabby gloom every day, he would subconsciously choose to speed up that timetable.

She studied the patterns and colors, seeking ones that would suit Easy, too often distracted by what would suit *her*. She'd once thought she would be living in that house, sleeping in that back bedroom with him, cramming kids into the other two bedrooms. She had amused herself through endless miles of travel by remodeling on a sheet of paper, adding a new bedroom and bath for them, enlarging and updating the kitchen, giving Easy an office where he could oversee his enormously successful horse business.

The exterior hadn't escaped her daydreams, either. In her mind she'd scraped every flake of that beige paint and dark-brown trim and painted the house white with classic black trim, or pale gray and dark smoky green, or the exact hue of a well-baked pumpkin pie, framed in crisp white. She'd chosen a dozen color schemes, depending on her mood, and painted the outbuildings and fences to match.

Of course, back then, she'd had the right to completely redo it. All Easy was asking for now was her advice, her shopping and her able-bodied help.

She wished he wanted more from her body than redecorating.

"Do you need help?"

The harsh voice was an unpleasant interruption that drew her features together in a scowl even before she shifted her gaze from the pattern books to the speaker. Jed Prescott, all six foot five of him, in the flesh. His scowl was as hard as hers, his expression accusing, as if every minute she sat there looking was costing him money.

"No, thank you," she said coldly. "I don't."

"Girl! What're you doing over there with your nose in a book while you've got a customer here?" he shouted loudly enough to make Shay cringe. "Get over here and do the job I pay you for."

She would have snorted if she hadn't feared it would make him even angrier with Grace. It was a well-known fact around Heartbreak that Grace had never received one dime in salary for the six-day weeks she put in here at the store. Prescott had boasted about it—how other businessmen had to pay their help when he had just *raised* his. He'd put food in her belly, clothes on her back and given her a bed to lie in for more than twenty years. Working for free was no more than she owed.

Bastard.

Shay got to her feet and fixed her chilliest gaze on him. "Grace has been most helpful. I asked her to leave me alone while I made my decisions."

"Have you made them?" he demanded.

Yes. I decided to go elsewhere. Shay bit back the automatic retort because, in Prescott's eyes, it would somehow be Grace's fault. Besides, she made a practice of supporting Heartbreak businesses as thanks for the support her own business received—not that Jed Prescott had ever set foot inside the café, and nor would he be welcome there.

Ignoring him, she turned to Grace, who'd scurried to his side like a frightened little mouse. "I'm going to collect some paint samples to show Easy. I'll be back after he chooses. Thanks for your help." Her smile slid back into a scowl as her gaze moved from the girl to the father, then she turned away.

The run-in left her feeling dirty and creepy the rest of the afternoon. After closing, when she drove out to Easy's with the samples, she told him about it.

"Why don't you get your daddy and Guthrie and some of their friends to take him out back and teach him a lesson?" he asked dryly as they polished off the leftovers from the daily special at his kitchen table.

"They can't do that."

"A hundred years ago they would have."

"A hundred years ago nobody would have cared how he treated his daughter. Jeez, the man calls his daughter by the same name he calls his dog. 'Girl.'" She shuddered with distaste. "He probably doesn't treat her any better than he treats the dog, either."

"I hate to break this to you, Shay, but…it's none of your business. She's an adult. If she doesn't like the way he treats her, she can quit her job and move out."

"No, she can't," she said quietly, sadly. "You haven't seen her, Easy. She's scared of her own shadow. Twenty-five years of living with that man has probably ruined her forever."

For a moment he sat in silence, watching her. Then he smiled the slightest of gentle smiles. "I'd forgotten you were so kindhearted. Lucky for me, you are."

"Lucky? You?" She feigned amazement. "Better watch it, cowboy. You say that too often, you might begin to believe it."

"Don't get smart."

"Too late. I was born smart." She stood up and began

gathering their dishes. When he caught hold of her wrist, she froze. Little chills danced up her arm and down her spine, followed immediately by tiny waves of heat.

There was something so incredibly sweet about touching—about him willingly, voluntarily reaching out and laying his hand on her. He hadn't touched her in more than six years, and she'd missed it every single day—missed the simple contact. The calluses on his hands. The strength in his fingers. Their incredible skill at turning simple touches into erotic ones. She felt as if she'd been in the desert all those years, given only the bare minimum of water needed to survive, and now found herself standing at the edge of a vast ocean. She felt parched. Greedy. Blessed.

His fingers flexed, the tips pressing against her skin, then his thumb moved fractionally, rubbing the inside of her wrist. She felt her heart rate accelerate and wondered if he felt it, too—felt her chest tighten and her knees go weak.

Under the gentle pressure of his hand, she released her hold on the plate, letting it settle back on the table with a thump. His fingers slid down to her palm, then made a slow journey up her arm to her shoulder as he got to his feet. In deference to the chilly weather, her T-shirt had long sleeves. More's the pity.

"Sit," he said, pressing down on her shoulder. His voice was husky, turning the single word into a hoarse command. "You wait on people all day at the café. You don't need to do it here."

"I don't mind—"

"I do." For an instant his hand remained on her shoulder, then he removed it to pick up his cane.

Sinking into the chair, she caught her breath, then twisted to watch him. He took the dishes to the counter in three trips, filled the sink with soapy water, washed each piece. "I like a man—" *who can make touching my wrist more erotic than the most intimate caresses any other man might offer* "—who knows his way around a kitchen."

"Considering how you cook, I bet you do."

''I could learn to cook if I wanted.'' She tossed her head with a haughty sniff and succeeded only in ruffling her short hair. ''I never thought culinary skills came high on your list of my attributes.''

''For me, they didn't. But frankly, I was a little worried about the kids.''

''What kids?''

He glanced over his shoulder. ''The ones we were going to have.''

The mention was enough to send a pang of hurt through her. For a time she'd been happy, so much in love, with a bright future ahead of her. For almost as long, she'd been miserable, with both her heart and her arms equally empty.

Rising from the table, she went to lean against the counter near the sink, her back to the cabinets. ''Now that I own the café,'' she said, carefully tempering her tone to sound as if it wasn't of utmost importance, ''you wouldn't have to worry about that anymore.''

He looked at her a long time before quietly agreeing, ''No, I wouldn't.''

When he turned his gaze back to the task at hand, she drew a breath, then walked to the back door. It was utterly dark outside. The light that had always shone outside the barn was off, the bulb probably burned out years ago. Though there'd been both moon and stars in the sky when she'd driven out, now they were hidden by clouds too heavy with rain to let light pass through.

''Easy?'' She continued to stare out as if the darkness out there made the conversation easier in here. ''Why didn't you ever want to marry me?''

He had promised her marriage when he'd asked her to run away with him. Of course, he'd promised her a lot of things—that he would love her forever, that she would never be sorry she'd chosen him, that he would never leave her.

At least he'd been right about one. She'd never been sorry.

He was motionless behind her. She knew the question had taken him by surprise. She could feel it. Then, after a moment, he finished rinsing the last dish, put it in the drainer and shut off the water. "I wanted to."

"But you never asked me. And when I asked you, you always said—"

"Later."

Yes, *later.* When he was through with the rodeo. When he'd earned enough money to give them a new start. When he'd be able to give her a home. He'd never understood—never wanted to understand, she'd sometimes thought—that those things weren't important to her. She'd wanted *him*, with his ring on her finger and his name for her own. She'd wanted to believe she meant enough to him to make it legal and binding. She'd wanted him to be *that* committed to her.

"Why?" she asked wistfully. "Why wouldn't you marry me?"

"Truth?" He came to the end of the counter nearest her, leaned against it and waited for her nod. "I wanted an easy out. Even from the beginning, I didn't believe it would last. I wanted you so much, but our being together was wrong. I didn't think we could ever escape that. When the end came, I wanted to it to be easy. No lawyers, no divorce, no hassle. I wanted you to be able to walk away, free and clear."

"Instead, it was *you* who walked away, with two last insults."

"What insults?"

She risked a quick look at him. His forehead was wrinkled in a frown, and he looked and sounded as if he didn't know what she was talking about. Smiling bitterly at the memory, she gazed out again. "Leaving that money on the night stand—payment for services—and replacing me with Clarissa."

"That money was to help you get back here. It wasn't meant as an insult. I was leaving you in Nowhere, Montana.

The least I owed you was a way home. Would you have thought more kindly of me if I'd left you there broke?'' He came a few steps closer, sending a shiver of badly needed warmth through her. ''Who told you I replaced you with Clarissa?''

She raised one hand to pinch the bridge of her nose, then spread her fingers to rub the outer corners of her eyes. It'd been a long day and an emotional one. She was bone tired. Soul tired. ''When I woke up that morning and found you'd left, I went to the restaurant there at the motel, hoping that maybe you'd just gone over for breakfast.''

In truth, she'd just been delaying facing the truth. His clothes were gone. Her belongings that she'd left in the truck had been neatly stacked inside the door. Her toiletries had been sorted out from his. And the money... She'd *known* he was gone for good. Oh, but she had hoped!

''Hank and Tracy were in there, and Tom and Mickey and some of the others. Tracy said she'd seen you and Clarissa come out of her room, get in the truck and drive off. Hank backed her up.''

''Hank,'' Easy repeated flatly. ''Who'd been trying for how long to get you into bed?''

Swallowing hard, she faced him. In those eight years, men had come on to her, but she'd paid them little attention. She'd loved Easy. What use could she possibly have had for any other man? But Hank had been one of the more persistent, which had led to bad blood between him and Easy.

And Tracy. Tracy the tramp, the wives had called her. She'd based her own worth on how many cowboys finishing in the money she could bed, and had done everything but dance naked on the tabletops to get Easy's attention.

Two losers with grudges against them both, and she had believed them on something so important. Groaning, she gave a dismayed shake of her head. ''God, how could I be so stupid?''

"Because I made it easy for you. It's not your fault. It's mine."

Her smile came with difficulty, but felt good. "Well, that explains why Hank volunteered to drive me all the way back to Heartbreak."

"You didn't let him, did you?"

She knew that tone—that darkly jealous, possessive voice men managed so well. It warmed her that it still came so naturally to him after all these years. "Of course not. I didn't like sitting at a table with him when you were between us. I certainly wasn't going to set off halfway across the country alone in a pickup with him. Whatever happened to him?"

"Last time I saw him, he had a broken jaw, a black eye and a broken arm, among other injuries. He'd gotten caught in bed with his girlfriend by the girlfriend's husband. He knew she was married, but she'd forgotten to mention that the guy was a body builder and was insanely jealous."

"Too bad," she said with a wince.

"It's no more than I would have done to him if you'd taken him up on his offer to bring you home."

Though she wasn't a proponent of physical violence most of the time, it was kind of nice to know that, even though he'd left her, he'd still thought of her as his.

But it would have been a whole lot nicer if he hadn't left her.

For a moment they remained silent. She listened to the old house, the long slow drip at the sink, the wind that had picked up outside. Easy seemed to be listening, too, his gaze on the wooden floor, his manner distant. The windowpanes rattled with a sudden gust of wind, jarring her out of her silence. "Shall we look at paint samples?"

The diversion jarred him from his thoughts, as well. He walked away, his limp more pronounced than usual—because he was tired or because of the dampness in the air? "Pick whatever you want. Except for this room. Make it yellow and white."

She thought of her own yellow-and-white kitchen and hid a smile. It was nice to know that something she'd done had impressed him. "Okay. With the bedrooms and the living room having been papered, it would probably be best to stick with paper again. If we chose to paint them, we'd have to strip off the old paper, then repair all the imperfections in the wallboard, which is a nasty job. Take my word for it. I did it in my bathroom."

"Is that why you painted it shocking blue? So no one can bear to look at the walls long enough to see if they're perfect?"

"Hey, I like bright blue. It helps get me going in the morning." They picked up their drinks from the table, then as they started slowly toward the living room, she returned to the subject. "If you really want paint, they make this textured wallpaper that, once it's painted, looks like a textured wall. Since we'd be both papering and painting, I assume it's a little more expensive, though I haven't priced it."

"Do whatever you want. I won't complain."

She circled the coffee table to sit at one end of the sofa while he eased onto the near end. "How do you know you won't hate what I do? It could be pink and ruffly or lime-green and fluorescent."

"You're not a pink or lime-green sort of person. And I know I'll like it because I like your house. It's comfortable. It feels like a home. That's what I want here. Do this house as if it were—" Flushing, he broke off and looked away. "I'm sorry. That was…"

As if it were your own. As it would have been, if only he'd been able to stop blaming himself for hurting Guthrie. As she'd been thinking of it off and on all afternoon. "It's okay," she said with a careless shrug that was all pretend. "But let me warn you—if you bring somebody like Clarissa here to live, I'm coming back and ripping it all out."

"You don't have to worry," he said with a dark scowl. "I won't ever be bringing anyone here to live."

Not even her.

The wind shook the old house on its foundation, drawing their attention outside once again. In the dim light that spilled through the windows, she could see leaves swirling in the air before settling to the ground once again.

"You'd better head home," Easy said quietly. "It's late, and there's a storm blowing in."

Her hands were suddenly clammy as she turned to look at him, as she prepared to make a suggestion that he was far likelier to turn down than agree to. She debated making it at all, then, with a deep breath and a measure of his old brashness, she went ahead. After all, nothing ventured, nothing gained. "Or I could just stay here," she said, her voice equally quiet, and more sultry than she'd intended. "After all, it's late, and there's a storm blowing in."

The first emotion to cross his face was desire. It was fleeting, there and gone almost too quickly to identify, but having seen it there thousands of times before, she recognized it easily. The second was embarrassment. Because she'd invited herself to spend the night when he didn't want her? Or because spending the night with her was an intimacy he wasn't yet ready for? The part of her that remembered too clearly being left in Montana hoped for the second, but feared the first.

"Shay—" He swallowed hard and couldn't meet her eyes as he bluntly, flatly answered, "No."

It was a simple answer that gave her no clue to the reason behind it, and it stirred her own embarrassment. "Then I guess I should go." Setting her glass on the table, she stood up, claimed her purse and jacket from the rocker, then headed for the door while shrugging into the jacket. "I'll pick up the paint and get started on the kitchen as soon as I can. It shouldn't take too much preparation since it's not papered. And I'll see if I can get a sprayer for the cabinets. It's always easier than—"

She was reaching for the screen door when he caught her arm and pulled her around. Before she could react, before she could even think, she was leaning with the door frame against her back, his body was so close that she could feel its heat, and he was kissing her. It wasn't the wild, hot, passionate kisses she remembered best, but tentative, hungry little tastes, as if too much at once might be too much to bear. They were sweet kisses, and cruel, too, because for every need they satisfied, they awakened another. She wanted more. She wanted wild, hot, passionate. She wanted greedy demands, hungry promises, savage pleas. She wanted *him,* all of him, body and soul.

And all she got were sweet, cruel kisses.

When he pulled away, she touched him, her fingers twisting in the soft cotton of his shirt. ''Please, Easy,'' she whispered.

''I can't,'' he whispered back. ''Damn it, I can't.''

She was tempted to slide her hand lower, to prove to herself and to him that he most certainly could—that the body was willing. He just needed to work on the mind.

She didn't, though. *Seduce him,* Reese and Olivia had advised, but seducing him against his will wouldn't prove a thing, except that he was human. They both already knew that. He was human enough to fall in love, to make mistakes, to hurt others. Now he had to learn to be human enough to forgive himself.

With a sorry, sorry sigh, she slipped out of the small space the jamb and his body had left her and out the door. With the screen door safely closed between them, she looked back long enough to see him leaning his forehead against the door frame, his eyes closed, his expression exquisitely troubled. Then she hurried to her car.

Nothing ventured, nothing gained, she thought scornfully as she drove away. Well, she'd ventured something, and what had she gained? Nothing.

Just his too-sweet, too-brief kisses.

Which were more than she'd hoped for when she'd come here.

More than she'd had for six years.

In fact, right now they were damn near everything.

Chapter 7

Wednesday night's storm had amounted to nothing—a flash or two of lightning, a few sprinkles of rain and a lot of wind that had blown in, rattled things around, then blown out again. Thursday was bright, sunny and hot. Easy watched TV, took a nap, read a book, fixed both breakfast and lunch and cleaned up each time, and still had endless hours to go before Shay might return. He wanted her here—and was glad she was gone. He wanted to kiss her again and wished he never had.

He wanted to make love to her but didn't know if he could. If he should.

No, that wasn't true. He knew for damn sure he shouldn't. He'd never deserved her, had never been good enough for her, but that was even more true now. She needed someone to love, to share her life, to give her a family. Not someone trapped way out here by his own fears. She needed someone who would take her out, dance with her, spend time with her family and friends, help her in the café when necessary.

She needed someone who could lead a normal life, and that put him out of the running.

Impossibly bored, he shut off the TV and went onto the porch. He'd been up ten hours, and only one car, the mailman, had passed by on the road out front. Neighbors were scarce out here, which made the chances for company even scarcer. Not that he was looking for any—at least, none besides Shay.

She hadn't said she would come back this evening. If she didn't, he would drive into town, which would probably be better for her anyway. He didn't like her driving home alone at night, while he was most comfortable in the night. Plus, she had to get up early for work, while he was free to sleep until noon. Hell, for all the demands on his time, he could sleep around the clock.

For the first time in years, he'd had enough sleep.

He descended the steps, got his hat from the truck, then started walking. He had no destination in mind. He just wanted to go *somewhere,* to *be* somewhere besides there. Following the driveway, he counted his progress by sections of broken fence. By the time he reached the road, he'd counted eleven, and he'd uncovered a faint desire, buried deep inside, to fix them, to see the fence the way it had always looked before. He wanted to see the pastures filled with grass, not overgrown with weeds, and the barn standing straight and the yard as neat as his mother had once kept it.

Hell, he wanted his dream, with a few important omissions—no horses, no kids, no Shay. But without them, what was the point?

He looked down the empty road to the right, where it ran a half mile before disappearing into trees and hills. To the left it ran straight, too, almost all the way to Shay's little house—and to the left, it wasn't empty.

The three riders stayed together, though one's mount was capable of leaving the other two in the dust. He thought about turning and beginning the long journey back to the house, but one of the smaller figures chose that moment to stand in the stirrups and wave a red-and-white cowboy hat high above her head in greeting. Since it would be rude to walk away after a greeting like that and since they could catch him in no time, he leaned against the sturdiest of the fence posts and waited.

Elly and her sister urged their ponies into a trot and reached him a minute before their mother. "Hey, Mr. Easy," Elly said breathlessly. "Whatcha doing?"

"Taking a walk. I figured you'd be locked up in jail somewhere." And closer to twenty-one than five the next time he saw her. "Did you escape, or were you reprieved?"

She grinned ear to ear. "They don't lock little girls in jail. Hey, this is Emma. Don't she look just like me?"

He looked from one girl to the other. They might have been identical twins, but there were enough differences to easily tell them apart. Elly, he suspected, had never known a shy day in her life, while Emma was timid. Elly's hair stood on end, her clothes were mismatched and her face was dirty. Emma's outfit was color coordinated, her hair neatly braided like her mother's, and she could go straight from the pony's back to a birthday party without pause. Elly was a loud, bold tomboy, and Emma was a quiet, demure china doll.

"Say hello, Emma," Elly commanded. When her sister didn't obey, she leaned across and poked her.

"Hey, no playing until your feet are on the ground," Olivia warned as she reined in Buck beside them.

Easy shifted his gaze from the girls to their mother. "Are you lost?"

"Of course not," Elly exclaimed. "We just live right down there. And that land across the road is my daddy's— well, actually, it's my mom's—or maybe it's my uncle Ethan's. I don't exactly know."

"Elly." Olivia waited until her daughter looked at her, then politely, gently said, "Hush. Why don't you girls take this—'' she offered a backpack she'd slung over her shoulder ''—and ride up and leave it on Mr. Rafferty's porch?''

Once they'd started away, he asked, ''What is it you're leaving on my porch?''

''Apple butter, applesauce, apple pie filling. We had an abundant crop this year.''

He understood abundant crops. Even with only two trees out back, there'd been years when his mother had despaired of ever making it through their apples. She'd canned what she could, served them in some fashion at every meal and given them to the horses by the bushel. He also understood the work that went into canning apple butter, applesauce and apple pie filling. ''Thanks. I appreciate it.''

She nodded in response. After an awkward moment, he said, ''I was under the impression that I wouldn't see any of you again for—oh, I don't know, fifteen or twenty years.''

''You were mistaken. Guthrie doesn't pick my friends.''

He smiled faintly. ''And he also doesn't know you're here, does he?''

Her answering smile was brighter, more genuine. ''I'll tell him when he gets in tonight. I thought I might tell him something else, too. In fact, that's really why I'm here.''

''So it's not just the abundance of apple products.''

She dismounted and held Buck's reins loosely in one hand. ''I wanted to invite you to dinner.''

Rather than push his hat back so he could see her more clearly, he tilted his chin up and studied her from under the brim. Her face colored delicately under the intensity of his stare. ''To dinner.''

She nodded.

''With Guthrie.''

Another nod. ''I would invite Shay, too. And maybe Mary and Jim. And Reese and—''

''How many people do you think you can get in that house?''

Her blue gaze became steady, serene...and determined.
"As many as it takes."

To do what? That was the next natural question, but he
didn't ask. She would invite as many people as proved
necessary to pressure Guthrie into behaving civilly toward
him. And that, he suspected, was far more than the Harris
house—hell, than the whole damn town of Heartbreak—
could accommodate.

"I appreciate the gesture," he said quietly. "But forcing
him to be around me isn't going to settle anything. You
can't *make* him get over hating me."

"He doesn't—"

"Yes, he does. And I don't blame him. If he'd stolen
Shay from me, I'd feel the same way."

Now it was her turn to raise her chin. "He doesn't still
love Shay."

"I didn't mean to imply that he does."

"Or, I suspect, to imply that *you* do," she said with a
gentle smile.

Love Shay? Only for the best, and the worst, times of
his life. But how he felt about her now didn't matter. It
didn't change the fact that he had nothing to offer her or
anyone else. It didn't change the fact that life as he knew
it was over, that he hadn't yet found another life he could
live.

Scowling, he tucked his chin so he couldn't see her face
and she couldn't see his. "We're not talking about me.
We're talking about Guthrie."

"You two were so close and had such an impact on each
other's lives that I'm not sure it's possible to talk about
one without the other. So...dinner at my house Saturday
night. We'll make it a party."

"I don't do parties. I don't do people. And I don't force
someone who's made his feelings about me very clear to
deal with me in his own house."

"As I understand, in those fourteen years you were gone,

you did an awful lot of partying. You took an awful lot of chances.''

''And look at me now.'' *Better yet, don't look.*

She led Buck to the nearest fence post and looped the reins around it. Finding the animal uncomfortably near, Easy moved to the next section of fence to lean.

Pushing her hands into her pockets, she followed him. ''Whenever people in Heartbreak talk about you, the words they use most often are brash, reckless, cocky. When did you become afraid?''

Unconsciously his breathing had turned shallow. He deepened it, forced one long breath, then another. ''Accepting someone else's opinion doesn't make me afraid.''

''What *does* it make you?''

''An intelligent adult?'' he asked dryly.

''Don't you want this resolved?''

Of course he did. Shay and Guthrie had always been the two people he loved best, and the years without them had been miserable. But some things were impossible to forgive. If he couldn't forgive himself, how in the hell could he expect Guthrie—the real victim in this mess—to ever manage?

It was with relief that he watched the twins approach on their ponies. ''Look, Olivia, I appreciate the thought, but this isn't going to be resolved. Guthrie's not going to forgive and forget. He's not going to trust me or be friends with me again. He's a smarter man than that. And I would appreciate it if you wouldn't come back here again. It's not fair to him.''

She untied Buck and led him into the driveway again before gracefully swinging onto his back. Then she gazed down at him. ''You're a stubborn man.''

''These days that's about all I've got.''

''No, it's not. Play your cards right, and you can have Shay.''

He thought about last night, those kisses and her husky suggestion. *I could just stay here.* In his house, in his bed.

She hadn't known how badly he'd wanted to say yes, hadn't known that he'd wanted her more than he'd ever wanted. Even now he could feel her skin, so soft against his. He could hear her plea, taste her mouth, feel the heat.

Olivia was right. He could have Shay—at least for a night, maybe longer.

She was also right that he'd become afraid.

She gave a delighted laugh that drew him back into the moment. ''Judging from that look you're wearing, Shay's been holding out on me. And here I tell her *everything*.''

''We lefted the apple stuff on the porch, Mama,'' Emma said as she brought her pony to a stop. She shifted her gaze from Olivia to him, quickly away, then back again for another instant.

He wondered if it was the scar that made it impossible for her to hold a steady gaze, then reluctantly admitted that it was more likely his scowl. He'd managed to intimidate plenty of adults with it. What chance did a shy little girl have against it?

''Thank you, Emma. Mr. Rafferty, think about my invitation, will you?''

''You can call me Easy...and thinking about it won't change my answer.''

She smiled a pretty, womanly smile that reminded him of Shay. ''I don't believe I've ever called a man Easy before. At least, not to his face.''

''It's a nickname for 'Zekiel,'' Elly volunteered. ''See, Mom? E-Z-kiel. Easy.''

''I see, babe. Let's go, girls.'' She waited until the twins had moved on, then urged Buck forward. As she passed him, though, she got in the last word. ''Maybe thinking won't change your answer. But maybe *Shay* will.''

The café closed at eight o'clock. By 8:03 Shay was out the door. Her first purchase of supplies for Easy's house waited in her car, along with a change of clothes. Manuel's last order for the day, a large pizza loaded with everything, was tucked under her arm, the cardboard box braced between her wrist and hip. She quickly covered the distance to her car and was about to climb into the driver's seat when an old station wagon pulled in beside her.

Joelle Barefoot leaned across to roll down the passenger window. Shay bent down, arms resting on the door so she could see her. "How's it going, Joelle?"

"I can't complain. Are you, by chance, going to see Easy?"

"Yes, I am." She intended to have dinner with him, work on his kitchen awhile, see if he would kiss her again. She hoped he would, but she wouldn't be surprised if he refused. He was so damn stubborn.

But so was she.

"Can you take some stuff to him?" Joelle gestured toward the back seat, where a small square basket and three grocery bags leaned together. "I was planning to, but something came up."

Judging by the faintly embarrassed, faintly flustered look the normally unflappable Joelle wore, it was something involving Vince Haskell, Shay suspected. "I'd be happy to." She transferred the items from car to car, then bent at the window again. "Whatever came up, I hope it turns out well."

Joelle's smile was nervous and quickly faded. "I don't know. I guess we'll see. Thanks, Shay."

After she drove away, Shay slid behind the wheel, started the engine, then glanced at the items. There were groceries in the bags, clean laundry in the basket. She rubbed one hand over the jeans on top—faded, soft enough to mold perfectly to long legs, narrow hips, slender waist. In the first years they were together, she had liked doing his laundry. There had been something so intimate about their clothing being in as close contact as their bodies often were. At some point, though, the romantic foolishness had disappeared and laundry had become just a chore that had to

be done every week or so, always in a different town, often
in a different state.

Evidently the foolishness was back, because doing his
laundry held a certain romantic appeal again.

Smirking at her own thoughts, she drew her hand back
and heard the rustle of paper. She lifted the jeans and found
a small stack of letters. Placed under the jeans for safe-
keeping, to keep them from possibly falling out or blowing
away? Or hidden from a nosy delivery girl?

There were two letters addressed to him in care of Joelle,
both bearing Betsey's return address in the left corner. The
other items had been forwarded from the Raffertys' Houston address—a bank statement and a flat pink envelope of
the sort greeting cards came in. Shay fingered the edge of
the card. The writing was definitely feminine—lots of
swirls and loops—and the return address was South Dakota.
Hermosa.

Clarissa was from Hermosa.

Of course, she chided herself in all fairness, there were
a lot of cowboys from the Dakotas, and they'd known a lot
of them, just as they'd known plenty over the years from
Oklahoma. The rodeo circuit was a pretty small commu-
nity. If you spent enough time there, you met everyone.
And even if Clarissa had sent the card, it was none of
Shay's business. Even if he'd chosen to give her his address, while Shay had scrambled like mad and never uncovered it.

She carefully returned the mail to the basket, tucking it
between the woven side and the clothes, then backed out
of the parking space. She wasn't going to be jealous, she
counseled herself. After last night's conversation about
Clarissa, Hank and Tracy, she'd assumed that Easy had
never had a relationship with Clarissa, but all he'd actually
said was that he hadn't taken her with him the day he left
her. That didn't mean they hadn't hooked up later—and he
would have been perfectly within his rights to do so. He'd
been a free man, unattached and uncommitted to anyone.

She couldn't be jealous, not under the circumstances, certainly not with her track record.

And, truthfully, it wasn't jealousy curling inside her. It was hurt that he'd been reachable for other people, but not for her. He'd gone through a horrible, life-altering experience, and of all the people he hadn't wanted contact with, *she* had topped his list.

By the time she parked beside his truck, she was feeling more than a little blue. Still, she pasted on a smile as she carried the basket and the pizza to the door, where he met her. "Why don't you get some napkins and pop and we'll eat before we work," she said, handing over the load. "Oh, by the way, you've got mail in the basket."

She unloaded the groceries and supplies, put away the perishable food, then sat down at the table. The letters lay beside his plate, his mother's unopened, the other two neatly slit. While she chatted about her day and the customers she'd served that he knew, her gaze kept slipping to the pink envelope. She didn't mention it, tried to avoid even noticing it, but it commanded her attention, seconds at a time.

Finally, when the pizza was gone, he pulled the card from its envelope and handed it to her. Embarrassed that he'd noticed her interest, at first she couldn't bring herself to take it. "What—?" She tried to feign curiosity at his action, nothing more, but failed.

"It's a nice card. Look at it."

Slowly she took it. It was a very pretty card—pink flowers, crystal vase, lace tablecloth, with the sentiment, "Hope you're feeling better," in flowing script across the bottom. Inside was a poem better suited for a grandmother than a thirty-something cowboy, and it was signed in that same feminine hand. "Leo and Marnie."

She didn't know whether to feel relieved or embarrassed. She settled for both. "Who are Leo and Marnie?"

"A couple I met a few years ago. He's a bull rider. She's a rich kid from back East. They met when she was visiting a friend in Dallas who dragged her to Mesquite. They got married about three weeks later and have been traveling together ever since."

Closing the too-frilly card, she laid it carefully on the table. "I thought—"

"I know what you thought. You come in here babbling about everything in the world except the card you can't keep your eyes off. You thought it might be from Clarissa." Twining the fingers of his left hand around her right hand, he gave them a squeeze. "Apparently, I didn't make myself clear last night. I never had an affair with Clarissa. I never wanted one. I can't even remember the last time I saw her because it wasn't important. *She* wasn't important. Understand?"

She nodded, grateful for the assurance. Then, to cover her gratitude, she defended herself. "I don't babble."

"You always babble when you're nervous or upset."

And he knew exactly how to calm her. But there was no offer of kisses tonight. No gentle seduction. No giving her some other way to burn that energy. At least, not yet.

Tugging her hand free, she busied herself gathering napkins and emptying bits of crust into the empty box. "Even if it were from Clarissa, it wouldn't be any of my business. None of your affairs after I came home are my business."

"None of my affairs?" he echoed. "You make it sound as if I'd been as busy as you were."

She stilled, her hand hovering in midair over the table, the lingering echo of his words slicing through her, leaving hurt and shame in its wake. He muttered a curse, but it barely registered as she forced herself to think, to function.

"Jeez, I'm sorry. That was uncalled for."

Was it? she wondered as she carefully crushed the pizza box in half to fit into the wastebasket under the sink. Or was it nothing more than truth? She *had* been busy the last six years and had told him so herself. Busy trying to forget him. Trying to ease the pain. Trying to convince herself that *somebody* wanted her, even if he didn't.

When she faced him again, she gave him a tight smile. "It's okay. I chose to be less than discreet in my relationships. I can't complain when someone brings them up."

"Yes, you can. Shay—"

Faking a casual tone, she interrupted him as she began removing dishes from the cabinet. "I talked to Olivia today. She invited us to dinner Saturday."

His remorse faded under a fierce scowl. "I'm not going. I've already told her."

"I think it might be fun."

"*Fun.* Forcing Guthrie into a situation where he has to be friendly to someone he hates, and it might be fun." He shook his head grimly. "You do have a sick sense of humor."

She crouched on the floor beside him. "Don't you miss him, Easy? Don't you miss all the time you spent together, talking, dreaming, planning, doing nothing at all? Don't you miss knowing that he's there for you, that he'll *always* be there?"

"Of course I do," he said sharply as emotion bronzed his cheeks. "More than almost anything in the world."

Briefly she wondered if she might be the *almost,* if he missed her more than Guthrie. She wanted him to, wanted him to hate every hour that they weren't together—not physically, but emotionally. Mentally. Spiritually. But she put the selfish thoughts aside for the moment and concentrated on the issue. "Then go to him and tell him. Tell him you're sorry. Tell *him* you've missed him. Tell him you need him."

For a long moment he stared at her as if she'd just suggested that he dance naked down the streets of Heartbreak. Then his expression turned flat—empty and accepting—and he shook his head. "I can't."

For a time she stared at him, then abruptly she got to her feet and began removing dishes from the nearest cabinet. His short, stiff refusal wasn't born of stubbornness or pride. It was, very simply, God's honest truth. He literally *could not* go to Guthrie and say, I've missed you and I need your friendship now more than ever. Words were hard. Emotions were harder. And his absolute conviction that he didn't deserve forgiveness or Guthrie's friendship was hardest—most unyielding—of all.

Taking a deep breath, she let go of the subject, let the tension seep out, then turned with an armful of plates, saucers and bowls. "Where do you want this stuff?"

He shifted in the chair to fix his grim gaze on her. "How about in the cabinet where it belongs?"

"We're going to start on your kitchen tonight. We need to move everything out, at least for a day or two."

He looked so ill-tempered that at any moment she expected him to grumpily order her to forget the project, go home and leave him alone. She felt so blue that if he did, she would probably obey, go home and sulk in her bed about the decisions he'd made in their years together, the ones she'd made in their years apart.

But he didn't try to send her away. He got to his feet, pulled both chairs away from the table, then lifted one end and waited. She set her load on the counter and picked up the end closest to her, and together they carried it into the dining room next door.

It didn't take long to empty the cabinets. While he removed the last few loads, she brought in everything from the car, then went into his bedroom to change into old shorts and a paint-stained T-shirt. She came back prepared to work, kneeling on the bare wooden floor with a supply of sandpaper. She'd barely started before pausing to give him a look over one shoulder. "You're not helpless. Grab some sandpaper."

For an instant the expression on his face was startled, almost comical. Then he pushed away from the doorjamb where he was leaning and hobbled across the room. "What are you doing?" he asked grudgingly.

"*We* are roughing up the surface a bit so it'll hold the paint better. Just give it a light sanding." Keeping her gaze on the cabinet door in front of her, she conversationally pointed out, "You *aren't* helpless, you know—unless you choose to be."

He didn't say anything, but started on the upper cabinet at the end.

"Yes, you have some physical limitations, but who doesn't? I mean, there are things *I* can't do, or my mom or my dad."

The sanding from his end seemed to grow a little louder.

"It's only natural. We get older. We slow down. We—"

"Get three fingers amputated and God knows how many pins in our hips," he added snidely. "I thought you quit being a cheerleader sixteen years ago."

She wagged her square of sandpaper in his direction, shaking bits of dust into the air. "Not true. I was your own personal cheerleader for eight years."

For a time he was silent, paying particular attention—or so it seemed—to the corners of the raised panel that fronted the cabinet door. Then he glanced at her. "That's true. You were always there."

Always. For every rodeo, from the tiniest little makeshift show to the biggest, grandest National Finals performance of all. For eight years he had never climbed onto a horse or roped a calf without her right there, cheering him on. She had celebrated with him when he won, commiserated with him when he lost and prayed for him every time. *Please keep him safe. Please don't let him get hurt.*

Then he'd gone off without her and look what had happened.

"It meant a lot to be able to look up in the stands and see you there. I never had to worry because I knew you were worrying for me. And I always wanted to do my best because I knew you were watching. I wanted—" the sanding slowed, stopped, then started again "—I wanted you to be proud of me."

"I *was* proud of you." But the rodeo—the winning

times, the championships, the payouts—had been the least
of it.

"At the first rodeo after—" another pause in his work
accompanied the hesitation in his speech "—after I left
you, it came my turn. I was sitting there on Gambler, and
I looked up to the center left where you always sat, and I
couldn't find you. It seemed so odd—so *wrong*. I kept looking, and they released the calf, and Gambler shot off. He
unseated me right there." He gave a shake of his head. "I
didn't win a dime that day or any other for more than a
month."

She finished the front of the cabinet door, opened it, then
scooted around to do the back. Conveniently, it gave her a
clear view of him. "So why didn't you come back for me?
You knew where I would be. You knew where to reach
me."

"Because nothing had changed. I still felt guilty. I still
believed we didn't have the right to be together. I still
would have hurt you." His smile was crooked, unsteady
and short-lived. "Besides, you were home, where you
wanted to be. You'd bought the café. If I'd called and said,
'Hey, I can't rope worth a damn because you're not here.
Please come,' would you have given all that up and gone?"

She didn't hesitate, didn't dither over her response. She
looked him in the eye and quietly, deliberately replied, "In
a heartbeat."

In a heartbeat. Easy's fingers curled around the edges of
the sandpaper as he repeated the words silently to himself.
In a heartbeat he'd fallen in love with her, driven away
from her, damn near killed himself. In that same heartbeat—in less than a second—he could have gotten her
back. If he had picked up the phone, if he had called her,
if he had only asked…

The last six years would have been worth living. They
would have had some bad times, of course, but they'd always had more good ones. Maybe he would have retired.
Maybe they would have come back here, made their peace

with Guthrie, gotten married and started that ranch, that family. Maybe he would have been whole and healthy, with every dream he'd ever had. Maybe the accident never would have happened.

Or maybe it would have, and instead of injuring only himself and Gambler, he would have hurt her, too. The guilt surely would have killed him.

"Would it make you feel better if I told you, No, I wouldn't have gone?" she asked quietly.

He shook his head without looking at her.

"Good, because I'd rather not start lying to you at this late date."

Silence settled between them, broken only by the refrigerator's hum, the drip in the sink and the soft, regular scratch of sandpaper on wood. When his left arm grew tired—much quicker than should ever be the case for an able-bodied cowboy, he thought grimly—Easy looked at Shay, absorbed in her own work, then switched the paper to his right hand. It was an awkward process and the initial results were lopsided. Without three additional fingers to provide even pressure on the sandpaper, he was taking off the finish in uneven layers.

"I have a sanding block." Shay scrambled to her feet, dug in the bag she'd carried in and pulled out a wood block and a utility knife. She left them on the counter near him, along with a couple sheets of paper, then returned to her cross-legged position on the floor.

He ignored the block and concentrated instead on the paper he held. As long as the surface was flat, he could manage, he realized. It was a simple matter of laying the paper against the wood, then using both finger and thumb, along with his palm, to move it. It required no more effort than the usual way and gave the same results, and when he was finished, he felt as if he'd almost accomplished something.

Sure, he had. He'd sanded a lousy cabinet door. A four-year-old could have done the same, and faster. And it was a hell of a long way from sanding a cabinet door to doing anything that mattered. Like working with his horses. Roping a calf. Touching a woman.

Touching Shay.

The thought made his body tighten with desire, but the image that sprang to mind filled him with revulsion. Her body was so beautiful, her skin so perfect. She had escaped a rough-and-tumble childhood without even the tiniest of scars, while he... His mangled, deformed hand touching her smooth, unblemished skin would be an obscenity. She wouldn't welcome it. He wouldn't endure it.

Scowling, he switched the sandpaper to his left hand, shoved his right hand out of sight and wished, not for the first time, that he'd died in that damn crash.

But honesty forced him to admit that that wasn't true. The pain, the shock, the bitter disappointment, all of it had been worth seeing Shay again, talking to her, kissing her, watching her smile. If he'd died, he could have been spared a lot of suffering—his own and others'—but he would have died believing that she hated him. It was worth more than he could say to know that she didn't.

By nine-fifteen she was slowing down, and he caught her hiding more than one yawn. Tired himself, he put the sandpaper down, brushed the dust from his hands and clothes, then limped toward her. "Let's call it a night," he suggested, offering his left hand.

She wrapped her fingers around his and let him pull her to her feet. "We made pretty good progress."

"You did." She'd done two cabinets to every one of his and still had more energy. His arms felt as if they weighed a ton each, and his hip was throbbing from too much time on his feet.

"We did," she repeated, brushing her palms briskly over her clothes. "I'm going to change into my other clothes and wash up."

He watched her go into the hall, then turned to the sink to wash his hands and arms and splash cool water over his face. After drying off, he went to the bedroom to trade his dusty shirt for a clean one—and came to a sudden stop in the doorway.

He had assumed earlier that she'd changed clothes in the bathroom, that she would change there once again. He hadn't expected to find her standing beside his bed, her back to the door, her work shirt on the floor and her hot-pink T-shirt in her hands. As his throat went dry, she cocked her head slightly, made aware by something that he was there. The intensity of his stare? The sudden heat radiating from his body?

Or the sudden cessation of that damn shuffle that was his pathetic version of a walk these days?

He tried to turn away, but his feet wouldn't obey. His body wouldn't move. All he could do was stand there and stare at the long line of smooth, golden skin that curved and enticed its way down to the waist of her shorts. All he could think was that she was half-naked and right beside his bed. All he could want was her—to see her breasts, to watch while her nipples swelled and hardened, exactly the way his own body was swelling and hardening. He wanted to go to her, lower her to the bed, to sink deep inside her and fill her so full that all the men, all the hurt, all the years, were wiped away forever. He wanted to make love to her until they were too weak to move, and then he wanted to do it again. He wanted...

Slowly she turned, holding the T-shirt to her chest. Just as slowly she let it fall away. He stared. Didn't breathe. Didn't move. Didn't reach out in silent plea. He simply stared, like an adolescent confronted with his first living, breathing, half-naked goddess.

With slow, easy, achingly graceful steps, she closed the distance between them—walked right up to him, slid her arms around his neck and kissed him. Stunned, he kissed her back, sliding his tongue inside her mouth, greedily savoring the taste of her. He'd been so empty for so damned long, and she was so sweet, so hot and demanding, and he needed her so damned much!

He shifted so he leaned against the wall, and she moved with him, clinging to him, her breasts flattened against his chest, her long, lean thighs trapped between the heat of his. He was hard enough to fragment with one wrong—or very, very right—touch, hot enough to steam, needy enough to beg. For six years he'd been haunted by memories of this— tormented by the need for it. For six years he'd wanted her desperately, and now he could have her.

He raised his left hand to her bottom, lifting her against him, rubbing his arousal hard against her. With a groan of pure, raw pleasure, he raised his other hand to her face, to position her so he could deepen the kiss, so he could take her mouth as intimately, as completely, as he would take her body.

But something was wrong. Cold panic raced through him, warring with sexual torment. Freeing himself of the kiss, he dragged in a deep breath, then forced his eyes to open, forced them to focus on the source of the panic—on his hand, scarred, disfigured, offensive against the smooth, pale gold of her cheek.

Shuddering with revulsion, he moved her away. For one moment she clung, but he lifted her fingers one at a time, then pushed her an arm's length back. "Go home," he demanded, his voice harsh, louder than necessary.

For a time she was still, quiet. Then, her own voice heavy with certainty, she said, "I don't want to go home. I want to stay here. I want to make love with you."

"You don't know what you're saying." He stared at the floor, unable to raise his gaze, to see her so beautiful and half-naked and promising the very thing he'd wanted for so long. He didn't want to find out exactly how weak he was, to see exactly how little pride or dignity he had left to sacrifice to bring her back into his arms.

"I know exactly what I'm saying, Easy, but if you're having trouble understanding, I'd be happy to show you."

Her hand—slim, delicate, too damned perfect—came into his field of vision, and he snapped, "Don't touch me! Just get out! I don't want—"

She touched him anyway, her hand brushing his chest, cutting off the lie with a sharp intake of charged air.

"You don't want what, Easy? This?" She slid her fingers lower, over the waistband of his jeans, to his abdomen. "Or this?" For one torturous, all-too-brief instant, her hand cradled his arousal. The sensation was so foreign and yet so familiar, intimate, agonizing and incredibly sweet.

Then, in a withdrawal that made him groan, she pulled back. "Or do you just not want it with me?" she asked flatly.

Amazed that she could ask such a question, he raised his gaze to hers. "Look at me, Shay," he commanded, yanking his T-shirt over his head, unfastening his jeans and awkwardly stripping them off along with his briefs. He stood naked in front of her, feeling so angry, so cheated, that he trembled. "Take a good look at what you're asking for, and then tell me you still want it. Tell me the scars don't bother you *now*. Tell me that the idea of *this*—" he thrust his mangled hand in her face, forcing her to retreat a step "—touching you doesn't make you sick, because it damn well makes me sick! Wanting you makes me sick! Knowing that I could have you—" His voice quavered and dropped to a harsh whisper. "That makes me sickest of all."

She stared at him as the moments slid past, then slowly began shaking her head. "You're right, Easy. I don't want you like this. But the scars have nothing to do with it. I don't want a man who can pity himself the way you do, and I don't want a man who values physical perfection as much as you do. What if *I* were the one who'd been in an accident, if *I* had the scars and the hand and the limp? Would you find me so repulsive? Would the idea of making love with me sicken you?"

"Of course not—"

"So you're just such a better person than I am. It's nice

to know what you really think of me.'' Spinning around, she grabbed her shirt from the floor and pulled it on, then stopped beside him and for a moment just stared. ''We've always been damned good together, but you know what, Easy? Tonight could have been the best night of your life.''

Bending, she picked up the cane he'd dropped earlier and braced it against the wall, then fixed that cool, wounded gaze on him again. ''If you ever get over feeling sorry for yourself, give me a call. You know where to find me.''

As she walked away, he reached for the cane and curled his fingers around it so tightly that he thought the wood might splinter, but that was all he did. He didn't yell her name. He didn't go after her. He didn't beg her to stay.

He just held on to the cane and damned himself to hell.

Chapter 8

Shay held her emotions tightly in check. She drove a safe speed all the way home, closed the car door quietly behind her, walked sedately to the door and let herself in without slamming it behind her. Then she undressed, got in the shower and let out a scream that ricocheted off the tile walls before fading away.

He was an idiot. She was in love with an idiot, plain and simple. How in the hell could he care so much about his perceived lack of perfection that he would turn down the most exquisite lovemaking either of them had ever known?

Unless he didn't really care so much.

Unless it was her that he really hadn't wanted.

But he'd damned well wanted *someone*—and at the moment, she was the only one offering.

And he'd turned her down. He'd said the idea sickened him.

Tears filled her eyes and the knot in her throat threatened to choke her. She swore aloud, then viciously narrowed her thoughts to only what she was doing—scrubbing her hair, her face, her body. Drying herself, fixing her hair, redoing her makeup. Dressing in her sexiest, skimpiest barely there outfit. Driving twenty miles to Buffalo Plains and the loudest, busiest, most popular bar in town.

She eased onto a bar stool and ordered a beer before swiveling around to look over the crowd. It wasn't too shabby for a Thursday evening, and most of the men in the place, whether alone or with someone, were looking at her. Instead of getting an ego boost from the obvious interest, though, she just felt empty. She'd spent too many evenings in places like this. For eight years she'd always left with Easy. In the next six years, she'd been far less discriminating, and what had she proven? That other men wanted her even if Easy didn't. And what did that matter when *she* wanted only *him?*

The bartender brought her beer, and she turned back to pay him, then stayed in the same position, her back to the crowd. She shouldn't have come here. It was an old habit—a bad habit—that could only make her feel worse. She should forget the beer and go home and—

"Shay Stephens is back on the prowl. I thought I felt something different in the air tonight." Reese Barnett, still in uniform, slid onto the stool beside her. "I would ask how things are going with Easy, but the fact that you're here dressed like that is answer enough."

Though there was no censure in his voice—Reese had an appreciation for her look-at-me! clothes that Easy had never developed—she suddenly felt cheap, even vulgar, in the tight green dress. She wished for a jacket—or better yet, a heavy blanket—to hide under.

"Don't get too comfortable," she said. "I was just leaving."

He smirked. "I'll walk you to your car."

It felt as if every eye in the room was on her when she slid to her feet. She resisted the urge to tug the dress's hem one inch lower, knowing it wouldn't go one inch lower, as she led the way out of the bar. Outside, the chilly air made her shiver and cross her arms over her too-exposed chest.

"You want to talk?"

Not really, but Reese could offer something she was lacking—a male perspective—and so she accepted his offer none too graciously, along with a suggestion that they talk inside her car. There she started the engine, lowered the volume on the radio, then stared at the lighted gauges on the dash without really seeing them.

After a few moments Reese chuckled. "Okay, darlin', let me explain this concept of talking to you. You tell me what's wrong, and I give you my brilliant advice, and you say, 'Oh, Reese, you're so wonderful. Thank you for saving my life.'"

She leaned her head back and listened as a melancholy George Strait tune ended and a melancholy Garth Brooks began, then exhaled loudly. "Is looking the way you do really important to you?"

"Looking the way I do?" he repeated.

"The face, the body, the great hair." She made a sweeping head-to-toe gesture with one hand. "The package."

He was silent for a moment before responding. "I take it Rafferty's having a little trouble adjusting."

"He won't—" She sighed wearily, then blurted out, "He won't make love to me because he's not perfect. Because he's got all these scars and I don't. Because I've got all my fingers and he doesn't. Because I don't need a cane and my hip's not held together with pins and my hand's not ugly and his is. As if any of that matters! It's just so damned ridiculous."

"No, it's not."

His disagreement startled her, made her turn her head to stare at him.

He offered her a faint smile in the night. "It's pretty easy to reveal your imperfections to a stranger whose opinion means nothing to you, Shay, but it's damn hard with someone you care about. If a stranger's turned off by your injuries, so what? But if the person you love is turned off by them— Hell, where do you go from there?''

Did Easy think that was what had happened? *Take a good look at what you're asking for,* he'd demanded, *and then tell me you still want it. Tell me the scars don't bother you now.* And she hadn't told him. Instead she'd acted sanctimonious and hurt and stormed out. Why hadn't she simply done as he wanted—looked, and then said, Yes, I want you. No, they don't bother me.

Because her feelings had been hurt. Because he'd thought she was shallow enough to care whether his hand, when it caressed her, had five fingers or only two. Because he'd thought she could look at him and see only the scars and not the man she'd loved damn near half her life.

Because he'd made her wonder what he saw when *he* looked at *her.* Did he see the woman he'd once loved…or simply someone he found attractive? And if it was the latter, how would that look change, how would those feelings change, if she gained weight? When her hair started turning gray? When wrinkles began forming around her eyes?

''He's lost a lot, Shay,'' Reese said quietly. ''I'm surprised he's dealt with it as well as he has. Cut him some slack. Give him some time to realize that you're accepting him the way he is. Give him some time to accept himself the way he is.''

''He's just so damn stubborn.''

''Good. In his situation, that's got to be a major plus.''

It probably had been, she reflected. Granted, he'd been too stubborn to stay in the rehab hospital as long as they'd wanted, but he'd also been too stubborn to die when his injuries would have made it so easy. He'd been too stubborn to accept the doctors' prognosis that he would probably never walk again. He'd been stubborn enough to survive this whole horror.

Now he just needed to be stubborn enough to start living.

''Patience is a virtue, Shay. For once, be virtuous,'' Reese said, then added with a grin, ''And when it finally pays off, remember that there are definite advantages to being on top.''

Especially with a man whose hip was held together with hardware not normally found in the human body. And was that another part of Easy's rejection? she wondered. Uncertainty over how well his battered body would function at that particular activity?

Easy Rafferty suffering performance anxiety? her little voice gasped. But why not? As ludicrous as it seemed—after all, he was the best lover she'd ever had—it was possible. If the man could think that a few scars and handicaps could make her not want him, then anything was possible.

Including dealing with those insecurities.

Straightening in the seat, she then batted her lashes. ''Oh, Reese, you're so wonderful. Thank you for saving my life.''

''That's what the county pays me for.'' He climbed out of the car, then bent low to look at her. ''Stay out of places like this, would you? It won't help, and it does nothing for your self-esteem.''

''I won't be back.'' She waited until he closed the door and stepped clear, then backed out of the parking space and headed back toward Heartbreak. She took her time, giving up the highway for back roads that meandered through woods and pastures and circled Buffalo Lake. By the time she reached Heartbreak, she was calmer, not much happier but a little more hopeful.

Make that a lot more hopeful, she thought as she turned onto her block. The black pickup in her driveway was impossible to mistake, even in the night. She pulled into the driveway, then eased onto the grass beside the truck.

He wasn't inside the truck or waiting on the porch. There were no lights on in the house—besides, no one had a key but her and her mother. She went around back, the dew soaking her heels, and found him on the tiny square of patio that opened off the kitchen, hands in his pockets, staring at the horses in the pasture out back. The moonlight showed them clearly—three quarter horses, three paints. It also showed the longing on his face as he watched them.

Hugging herself against the cold, she stepped onto the patio, and he immediately turned toward her. The longing didn't disappear. If anything, it grew stronger, deeper, even more wistful.

"Hi," she said, her voice little more than a husky whisper.

Reclaiming the cane from the lawn chair beside him, he took a step toward her. "You were right. I did know where to find you...sort of. You've—" he indicated her clothes with a gesture "—been out."

"Yes. I needed—"

"Someone who—who makes you feel wanted." He swallowed hard, but it didn't change the unsteadiness of his voice. "You don't have to explain." He moved as if he intended to leave. She quickly stepped to the side to block his path.

"I went to a bar in Buffalo Plains. I ordered a beer and didn't drink it. I didn't speak to anyone in there except Reese, who escorted me to my car and told me to stay away from such places." Among other things.

He accepted her explanation with a nod, then his gaze slowly moved down all the way to her feet before coming back to rest on her face. "You're a beautiful woman."

She didn't respond. She'd been fortunate enough to hear the words before, but the only time they'd really mattered, the only time they'd made her *feel* beautiful, had been with him.

He gestured toward the steps leading to the back door. "Can we sit down?"

"Why don't we go inside?"

"I—I'd rather talk out here. Why don't you get a coat?"

She found the back door key on her ring, let herself into the kitchen and walked through the darkness to her bedroom. Instead of a coat, though, she took the comforter from her bed, wrapped it around her and returned. He was already seated on the steps, his left leg stretched out. There was just enough room for her and the comforter to join him.

As warmth seeped through her, she waited for him to speak. Of course, the words didn't come easily. Important words didn't, she'd discovered in their years together. Words like *I'm sorry, I love you, I need you, please forgive me*. Words like, *Forget Guthrie and come away with me*. And *Goodbye* must have been extraordinarily hard for him, because he hadn't said it at all. He'd simply let his leaving speak for him.

Finally, his gaze still on the horses, he broke his silence. "Do you remember when you first started traveling with me?"

Though he paused, an answer wasn't necessary. How could she possibly forget the most incredible time of her life—the happiest, the saddest, the most promising.

"One night I'd won a hefty payout—somewhere in Idaho, I think—and we'd gone to a party with friends to celebrate. After watching me with them for a couple of hours, you made the comment that I was all surface and no substance."

The memory brought a faint smile that she tried to hide by dipping her chin deeper into the covers, but he saw it. "What? You didn't remember that?"

"I did. I'm surprised you did. After all, at the time, you were, ah, otherwise occupied." They'd *both* been occupied—parked on a side street, too eager to wait the ten minutes it would take to reach the motel. She'd been sitting astride his hips, riding him as surely, as easily, as any cowboy had ever been ridden, and he...he had been enjoying it. *Tremendously*.

For the first six months they'd been like that all the time—greedy, impatient, tearing off each other's clothes whenever they'd had the slightest chance of privacy. At first she'd mistaken their constant craving for passion, for proof of how deeply they loved and needed each other.

Later she'd realized it had been something darker that drove Easy—the need to assure himself that they'd done the right thing in running off, the effort to keep the guilt and the doubts at bay.

He smiled faintly, too, no doubt remembering exactly what he'd been occupied with. But his smile faded more quickly than hers when he returned to the subject. "You were right. With me, what you saw was all you got. No commitment, no friendship, no loyalty, no affection beyond the most superficial. Men liked me because I was damn good at what I did. Women liked me because I was handsome and charming and looked like I could show them a good time. It was all surface."

His voice quavered, and he broke off to steady it with a couple of deep breaths. Before he started again, he turned to look at her. The bright moon showed the scarred side of his face in exquisite relief and cast the handsomely perfect side in shadow. "I'm not good at anything anymore, Shay. I'm not handsome, I've forgotten how to be charming, and I don't know if I can show *anyone* a good time. The surface is destroyed, and you were right. That's all there was. There is no substance."

She shifted to the right so she could gaze at him. "For the record, Easy, I said you were all surface with *them*. You wanted to be that way with them, because if they didn't get close, then they couldn't hurt you, and you'd already been hurt too much."

After a moment's silence she asked, "Do you know when I realized how incredibly handsome you were? It was my birthday—when you kissed me in my mother's kitchen. Until that moment, you were just Easy—my buddy, my partner in crime, the kid I used to take baths with when we were little. If I'd given it any thought, I would have said you were cute—not my type, but cute. It wasn't until I realized that I had feelings for you that you became not only my type, but downright handsome. The more I loved you, the more gorgeous you got."

The look on his face was thoughtful, as if she'd scored a few points, but also wary, as if he still had plenty of doubts.

Taking a deep breath, she tried again. "Do you know why I loved you?"

"Because you were young and foolish, and I made you promises I couldn't keep."

She elbowed him gently in the ribs. "Because when I walked into a room, you got this look as if my simply being there made your life better. Because we could drive two hundred miles without saying a word and it was a sweeter, more satisfying way of passing the time than anything I'd ever done before. Because every time we made love, you acted as if I'd given you something you'd always, always wanted, something so precious you couldn't put a price on it. Because you treated your horses with gentleness and respect, and because you treated the people you came across just as well."

She leaned against his shoulder, and he automatically raised his arm to wrap around her. That single act did more to raise her temperature than all the comforters in the world. "People didn't like you because you were handsome and charming and good at what you did, Easy. They liked you for the same reason I loved you—you were a good man. You *are* a good man."

Easy silently coaxed her head onto his shoulder, then rested his cheek against her hair. Gleaming with moonlight, it felt like cold silk and smelled of fond memories and old sorrows.

He felt awed that she could speak so well of him after all his mistakes, and blessed that he could hold her like this after all the times he'd pushed her away. He wished she was right, though, wished he really was a good man, one who deserved a woman like her.

He wished he wasn't greedy enough, needy enough, to take her anyway.

"I drove past Buffalo Lake tonight," she murmured.

"You know what? I wouldn't change a thing. Even knowing how it would end, even knowing that we were both going to get our hearts broken, I wouldn't change it at all."

She was more generous than he was. If he could, he would change a lot of it—every harsh word he'd ever spoken, every time he'd hurt her, every time he'd made her cry. He sure as hell would have changed the way it ended. Given the opportunity to live it again, he would never let it end. Not until—as the wedding vows he'd refused to take had promised—*death do us part.*

Swallowing hard, he lifted his hand—his ugly, disfigured hand—and raised her chin. She didn't flinch when it— when he—touched her. She didn't pull away or startle or even seem to notice anything except that he was touching her.

"Shay…" He stroked her jaw with his thumb, brushed it across her full bottom lip, watched her lashes flutter. "I want to make love to you, but I don't—I don't know—my hip—"

She rubbed her cheek against his palm, reminding him of a cat seeking pleasure. "Remember Custer?"

"The general, the town or the bull?" He remembered— sweet hell, yes. That one night had given him a whole new appreciation for the state of Oregon. When it was over, he wouldn't have been surprised to find scorch marks on the sheet and singed places on their bodies.

Wearing a smug smile, she rubbed again. "You were so banged up that night that you could barely move, but you told me what to do and how to do it. All you had to do was lie there on your back, and it was amazing. Well, darlin', all you have to do tonight is lie back. I'll handle the rest."

Lie back. I'll handle the rest. And how much pleasure would she find in that? Doing all the giving while he did nothing but take?

In Oregon, he remembered, she'd found enough pleasure to make her weep.

"It's late," he murmured, gazing into her eyes, "and there's a storm blowing in. Maybe I could stay here tonight."

Her gaze never left his as she replied, "The sky is as clear as a bell. See?"

"Wrong kind of storm. Se—" The last word was lost as he kissed her, taking her mouth gently when gentleness was the last thing in the world he needed. She opened to him, welcomed his tongue, brought her hands up to touch him. Gentleness was the last thing she needed, too, he thought as she sucked hard at him, as her hands immediately sought bare skin under his T-shirt, as she struggled out of the confining blanket to strain against him. His fingers aching for the warmth of her skin, he fumbled with the blanket and her dress. She fumbled with his own clothes.

After a moment he ended the kiss, touched his forehead to hers and laughed. He hadn't laughed in so long, and it felt almost as good as her body, long and lean, against his. "Is it just me, or were we better at this clothing thing when we were younger?"

Slowly she stood up, sliding over him all the way. "Come inside—" she invited "—and I'll show you just how good I am at this clothing thing."

While he eased to his feet, she climbed the steps and sashayed through the door. Inside, she turned on one dim light—for him, he knew, since she knew her way through the dark—then started for her bedroom. He stayed far enough behind her to appreciate the view, and with her mile-long legs and that impossibly short dress, it was quite a view. If he hadn't been hard already, one look at her would have done it for him.

He followed her into the bedroom, where she was closing the blinds at the windows. When she finished, she turned to face him, and for a moment they simply looked at each other. There wasn't much light in the room—just what spilled in from the kitchen—but it was enough to see. Enough to feel vulnerable.

"If you have any second thoughts…" He watched her jaw tighten, saw the glint come into her brown eyes and changed the last part of his sentence. "I'd be happy to dispel them for you."

Her jaw relaxed, her eyes softened, and her mouth curved up in a sensual smile. "No second thoughts," she promised. "Not for either of us."

He crossed the room to her, and she moved, too, meeting him at the bed. His arms went around her waist, hers went around his neck, and they moved together naturally, perfectly. She pressed a kiss to his jaw. The next landed on his cheek, and the third landed on his ear, where her mouth lingered, tracing, nibbling, biting, sending shivers down his spine.

Cupping her face in his hands, he took her mouth again, greedy, demanding. It was a brief kiss, followed by more— hot, quick, hungry. Together they maneuvered closer to the bed until he felt the mattress bump against his knees. After pulling his T-shirt over his head, she urged him down onto the bed. He lay back, the sheets cool against his heated skin, and her perfect, slender fingers unfastened his jeans, guided them down, treated him to a fleeting, intimate caress that dragged a groan from deep inside.

Once he was naked, she joined him, one knee on either side of his hips, still fully dressed. Leaning over him, she left kisses along his chest, suckled his nipples and made them swell, tormenting him with full-body, silk-and-satin caresses so soft, so tantalizing, that he couldn't tell where her dress stopped and she began, where she stopped and he began.

When the pleasure became more than he could bear, when he thought he just might explode right there, she sat back, her bottom snug against his groin. Her fingers curled around the hem of her dress and his fingers curled into the sheet underneath him. She slowly peeled the dress away, revealing slender hips clad in deep crimson silk, a narrow waist, full breasts, long, strong arms. When she pulled the dress over her head, it left her hair looking as if she'd just crawled out of bed after a long, hot night.

She looked damn beautiful. Sexy. Too good for him.

But he could damn well try to be better.

She had to move aside to slide that bit of crimson silk off, then she eased, inch by inch, back into place, took him breath by breath deep inside her. Her body clenched around his, stretching, yielding to fit him snugly. If he were a lesser man, that alone—those exquisite little tremors—could finish him. As it was, they made him groan, made a cold sweat pop out across his forehead even as they turned up the heat.

Once she'd taken him completely, she leaned forward, resting one hand on either side of his head. "What do you want me to do?" Her voice was soft, thick, and her brown eyes were hazy.

"D-do?"

"Do you want me to stay like this? Or would you prefer that I do *this?*" She moved her hips in one long easy stroke, withdrawing until they were barely touching, then taking him again in another long easy move. "Or maybe you'd like—"

He grabbed her hips with both hands and guided her into a torturous rhythm that made her breath catch in her chest, that made his nerve endings start to quiver. With his lungs burning, his muscles straining, he didn't even consider trying to hold out. His eyes open just enough to see her, he surrendered to the torment, surrendered to her. He did exactly what she'd advised.

Lie back. I'll handle the rest.

And she did it exquisitely.

"'Handle the rest.'"

Shay thought about lifting her head from Easy's shoulder to give him a questioning look, then decided it would require too much effort. She considered moving to the side to curl against him, but had spent too many years missing this sort of full-body contact with him—and she did mean *full.* He was still hard inside her in spite of that terrific climax that had made him cry out and arch against her, that had been sweet enough to bring tears to her eyes.

So instead of moving, she settled for turning her head to the side enough to see him through a fringe of her hair. "Hmm?"

"You said you would handle the rest. You didn't say that that translated to damn near killing me with pleasure."

She managed to raise one hand enough to shove her hair back before she smiled sleepily at him. "You complaining, cowboy?"

"Hell, no," he said fiercely. "I've waited six long years to feel that way again."

Six long, lonely years—longer for her, lonelier for him. She wished she'd waited, too—wished she hadn't tried to replace him with any man foolish enough to try. She'd known from the start that it was impossible, but she'd kept trying and failing.

She hoped to God she wouldn't ever have to try again.

"Shay." He brushed his hand over her hair, then let his fingers slide over her jaw. "I'm so sorry. You're the one person in the world I should have bent over backward to make happy, and instead I went out of my way to hurt you. It seemed so wrong that we should be happy at Guthrie's expense. If he was suffering, I thought we should suffer, too, and so I..." He drew a shaky breath. "I treated you badly, and I regret it more than I can say. I'm sorry."

She blinked to keep the tears from seeping into her eyes. "So you didn't find me pathetic, after all."

Even in the dim light, it was easy to read the astonishment in his expression. It turned to shame when he remembered the comment he'd made the first time she'd found the courage to visit him. *No matter how badly I treated you, you kept coming back for more. You always were pathetic that way.* "God, no. I was just trying to make you go away. I didn't want you to see me like this. You're so beautiful, and I'm— I didn't want your pity. I couldn't bear it.''

She carefully eased into a sitting position, braced her hands lightly on his flat belly, shifted her hips slightly along the length of his arousal. ''The only pity I'll ever show you is when your skin is slick with sweat...'' She bent to kiss his chest, to make his nipple pucker.

''...and your heart's about to pound right out of your chest...'' Lengthening her strokes, she withdrew farther, took him deeper, held him tighter.

''...and your muscles are taut and your nerves are wound tight...'' Trailing her fingertips across his stomach, she watched the bronzed skin ripple and quiver.

''...and you can't see...or hear...or feel...or think...or know anything...'' He raised his hands to her breasts, rubbing, teasing, and her own vision went blurry. Her tongue felt thick, and the words kept slipping from her grasp as she took him faster, as *he* took *her* harder.

''...except...'' She dragged in a deep, desperate breath of superheated air that threatened to make her melt and searched for words lost in a rush of helpless, whispered pleas as he slid one hand between their bodies.

''...except how good it feels—oh, yes, there—'' She gave a great sigh as he found the one tiny place where she needed him most, and bliss turned quickly to pain, then back again.

''...and how much you want it...'' His muscles clenched. Hers were throbbing. Holding her hip with one hand and pleasuring her with the other, he thrust heavily into her, driving her closer, closer...

''...and how—'' her voice was frantic ''—you're going to—please, Easy, oh, please—''

And, taking pity on her, he did.

When the bedside alarm went off early Friday morning, Easy knew immediately where he was, and with whom, and why. Without opening his eyes, he flung one arm out, located the alarm and punched buttons until the beeping stopped, then he carefully eased onto his left side to face the woman who'd slept the last few hours curled against his back.

She looked tired, gorgeous—like the answer to every dream he'd ever dreamed, to every prayer he'd ever prayed. She was an incredible woman, and she'd long been *his* woman. *If* he could be man enough to claim her.

His mouth quirked in a half grin. She'd put more than a few doubts about his manhood to rest last night. He *could* make love to a woman—maybe not in the same way he used to—but he could do it quite well.

Maybe that was the key to the life he was looking for. Maybe it would be different from his old life because of his injuries and limitations, but maybe it could be a *good* different. Maybe it could even be better than his old life.

Behind him the clock began beeping again. He reached back, found it, followed the cord down and yanked it from the wall. Letting it fall to the floor, he settled in again to watch Shay sleep. He would wake her soon—wouldn't make her late for work, unless of course, she wanted to be late—but he needed these few minutes. Needed to think. Needed to marvel.

Three, maybe four minutes had passed before he realized that she was awake. It wasn't anything overt—her eyes didn't move underneath her closed lids, her lashes didn't flutter, her breathing didn't change. It was an awareness— hers, his, both. He *knew* she was awake.

"If you don't open your eyes, I'm going to kiss your nipple," he warned in a husky, heavy voice.

She didn't open her eyes, but pushed back the covers, reached blindly for his hand and guided it to her breast. "Please do," she whispered. "Make it hard. Then *I'll* make *you* hard."

"You already did that, darlin'." The instant he'd awakened and felt her warmth against him, the ache had started. Her breast was soft, her nipple flat and even softer. He caressed around it, awakening it, rousing it, then, careful to touch her nowhere else, he dragged his tongue across it. Instantly it swelled, straining to meet his next slow stroke.

Shay's sigh was full and satisfied. "I love when you play with my breasts," she murmured sleepily.

"We could play all day if you didn't have to get ready for work soon."

"Says who? I'm the boss, remember?"

"And what would you tell your employees?"

"That I got lucky. I got Easy."

He licked her nipple again, then watched it pucker. "Are you sure—" taking it in his mouth, he scraped his teeth across it, then gently bit it "—you want to tell them that?"

She smacked him on top of the head, making him release her nipple to yelp. "Hey, what was that for?"

"For asking a stupid question. I don't care if everyone in the county knows what we did here last night, because one of these days, Easy Rafferty, I'm going to marry you."

He propped his chin on his hand and looked at her. "Is that right?" he asked mildly.

"Yes, it is. When you're marriage material, of course, which you're not now."

"And what would it take to make me marriage material?" Though he asked the question lightly, he was dead serious about the answer. He'd loved her damn near half his life. Every dream he'd ever had involved her, marriage and kids. Every life he'd ever wanted had included her in his bed, at his side, part of his soul.

He didn't know if he could become what she needed, but he damn well intended to try.

"First—" With gentle fingers, she guided his mouth back to her breast, then shuddered as he suckled her. "Second, you've got to accept yourself the way you are and stop regretting that you're not the way you used to be. Third—"

Moving carefully, testing his usual morning stiffness against a-long-night-of-incredible-sex stiffness, he braced himself above her, parted her thighs and easily sank inside her.

"Th-third—"

"Shh." He kissed her gently. "Set your rules later. Right now just let me make love to you."

"Oh, yes," she sighed happily as she wrapped her arms around his neck.

It was a not-entirely successful experiment. Slow and easy he could handle, but when it came to the serious, hard-and-deep-and-damn-are-we-going-to-survive-this part, it was Shay's turn to take control again.

But who did what didn't matter. What mattered was that they did it together.

And someday, he thought with a wry smile, he would say that and fully believe it.

Twenty minutes later he stepped out of the shower in her god-awful electric-blue bathroom and watched her apply makeup while he dried off.

"What are your plans for today?" she asked, putting on lipstick, then fluffing her hair with her fingers.

"I thought I'd do a little work in the kitchen."

"Don't overdo it. You're not as young as you used to be."

He stepped close behind her and breathed deeply of perfume, powder and all her other scents. "It's not the years, darlin'."

Holding his gaze in the mirror, she raised one hand to touch his throat. "I know. So take it easy. I'll come out when I get off work."

"I'll look forward to it." Easing away, he got his cane and left her to finish while he dressed in the bedroom.

He hoped none of her neighbors were out when they left. Luckily, they weren't. Shay walked to the truck with him, waiting patiently while he climbed inside. "I'll see you."

He nodded, let her walk away a few yards, then called, "Shay?" When she turned back, he swallowed hard. "Thank you."

''You're welcome. For what?''

Letting me back into your life. Making my life better. Making me feel like a man. Those were only a few of the answers he could give. He settled for the most basic of them all. ''Everything.''

She smiled brightly. ''You're welcome…for everything.'' She was still smiling when he drove out of sight.

So was he.

The day started early in Heartbreak. Though it was only six o'clock, lights were on in most houses and traffic was as steady as it ever got. Ranchers and farmers were up before the sun, so people who dealt with them were also up early.

As he passed the Rocking S, Shay's folks' place, he saw Jim Stephens out back by the barn. As he approached the Harris place, he knew Guthrie would be up, too—had probably already eaten breakfast, kissed his wife and kids goodbye and gone out to tend to the endless chores that ranching required.

If things had turned out differently, Easy would have been doing those chores with him. Sometimes he wished desperately that things *had* turned out differently. He missed Guthrie—missed the friendship, the bond, the shared history. Most of all he missed knowing that Guthrie was there for him, no matter what. He'd had that certain knowledge for twenty years and had found it impossible to replace.

But not even that kind of friendship would be worth giving up Shay.

As he came to the beginning of Harris property—he knew those two hundred ninety acres as well as he knew his own place—he moved his foot from the gas pedal. The five-strand barbed wire fence completely encircled the ranch except at the gate, where pipe replaced wire for a few yards. He and Guthrie had cut and welded the *H* that topped the arch in junior high, and they'd made it crooked, but Guthrie's mom had pretended not to notice and let them weld it in place, anyway.

He was a little surprised Guthrie hadn't junked it in the years since.

The truck rolled to a stop, and he realized his foot was on the brake. The few times he'd driven past, he'd made a point of not looking. Now that he was here, he did.

The house where he'd spent practically as many nights as in his own was little changed—older and a bit more worn, but weren't they all? The cabin Guthrie's stepfather had built for his old bat of a mother still stood at the west edge of the yard, and the barn and corrals out back were in as good shape as ever. While it didn't have the look of a particularly prosperous ranch, it looked settled and well cared for, which was a damn sight better than could be said of his own place.

With a sorry sigh, he moved his foot from the brake to the gas, ready to go on home and spend yet another day without Shay. When the truck moved, though, it wasn't headed west. Instead, as if guided by hands other than his own, it turned into Guthrie's driveway.

He parked beside the pickup already there and reluctantly climbed out. At the sound of his arrival, the man he'd come to see had stepped out of the barn and now watched. Even across the distance, it was plain to see that there was no welcome in his expression.

Easy reached inside for the cane, then closed the door. Guthrie remained where he was, hands on his hips, not even interested enough to meet him halfway.

That was okay. It might take him a while, but he could walk that far.

He hadn't gone more than twenty feet when Guthrie turned away and went back in the barn. Easy's thin smile was tinged with bitterness. His dad always did that—always managed to be looking elsewhere whenever Easy was doing something. It had pained Bud to see his only kid, his rodeo-champion kid, moving like a cripple three times his age.

He thought his son's limitations made him less of a man. So did Betsey, and they'd treated him accordingly.

It was a damn good thing Shay didn't share their opinion. Even if Guthrie did.

Finally he reached the barn doors. He paused long enough for his eyes to adjust, then crossed the few feet to the tack room on the left.

Guthrie was there, his back to the door, his hostility as obvious as the dust that drifted in the air. Easy's hand tightened around the head of the cane. Now that he was here, he didn't have a clue what to say. *I'm sorry* seemed so damned inadequate, but what else did he have to offer?

Purring loudly in the stillness, a cat wrapped its way around and between his feet. He glanced down at a familiar orange body and found his voice—at least, a rusty version of it—to comment, "That looks like Ginger."

The cat had become tired of him and, with stately feline grace, crossed the room to Guthrie, leaping onto the bench he stood in front of, rubbing against his arm. "Ginger's been dead a long time," he said grudgingly as he stroked the cat from head to tail. "Pumpkin's probably related to her."

"Pumpkin?"

"She's orange. Pumpkins are orange." His tone was short, his manner sharp, even as he added, "The kids named her. They've named damn near everything around here—even the snake that visits Liv's garden."

Easy shifted to lean against the door frame, taking a little weight off his bad hip. "I can't believe you've got kids. It makes you seem...grown-up."

Guthrie flicked a scowl over him before turning his attention back to the saddle in front of him. "I grew up pretty quick. I didn't have much choice."

Feeling the sting of those last words, Easy drew a deep breath and smelled dust, leather and old wood. There was hay at the far end of the barn, stalls that needed mucking and feed for the horses—all familiar smells that brought back fond memories. They made him feel homesick, not for a place, but for a time.

But they couldn't go back in time. The best he could hope for was an adult version of the best years—and friends—of his life. At the moment it didn't look encouraging.

Seeking another reason to break the silence, he glanced around and caught a glimpse of the horses outside in the corral. "Buck looks good."

"He *is* good—the best I ever had."

"Remember the day I brought him home? When we unloaded him from the trailer, everyone scattered for the nearest fence."

"Except you."

Easy smiled faintly at the memory. Buck had been wide-eyed and terrified that cold January morning. All he'd ever known from the humans in his life was pain, and he hadn't expected anything else from Easy. He'd done his share of harm to the men foolish enough to think that training a horse meant breaking his spirit, and he'd been ready and willing to defend himself that day. It hadn't been necessary.

"You bet twenty bucks that I couldn't calm him," he said quietly.

"And Shay bet twenty bucks that you could." Slowly Guthrie turned, leaning back against the bench. Face-to-face, the tension between them seemed to double in intensity. "Were you involved with her then?"

His fingers clenching the cane tighter, Easy resisted the urge to hedge. "I was in love with her," he admitted, his gaze steady and unflinching. "We hadn't done anything about it."

"And when *did* you do something about it?"

"The day we left."

"So you were in love with her at least four months, and you never slept with her, never kissed her, never did *anything?*" Guthrie sounded skeptical and looked it, too, as he shook his head in disgust.

"I kissed her once...on her birthday. I never touched her again until the day we left. How could I? She belonged to you."

"Yeah, right." Guthrie's snort was scornful. "That didn't stop you from running off with her."

Easy pushed away from the door's support and crossed half the room before stopping. "I came here for the wedding fully intending to watch her marry you, and then I was going to leave and never come back. But that day... I saw her alone for the first time in six months, and she— We—" He took a ragged breath. He was none too proud of what he was about to say, but it needed saying. "She would have gone through with the wedding, but I couldn't bear it. I begged her to leave with me—to leave you for me. I know it was wrong—I knew it when I did it—but I loved her and wanted her, and I didn't give a damn who got hurt if I took her."

After a long hard look, Guthrie turned back to the saddle. "Why didn't you come to me? Why didn't you tell me?"

"How do you do that? How do you tell your best friend you're in love with his girl?"

Abruptly Guthrie turned to face him again. "You don't fall in love with your best friend's girl—not if you give a damn about that friend."

"You think I did it on purpose? You think I *chose* to betray you like that? I would have given *anything* to not love Shay. I would have given *everything* to not do that to you. It wasn't my choice. It just—" His shrug was helpless, exactly the way he'd felt that day fourteen years ago. Helpless and frightened and ashamed...and relieved. So damned relieved that he wasn't losing her. "It just happened."

His words didn't ease Guthrie's skepticism. That was clear in his expression, his voice, his impatient gesture. "You loved her so much, but you couldn't marry her. You couldn't be faithful to her. You couldn't help but break her heart."

Regret warmed Easy's face and tightened his chest.

"You're right. I did hurt her. I just didn't seem to be able to stop it. Every time things got really good between us, I'd think of you and— It was wrong for us to be together, wrong for us to be happy when we'd had to hurt you to do it. So, since you weren't there to punish us, I had to do it for you."

All the fights they'd had, all the tears she'd cried, all the times he'd tried to drink away his guilt. It was a wonder anything had survived. They'd had so little good and he'd created so much bad. But he still loved her. She still wanted him. They had a chance, if he could put the past, and Guthrie, behind him. "For whatever it's worth," he added as he rested his hand on the saddle beside him, "I was never unfaithful to her. She knows that now."

Guthrie's gaze dropped to the saddle and Easy's hand. Resisting the urge to hide it, Easy left it where it was and let him look. He looked, too, rather than see the emotions— disgust, pity—that were sure to be on Guthrie's face. "Sometimes when I see that hand, I think it can't possibly be a part of *me*," he said with a little less bitterness than he usually felt. "But when it hurts, I feel the pain. When it can't do something, I get frustrated. It's mine, all right— the whole two worthless fingers."

"I was sorry to hear about the accident," Guthrie said quietly, and when Easy risked looking at him, that was all he saw—regret. Not pity. Not disgust. "Elly says you can't work with horses anymore. I'm sorry about that, too."

"That was all I ever wanted," Easy murmured, raising his hand, turning it to look from different angles. "To marry Shay, raise horses, raise kids."

"How many fingers you have doesn't have anything to do with marrying Shay or raising kids," Guthrie pointed out.

"I don't deserve her."

"You think I deserve Liv?"

"Yeah, I think you do."

"Lucky for me, she agrees with you." Guthrie's smile

faded as quickly as it had come. He picked up the saddle, snagged a bridle from a hook on the wall, then circled around Easy on his way to the door. There he turned back. "For whatever it's worth, I don't think there's any need to punish anyone for anything. I'd say we've all suffered enough." He looked away, then back and said the best thing he could have said—words Easy had needed for fourteen long years.

"If you love Shay and she'll have you, marry her and have those kids. Mine need someone to play with."

Chapter 9

Shay woke early Saturday morning, but not early enough to catch Easy asleep. Though the room was cold—they'd opened all the windows in the house last night to air out the smell of fresh paint in the kitchen—he stood at the window, wearing jeans and nothing else. He was staring out with that same wistful expression he'd worn when she'd found him watching Pete Davis's horses at her house Thursday night. She knew without looking what gave him that look—the empty corrals, the ramshackle barn. The broken-down home of his broken-down dreams.

Wrapping the blankets around her, she left the bed to stand behind him. His back was cold. Even the denim against her legs was cold as she opened her covers, then wound both arms and blankets around him. He cupped his hands over hers, turned his head to press a kiss to her forehead, then directed his attention outside again.

"Where is Gambler?"

The muscles in his back tensed, and the pressure his

fingers exerted over hers increased fractionally, then relaxed. "He's at my uncle's place in Texas."

"Why don't you bring him here?"

The tension returned and stayed. "I can't."

Couldn't bring him? she wondered. Couldn't care for him? Or couldn't bear to see what he'd done to him? "Well, then, Jeff Hendrix has a couple of paints for sale. Why don't you talk to him?"

"What would I do with a horse?" There was a sharp tone to his voice—edgy, almost fearful. It made her ache deep inside to think of the rash, reckless cowboy she'd loved for so long now afraid to be around a horse.

"Oh, I don't know." She pressed a kiss to his shoulder, then a little lower. "Maybe train him. Maybe ride him. Maybe just admire him."

"I can't train them anymore. I can't ride. And I don't want to admire them."

She tucked the covers into his hands, freeing her own hands to stroke his chest, to unfasten his jeans and slide inside for an intimate rub. "Who says you can't ride?"

"I can't even walk—" he caught his breath in a sharp gasp "—worth a damn. How in hell could I ride?"

"You're walking better every day. Besides, walking involves weight-bearing muscles, joints and bones all working together. Riding involves sitting." A major oversimplification, she knew, but considering how he was responding to her caresses, she didn't think he would notice.

"I...I can't." His breathing was ragged, his body rigid. "I *can't*."

"Whether you think you can or you can't, you're probably right," she murmured before kissing his ear. "I think someone famous said that."

He yanked her hands free, shucked his jeans, then turned so she was perched on the windowsill, her legs around his hips, as he sank deep inside her. For a time he simply stayed there, his cheek resting against her hair, and then he

gave a great sigh that shuddered through his body into hers.
"You're the best part of my life."

"I know," she agreed without smugness, because *he* was
the very best part of her own life.

"And I know you mean well, but you're wrong."

"Wrong?" Experimentally she rocked her hips along the
length of his arousal. "Does that feel wrong?"

"No. Hell, no. But you told me yesterday that I have to
accept myself the way I am. Not able to work with horses
is the way I am."

She rocked against him again, sending shivers through
them both. "No, Easy. Afraid to even try—that's what you
are. You were afraid to try to make love with me, and look
how well it turned out. You were afraid to talk to Guthrie,
and that was great, too. Now you're afraid to even get near
a horse. You're so afraid of seeing exactly what you've lost
that you can't let yourself see what you might still have."

"You're wrong."

"Prove it."

He slid his hands to her bottom and thrust deeper inside
her. The angle and position were just different enough from
lying in bed that his hip didn't hamper him at all. It was
only a few minutes before he finished in a slow, lazy climax
perfectly suited to a chilly Saturday morning, and only a
moment later that she joined him.

She started to lower her foot to the floor, but he caught
her leg, curving his fingers to the back of her thigh, flexing,
massaging, caressing. "I don't have to prove anything," he
announced.

"You and I have spent half our lives proving everything.
When did you change?"

He ignored her question—and her point. "The simple
fact is—"

"Gambler should be here with you."

Shadows turned his already dark eyes practically black.
"And what would he do here?"

"I imagine the same thing he's doing in Texas. Laze and graze and take life easy."

Slowly he let her leg slide to the floor, then pulled away from her, letting her keep the blankets for herself. While holding on to her, he had maneuvered a few feet away from his cane. Now he took one tentative, halting step, then another, to reach it. It was the first time she'd seen him walk at all without it, but he didn't seem to even notice.

He walked—beautifully, impressively naked—to the doorway, then turned back. "I don't want any horses here," he said flatly.

"Then what about cows?" she called as he disappeared into the hall. "You can raise cattle without ever getting on a horse."

His only response was the closing of the bathroom door. She listened to the shower come on, then tucked the blankets tighter and turned to look out. The main corral was in pretty decent shape. It was overgrown with weeds, but the fence, for the most part, was intact. There were a few boards down here and there, but nothing that couldn't be easily fixed. The barn looked pretty shabby and might not survive next spring's storms, but for now it would probably keep the rain out and provide decent shelter in the stalls that opened off the corral.

The place needed stock—horses, cattle. Hell, maybe even llamas. Whatever it would take to get Easy out of the house and into life. But he wasn't going to get them on his own. He was probably satisfied with the life he'd confined himself to, especially now that sex was a part of the bargain. He had no reason to change anything—no reason to expand his life outside these four walls.

Unless she gave him one.

There was no way she was going to contact his parents herself, but they would probably be thrilled to hear from Guthrie. Betsey and Bud had loved him like a son, and they'd hated her almost as much for hurting him as for seducing sweet, innocent Easy. If she told them that she thought it was important to bring Gambler to Heartbreak, they would—well, they'd do nothing, because they would never stay on the phone with her long enough to hear her out. But if Guthrie gave them the same message, they would be more than happy to tell him where the horse could be found and to arrange for him to be picked up.

And once they got the quarter horse here? What if Easy continued to insist that he didn't want any animals on the place? What if he refused to take care of Gambler? What if the guilt of seeing his beautiful, beloved horse crippled at his own hand was more than he could bear?

Maybe she should back off. Maybe, if she gave him time, he would come around. After all, when he'd first come here, he hadn't given a damn about anything. Now he wanted the house fixed up and he wanted her at his side. Maybe, eventually, he would feel the urge to make repairs and put the ranch to good use again. Maybe, after a while, he would want to start living a real life again.

And maybe she couldn't wait that long.

He returned from the shower, his hair combed straight back, a towel knotted modestly around his waist. "You planning to sit there naked all day?" he asked as he took clean clothes from the dresser and the closet.

"I might. You have any better suggestions?"

"Not at the moment. Ask me again after breakfast."

She watched him get dressed. He was slower than he used to be, but there was nothing wrong with slow and methodical. He realized she was watching when he started to tie his work boot and gave her a mocking smile. "Hard to believe I'm the same man who could expertly truss a calf quicker than most people blink, isn't it?"

"But you've got the belt buckles, the bank balance and the newspaper stories to prove it." She paused before asking, "Where are the buckles and the stories?"

"At Mom's house. I didn't need any reminders of what I used to be. She did."

Shay felt a surge of anger at Betsey Rafferty. If she'd

been more accepting of Easy's injuries, perhaps he would have been, also. If she'd encouraged him to get out, to do things, to make an effort to fit in and feel normal, maybe he wouldn't have come here to hide alone for the rest of his life.

"She meant well," Easy said as if he'd read her thoughts.

"She always did. Like every time she tried to convince you to dump me. Every time she insisted I was no good for you. Every time she invited you to visit but made it clear that I wasn't welcome, too. She always meant well, Easy. It's just that she meant well for *herself.* It was always *her* welfare she was concerned about. Not yours. Certainly not mine." She tasted bitterness and tried to swallow it away. "In the end, she won. You dumped me."

"The end hasn't come yet, darlin'. I'm here. I intend to be here forever." He finished tying the second boot and let his foot hit the floor with a thud. "So much for the fastest hands in the West."

Her smile was sweet, warm and felt damn near womanly. "Who cares about the fastest, cowboy? Slow hands and a gentle touch have a hell of a lot to offer."

"Want to prove it?"

She walked to the bed where he sat, bent low to brush her lips across his, then dropped the covers in a pile around him. Sashaying across the room as naked as he'd been earlier, she stopped in the doorway and smiled back at him. "Ask me again after breakfast."

After a quick shower, she dressed and joined him in the kitchen, where a pot of coffee was brewing. The morning light through the windows glinted off white cabinets and sunny yellow walls and made the appliances, the countertop and the floor look ancient in contrast.

"We'll do the floors last," she remarked as she retrieved two cups and spoons from the dining room. "I'd recommend white countertops and replacing or reconditioning the appliances."

"Why don't you buy new ones?"

"Why don't we? Let's drive into Tulsa today—" The wary, stubborn look that came into his eyes made her break off and take a breath for patience. "Easy, this is your house. I'm perfectly happy to give advice, but you should make the decisions yourself. You're the one who's got to live with them."

"You'll have to live with them, too. You're going to marry me one of these days, remember?"

"If you become marriage material, remember?"

"And to do that, I have to be willing to make a spectacle of myself." His voice was sharp with loathing for the idea. "I have to be willing to go to Tulsa with you and let people stare at me—or, worse, ignore me altogether because they can't bear to look at me."

The coffee maker stopped percolating, and she poured two cups of steaming coffee, then left them to cool. "No, Easy. You have to be willing to live a normal life."

"This life *is* normal."

"Hiding in your house? Seeing nobody but me and occasionally Joelle or the Harrises? Relying on me and five-year-old Elly for your social life?" She gave a shake of her head. "Easy, this life isn't normal for *anyone,* certainly not a healthy grown man."

"I'm not health—"

She raised one hand to cut him off mid-denial. "I've made love with you. Don't tell me you're not healthy," she warned. "You have a few problems—the worst of which is that you're afraid."

"I'm not."

"You are."

Easy took an unsteady breath. He *wasn't* afraid. He just had no tolerance for being the local freak. There wasn't any reason to subject himself to the stares, the talk, the pity. Accept yourself the way you are, she'd counseled, when what she'd really meant was accept himself the way she wanted him to be. What gave her the right to decide what was normal for him?

Nothing. But she sure as hell had the right to decide what was normal for herself, and she obviously felt that living with a man who had become a virtual recluse wasn't normal for her.

So the issue here wasn't really him, but her, and what he was willing to do to have her.

What *was* he willing to do? Go shopping in Tulsa?

It wasn't a bad place to start. A city that size was filled with strangers. If he knew anyone there, what were the odds of running into them in a few hours spent at an appliance store? Slim at best.

He drank a gulp of coffee even though it was still hot, though he hadn't yet added sugar and cream, and then he looked at her. ''All right. Let's go shopping.''

The smile that brightened her face once the surprise disappeared was worth the decision.

The reality of finding himself an hour later in Tulsa's biggest home supply store among strangers wasn't. He couldn't honestly say that everyone in the store was staring at him. Some glanced at him with total disinterest. Others never noticed him. But the salesman certainly found it easier to talk to Shay than to him. The woman who was interested in the same model refrigerator kept giving him surreptitious looks from face to hand to cane, and he knew damned well she wasn't thinking she'd like a few hours to play rodeo queen with him. And when he tried to make out the check for the appliances and the new countertop Shay had chosen, he struggled with the ink pen and the checkbook while everyone—salesman, clerk and other customers—waited impatiently.

Frustrated, he tossed the pen on the counter, tore the check out and wadded it, then slapped down a credit card. After scribbling an illegible signature at the bottom of the charge slip, he took the paperwork and stalked off as best he could.

"Easy." Shay hurried to catch up with him and caught his arm just as he placed the cane tip on the concrete floor. It slid and he slipped, losing his balance. If not for a teenage boy passing by, he would have fallen.

"Are you all right, sir?" the boy asked, increasing the heat that was already burning through him.

"I'm fine. Thanks," Easy muttered, his jaw clenched, a fierce scowl locked in place.

"Easy, I'm sorry," Shay whispered, reaching out again.

He raised his right hand to stop her, caught a glimpse of it and returned it to his pocket. "Don't grab me. Don't touch me. Let's just see if we can get out of here without making me look like a complete fool."

It was a long way to the front entrance, made longer by the Saturday morning crowd. Once they finally reached the door, they still had to cover half the parking lot to get to his truck.

"If you want to wait here—"

He glared at Shay, and she broke off and lowered her gaze. She looked sorry—sorry for him, sorry to be here with him. Well, she couldn't possibly be any sorrier than he was.

He waited for a break in traffic and got it when a white-haired man stopped and waved them across, then tapped his fingers on the steering wheel, impatient with their slow progress.

"You know," Shay began when they were halfway down the aisle, "you can get a parking permit to—"

Slowly he turned a cold, angry stare on her and, once again, she clammed up. When she didn't go on, he finished for her. "To let me park up front with all the other cripples?"

"Easy—"

"Don't 'Easy' me! That's what you're talking about—a handicapped permit! To give me special privileges because I can't even park in a damned space like a regular person!"

"There's nothing wrong with having special privileges

when you're entitled to them!'' she argued. ''We're talking about a stupid parking permit! How does that diminish you? How does parking all the way out in the north forty make you any less—''

He stopped walking, and slowly she did, too. For a long still moment they stared at each other, then he finished the sentence for her once again. ''Handicapped. Go ahead and say it, Shay. You're obviously thinking it.''

''I'm not, damn it, Easy!''

Handicapped. By anyone's definition, he was, of course. He'd known it for months. Hell, his parents had never let him forget it for a minute. But it hurt more to know that Shay thought of him that way, too—way down deep in places that his parents could never touch. To her he wasn't merely a man she might love, but a handicapped man. Less than a man.

Right that moment, he felt it.

Unbearably weary, he started walking again, his gaze locked on the truck a hundred feet away. It took Shay mere seconds to catch up with him, took a conscious effort on her part to match her pace to his. Somewhere down deep inside, he hated her for doing it, almost as much as he hated himself for making it necessary.

They were mere feet from the truck when a woman headed inside backtracked and called Shay's name. ''Shay Stephens, is that you? Oh, my God, what did you do to your hair? It's so—so *short!*''

Shay's smile was strained, her response reluctant as she stopped. Though it would be easier to go on to the truck, though he *wanted* to go on to the truck, perversely, he stopped beside her.

''Hello, Chris,'' she said quietly, her voice noticeably lacking in warmth. ''Yes, I cut it this summer. It's so much easier to take care of.''

He'd thought the woman looked familiar, and the name clinched it. Chris Taylor had graduated the year after them and came from Heartbreak's wealthiest family. They had more money, more land and more cattle than anyone else in the area, and they'd thought it put them on an elevated social plane—that, and the fact that their heritage was untainted by Indian blood.

He never had liked her.

He remembered her as a thin, snotty redhead. Now she was a plump, overbearing redhead, and trailing along behind her was a thin, snotty kid who looked too much like her to not belong to her. The boy looked at him, staring openly at the scars on his face and throat, then lowered his gaze before tugging on his mother's sleeve. "Mom…"

"Hush, Devon. Mama's talking," Chris admonished without missing a beat in her conversation about some poor unfortunate she and Shay both knew.

"But, Mom…"

She brushed the kid off, continued her rapid speech, then abruptly drew a deep breath and turned her attention to *him.* "And who is this?" She squinted, stared, then gasped. "Oh, my God, Easy Rafferty. What have you *done* to yourself? Your poor face—"

She reached out, but before she could touch him, Easy deliberately caught her wrist with his right hand. Her gaze dropped to his hand, and revulsion crossed her face, followed by morbid fascination. "Oh, Easy, your poor hand," she murmured sympathetically even as she none-too-subtly twisted free so it wasn't touching her.

"That's what I was trying to tell you," the kid said. "His fingers are gone. *Gross.* Where are they? Like, did the doctor cut 'em off and give 'em to you to keep? Or, hey, I seen this movie once where this guy stole money from a drug dealer, and the drug dealer, he had 'em hold 'im down and he chopped off his hand with a machete." With one hand, he made a cutting gesture across the other. "Did you get caught stealin' from somebody?"

His mother recovered enough to give him a shake. "Devon McCloud, you hush up right now! It's rude to talk about a stranger's handicaps right in front of him!"

''But it's okay if you do it behind his back,'' Easy said sarcastically, then directed his next words to Shay. ''Or if you just think about it.''

Her face turned deep crimson, and hurt darkened her eyes. ''Chris, we've got to—''

Chris brushed her off. ''Easy, what did you *do?*''

''I was in a wreck.'' He forced the words out in a steady, indifferent tone—not easy with his jaw locked tight, with every muscle in his body straining to walk away before she could say anything else.

''Is it permanent?'' she asked, then added in a rush, ''Of course, you're not going to grow new fingers, but the cane... Are you ever going to walk normally again? And the rodeo—that *is* what you were doing, isn't it? I guess it's over for you.'' She shuddered dramatically. ''If I suddenly lost my career like that, why, I think I'd rather die! What will you do now? What *can* you do?''

''Not a damn thing.''

''Well...'' Looking as if the prospect repulsed her, she forced herself to pat his arm. ''Don't you lose hope. There are all kinds of programs out there to help—well, people like you. You know, disabled people, or physically challenged, or— What term do you prefer?''

His fingers were knotted so tightly around the head of the cane that he couldn't feel the tips anymore. ''I usually just say useless cripple,'' he said snidely. ''And what term do you prefer for yourself? Insensitive bi—'' He glanced at the kid and chose another word. ''Bigot?''

She looked flustered. ''Why—why, I can't imagine why you'd say such a thing, Easy. I've never shown any prejudice against you. I always treated you exactly the same as everyone else, even though you were Indian, and every year I make a donation to charities that help people like you. But—'' she gave a holier-than-thou sniff ''—I understand. You're bitter over your situation and you have to take it out on someone. I can forgive that—though it may take some time. Devon, let's go.''

"I don't *want* your forgiveness," he called after her, drawing the attention of other shoppers in the area. For once, he didn't care that they looked. He was too damn angry.

Chris and her son walked on as if they hadn't heard. Shay brushed past him and went to wait at the truck. Her head was down, and she looked...

Mortified.

He hobbled to the driver's side and climbed in, then tossed the cane in back. After starting the engine and fastening his seat belt, he simply sat there for a moment, breathing heavily. Maybe he owed her an apology. Maybe, for her, he should follow Chris Taylor inside and apologize to her, too.

But he didn't feel particularly sorry. He just felt hurt.

They drove home in silence. Finally, after what seemed like forever, he turned into his driveway and felt a rush of relief. The tension that had knotted his shoulders began to ease in a flood of heat, and his fingers, cramping from his tight grip on the steering wheel, flexed, then relaxed. It felt good to be home. It felt *safe*.

He parked beside Shay's car, and for a moment, even after he shut off the engine, they both simply sat there. Then, at the same time, they started to speak.

"I'm sorry," she began.

He asked, "Now do you under—"

They both stopped, and he drew a breath, then started over. "Now do you understand why I don't want to go anywhere? Why I'd rather stay here?"

"It was just Chris Taylor. You can't possibly care what Chris Taylor thinks."

"Yes, Shay, I can," he said quietly. "And it wasn't just Chris. It was *you*. You were embarrassed. You were embarrassed to be with me."

Shock darkened her eyes and rounded her mouth in a silent exclamation. After a moment she closed it, then opened it again. "I can't believe— That's the most ridiculous— *How can you say that?*"

"I saw your face." The bleakness he felt came out in his voice, making it quaver unsteadily.

"Then you saw what *you* were feeling—not me. I was sorry I talked you into going. I was angry about the way some of those people looked at you. I was angry with myself for making it worse, and I was sick about running into Chris because she's such an idiot and I knew she would say something to hurt you. But I *was not embarrassed,* Easy. Not for one second."

He closed his eyes and tilted his head back and to the side, stretching the muscles. After a moment he felt Shay's fingers close gently over his arm. Her touch was as tentative as Chris's had been, though for totally different reasons. Chris had been showing her open-mindedness, that she wasn't afraid to touch the Indian cripple, while Shay was expecting rejection. Truth was, he couldn't push her away to save his life. Hell, she was saving his life.

"You know what, Easy?" she asked softly. "People *will* look. That's their nature. All your life they've looked at you because you were so damn gorgeous. Some still look because you're gorgeous. Some feel sorry for you. Some feel uncomfortable. Some are even put off by your scars or your hand or the way you walk. But you're not the only one they look at. You're not the only one who gets judged unfairly. Everyone's got their prejudices. It's an unfortunate fact of life. But you can't let it determine how you live your life."

He let his head roll to the right and opened his eyes to look at her. "I'm not doing that again."

Her smile was faint and regretful. "I think it was enough of an experience for a while—"

"Not for a while, Shay. Not ever. I can't handle it."

"I won't ask you to." *For a while.* She didn't add the phrase, but he heard it. Even after this morning's disaster, she was still convinced that getting out and seeing people was best for him. He was more convinced than ever that she was wrong.

The pressure of her fingers around his arm increased, then eased. "Let's go in."

"Wait." He turned to face her, taking her hand in his good hand, sliding his fingers between hers. "You do think of me as being handicapped, don't you?"

He knew she was remembering almost saying the word in the parking lot when her hand tightened around his. "The simple fact, Easy, is that you do have a couple of handicaps, and they are permanent. They're as much a part of you as your black hair and your brown eyes and your smile. I think the problem here is in definition. You see *handicapped* as meaning diminished—less than before. I see it as having to make adjustments—different from before."

"Nice distinction." Unfortunately it wasn't one he could make just yet.

"And the first adjustment you need to make is your attitude. You might be amazed by what you can accomplish if only you believe you can do it."

Feeling marginally better in spite of himself, he teased, "Jeez, when did you become such a cockeyed optimist?"

"The day I invited you out to Buffalo Lake so I could seduce you and you came."

"The day you *invited* me? And *seduced* me? I don't remember it quite like that."

She smiled sunnily. "And how do you remember it?"

He pulled, and she slid across the seat to him, maneuvering beneath the steering wheel to sit on his lap. "Ooh, I've been here before," she murmured as she wrapped her arms around his neck. "Been there, done that, would love to do it again—but we seem to be wearing too many clothes."

He drew her head to his shoulder, then simply held her, rubbing her back, his every breath filled with her scent. She felt good—so soft and yet so strong—and she made *him* feel good.

After a time, with her mouth close to his ear, she murmured, "How *do* you remember that day, Easy?"

He remembered the way she had touched him, the way she'd all but whispered her plans—*I'm driving out to the lake*—and the way she'd managed to look frightened, excited and relieved all at once when he'd gotten there. Tilting her chin up, he pressed a single chaste kiss to her mouth, then replied, "I think of it as the best day of my life. Every day with you has been the best day."

For a long, still moment, she looked dazed. Then she gave a husky, delighted laugh as she began pulling at her clothes. "Easy Rafferty, you are too good. I want you— right here, right now."

He helped her with their clothing and showed her—or did she show him?—just how good *too good* was.

After making love in the pickup like desperate kids with no place else to go, they ate lunch, then started working in the living room. With music from the boom box in the kitchen for accompaniment, Shay wiped a tack cloth over the woodwork she'd sanded while Easy taped the window glass in preparation for painting.

She regretted the trip to Tulsa more than she could say, and she wished she could promise that she'd never ask him to set foot off the property again, but it was a promise that they would both know she couldn't keep. After all, going into Heartbreak would be different. The people there weren't strangers. They'd known him since he was a baby and would be too careful of his feelings to let any shock or dismay they might feel show. On top of that, most of them were just plain good folks. They wouldn't care that he used a cane or had lost his fingers. They didn't judge other people by such meaningless standards.

But, thanks to Chris Taylor, it would be a long time before she'd be able to prove that to Easy.

She finished just as he began taping the last pane of glass. Looking outside, he remarked, "We've got company."

She walked to the open door and saw three horses coming up the driveway. "They've got good timing. How about a break?"

"How about you keep them company outside while I put the first coat of paint on?"

She glanced at the paint sprayer, then nodded. As she went outside, Olivia and the girls dismounted in the driveway, then tied the horses to the fence there. "Hi," she greeted them.

Elly came tearing toward her. "Hey, Miss Shay. Where's Mr. Easy?"

She swung the kid into her arms, intercepting her on her way to the house. "He's started painting. You'd better stay out here or you might get paint all over you."

"That's okay. These is old clothes."

"Elly," Olivia admonished. "You and Emma go play."

"But, Mom, he come to our house yesterday and didn't even stop to say hello to me."

"That's because he came to see your daddy, not you." Olivia softened her words with a smile. "You'll get a chance to see him. Now go on and play—and stay out of trouble. And stay out of the house. And out of the barn. And—"

"But there's not anything else to get into," Elly protested as Shay let her slide to the ground.

"Why don't you go pick some apples for your ponies?" Shay suggested. "The tree's out back."

As the girls ran off, Olivia leaned against the pickup, hands in her hip pockets, feet crossed at the ankles. When she'd moved here back at the beginning of the summer, she hadn't owned anything more casual than an oh-so-feminine sundress or a perfectly matched designer short set, she'd worn a most fragile air, and her complexion had been peaches-and-cream pale. Now, in Wranglers, sleeveless chambray shirt and scuffed boots, she looked tanned, healthy and strong. "How's it going?"

"Pretty good."

"I see you've taken our advice."

"What ad—"

"Reese and I told you to seduce him, remember? And obviously you have."

"What makes you say 'obviously'?" Shay asked uneasily as she tucked her shirt a little tighter and combed her fingers through her hair.

Olivia laughed. "Ooh, obviously you seduced him *recently.* I wasn't referring to anything that might have happened in the last few hours. It's just that you've got this look…"

"What look?"

"The same one I have. The well-loved-woman look. Incredible satisfaction. Peace. Contentment."

Shay knew exactly what she was talking about. She'd envied Olivia for having it these past few months when she didn't—when she thought she had no hope of ever having it again. "You know, Magnolia," she said, feigning a sour tone, "I haven't exactly been celibate the past six years—not even the past six months—and you never suggested that I had *the look* before."

"Because before, I never saw you after you'd been with Easy. *The look* has as much to do with love as making love." Without missing a beat, Olivia changed the subject. "I persuaded my husband to knock off early today and celebrate the lovely fall weather with a cookout for our neighbors to the west. Will you and Easy come?"

"I'd love to…" Abruptly remembering her agreement only a few hours ago to not ask him to go anywhere—for a while, at least—she caught herself. "…ask him if he will. Hang on a minute." She retraced the trail, beaten in the grass, climbed the steps and pulled the screen door open, then came to a sudden, startled halt as a thin coat of white paint sprayed across her midsection.

"Sorry. I wasn't expecting you." Easy's expression wavered between amusement and contrition—with amusement winning out.

"Better be careful, cowboy. I don't have any other clothes here. Get too much paint on 'em, and I just may have to go naked."

"Well, it would be hard—" when she snorted, he rephrased "—difficult, but I think I could bear it."

"You could b-a-r-e bare it, 'cause, sweetheart, if I'm going to be naked, so are you. And if we're both naked, it damn well better be hard. Otherwise, what's the point?" She watched his eyes turn smoky as his mouth turned up in a sensuous smile.

"There'd be a point," he promised. "Speaking of…what was the point of your coming up here and distracting me at work?"

"Am I distracting?"

"Incredibly."

"Good." She smiled smugly. "Magnolia—that's Olivia to you—has invited us over for a cookout. I told her I had to check with you."

He looked past her, his gaze growing pensive, and she turned to see what he was looking at. The girls had returned with apples and were in the process of feeding Cherokee and Angel while Buck patiently waited his turn. Was it the horses who held his attention? The girls? Or all of the above?

"Does Guthrie know she's invited us?"

"Yes, he knows. It's okay if you don't want to go," she said, careful to keep her voice even and empty of emotion.

He looked back at her and grinned. "That'll work better if you poke your bottom lip out like this—" he gently pinched it into position "—and cast your gaze downward and add a brave sniffle or two."

She slapped his hand away. "I'm not trying to manipulate you into agreeing. I'm trying not to influence you in any way. It's your decision."

"But you would like to go."

"Sure. Magnolia's my best friend." Hearing her own words, she frowned. They sounded so strange…and felt so natural.

"You never had the chance to have a best friend, did you?" Easy asked quietly.

"Of course I did. I had you and Guthrie."

"A best *girl*friend. In school you spent too much time with us. Afterward, I kept you moving around so much that you never had the opportunity to get close to anyone."

"The only person I wanted to be close to was you. But now I have a best friend, and it's Olivia, and I would like to have dinner with them tonight if you don't mind."

He looked at the Harrises again, then back at her. "I'd like that, too." Taking her arm, he walked outside with her. "Olivia, what time do we eat?"

"How's six sound?"

"Fine."

"Can I bring anything?" Shay asked.

Olivia feigned a look of horror. "Oh, dear, please, no. I've heard about your cooking."

When Easy and the twins laughed, Shay treated each of them to an exasperated look. "For heaven's sake, I own the best café in town!"

"And it's well known that Manuel and Geraldine don't let you in the kitchen except to wash dishes," Olivia retorted. "Face it, Shay, your talents lie elsewhere."

Shay's smile was slow and womanly, and she directed it primarily at Easy. "They certainly do, and some folks around here are most grateful for it."

"I'm sure he is—I mean, they are," Olivia agreed. The flush that colored Easy's cheeks made her laugh. "You guys go back to doing whatever it was you were doing, and we'll see you at six."

"We'll be there," Shay said. A normal evening out with Easy, time with Olivia, and watching him with Guthrie. She wouldn't miss it for the world.

Chapter 10

They quit work at four-thirty and Shay went home to clean up and change for dinner. She had just dried off from her shower when the phone rang. Stretching across the bed, she snagged it on the third ring.

"If you're going to spend all your spare time at Easy's, then the boy needs to get a phone," her mother said.

"And hello to you, too, Mom."

"He needs a phone, anyway. What if he fell and got hurt? He'd just be stuck there until you get home from work—and you work way too late."

"You know what, Mom? We're not kids anymore. You don't have to worry about us," Shay said gently.

"Where in the world did you get the idea that a mother quits worrying when her kids are grown?" Mary sounded incredulous. "You've all given me more anxious moments since you turned eighteen than you ever did before."

"I'll talk to him about a phone," Shay conceded with a grin.

There was a moment's silence—the kind that meant her

mother was preparing to get to the point—then, "I got a call this afternoon from Inez Taylor."

Shay's grin slipped, then slid into a wry smile. "And how is Chris's mother?"

"Just like her daughter. Remember what I told you when you were little and you wanted to get back at someone who'd done you wrong?"

"You were full of advice when I was little. You'll have to be more specific."

"You never wrestle with a pig. You just get dirty, and the pig has all the fun."

"Mom, Chris Taylor is one pig I didn't touch. Easy may have had a few things to say to her, but nothing that wasn't well deserved. Under the circumstances, I thought he was generous in letting her walk away in one piece." She picked up the lotion from the night table, squirted out a palmful and began massaging it into her legs. "What's Chris's version?"

Mary affected Inez Taylor's style of speech, colored with her own dry delivery. "Why, she was just trying to be friendly to that poor, poor Easy Rafferty, and you and he like to took her head off. He's really very bitter—probably needs psychiatric help—why, he might be suicidal, maybe even homicidal. You know, with his emotional problems, along with his drinking problem—all his people drink, of course—it might not be safe for him to live here."

"Oh, *please!*" Shay exploded. "Easy's not suicidal or homicidal, he doesn't have a drinking problem, and to even suggest that it's not safe for him to be here—"

"Sweetheart, you don't have to yell at me. I'm on his side, okay?"

She took a deep breath, held it to the count of five, did it again and counted to ten, then sighed. "What did you tell Inez?"

"That I knew for a fact he wasn't homicidal, because if he was, Chris wouldn't have lived to tell the tale. Lord knows, *I've* wanted to wring her neck a few times. I also told her that she'd raised an idiot for a daughter, which wasn't surprising since she's an idiot herself.''

Shay's grin spread ear to ear. "Good for you, Mom. I'm proud of you.''

"Unlike Taylor women, Stephens women have brains and aren't afraid to use them.'' Then Mary echoed Shay's sigh. "I just wanted you to be prepared. Inez does like to talk. She'll probably be telling people that Easy's a menace to society. Nobody'll believe her, of course, but...gossip's gossip. It'll get around.''

"Well, since Easy has sworn he won't be going to town again, I don't think it'll get around to him. But I appreciate the warning. And if Inez Taylor says anything to me, I'll remember the pig lesson. I'll be on my best behavior.''

"Good. It'll look better if one of us shows some decorum before I snatch her bald.''

Shay's laughter gradually turned to tears. "Thanks, Mom,'' she whispered.

Mary sounded a little hoarse, too. "I figure it's the least I can do to make up for all those good-for-nothing cowboy remarks. You have a good time tonight, and be careful on your way to work in the morning.''

Shay hung up, then dressed in jeans and a sweater and started her makeup. For fourteen years, in her mother's eyes, Easy had been a good-for-nothing rodeo cowboy and Shay had been her empty-headed, fool-minded daughter. She'd told herself her mother didn't mean it, not really. Mary had just been so upset about her jilting Guthrie, and she'd been best friends with Guthrie's mother, who'd died only a few years later. But the remarks had still hurt.

Now she'd gone from empty-headed and fool-minded to a woman with a brain. Though she'd done nothing to earn it—she was still a fool for Easy and always would be—she liked the change in her mother's perception.

She left her house at five-thirty, and she and Easy arrived at the Harrises' place at exactly six o'clock. The twins met them as they climbed out of the truck, Elly skidding to a stop beside Easy, Emma coming to Shay.

"Where's your folks?" she asked as Emma sedately walked beside her.

"Around back. They're acting silly."

"What are they doing?"

It was Elly who answered. "*Dancing*. In the *grass*."

"Oh, darlin', dancing's not at all silly. Wait till you're older. You'll see."

As they turned the corner into the backyard, Elly asked Easy, "Can you dance?"

Shay glanced his way, expecting some discomfort, maybe a scowl or just a flat *no*. Instead, he shrugged. "I don't know, Elly. I haven't tried since the wreck."

"Maybe you can try tonight."

He looked up, caught Shay's gaze. "Maybe I can."

But if he did, it wouldn't be here, she knew. They'd never danced together unless they were feeling unusually strong or were reasonably close to a bed. Being so close, moving so intimately…it always did something to them…and it was always incredible.

The evening air was comfortable, though once the sun went down, the temperature would drop. It wouldn't get too cold—just enough to justify snuggling on the glider, Shay thought. The picnic table was set with a cloth and real dishes, and steaks were marinating in a covered glass dish at one end while the charcoal burned in the nearby grill. A radio in the open kitchen window was tuned to a country station, and Guthrie and Olivia were dancing—sort of—between the lawn chairs.

"They dance like we used to," Easy murmured in her ear.

"Hmm." Awfully close, barely moving, lost in each other.

The song ended, and the broadcast turned to news, but their hosts didn't seem to notice. After a moment Shay cleared her throat. "Don't let us intrude, Guthrie, Magnolia.

We'll just help ourselves to some dinner here, then run along. Or would you prefer that we stay here and watch the kids and let *you* run along?''

Slowly they separated, but neither looked the least bit embarrassed. And why should they? They were married, and they were in love, and she was very happy for them.

And very jealous.

But her time would come.

''What would you like to drink?'' Olivia asked. ''We have iced tea, soda—I'm sorry, make that pop—and beer.''

Shay requested iced tea, while Easy and Guthrie asked for beer. The girls instructed them to sit—Guthrie and Olivia on the glider, Easy and Shay in old wooden lawn chairs that still held the afternoon heat—while they served the drinks. Elly was giggling and acting silly, while Emma was a pint-size version of the gracious hostess her mother was.

They talked about nothing—the weather, school, both Shay's and the twins' upcoming birthdays. By the time steaks were grilled and dinner was served, Shay couldn't have repeated much that was said, but she treasured the time for that reason. Who ever would have believed that she, Easy and Guthrie could sit and talk for half an hour like friends about nothing?

''Is this your beef?'' Easy asked after tasting the ribeye. Underneath the table, Shay bumped her knee against his. Across the table Guthrie and Olivia exchanged glances, and at the end, both twins instantly tuned into the conversation.

''Did I mention that the girls have named everything around here?'' Guthrie asked. ''Everything—the bulls, the cows, the calves.''

''Yes,'' Olivia added with a smile. ''They haven't quite grasped the concept of what we raise cattle for. You see, when we send our calves away, we sort of adopt them out to new homes.''

''To people who don't got little calves of their own,'' Elly added helpfully. ''And then our mama cows have more babies so's they don't get lonesome, and when they're big enough, we adopt them out, too.'' She grinned ear to ear. ''When Mom has a new baby, we're gonna adopt Em out to someone else, and then I can be the oldest.''

''Uh-uh!'' Emma reached across to poke her sister even as Olivia said, ''I've told you before, Elly, we're not giving your sister away. Besides, you're already the oldest.''

''Only by eighteen minutes. If we adopt Em to somebody else, then I could be the oldest by five whole years. I could be the boss.''

''Like you're not bossy enough already?'' Guthrie asked. ''Besides, what would you do if the people decided they'd rather adopt you than Emma?''

Elly considered it a moment while chewing a bite of food. After washing it down with pop, she said earnestly, ''They prob'ly *would* want me, on account of Em's timid and prissy, and I'm a real cowboy.''

Emma's face screwed up as if she were about to cry, then suddenly she smiled. An instant later Elly popped up off the bench, hopping on one foot. ''Ow! She *kicked* me! Mom, Daddy, she *kicked* me *really* hard!'' She ducked to look under the table, then came back up, her hair mussed. ''Wow, and with sandals, too. Good kick, Em.''

Olivia smiled her sweetest smile at Shay and Easy. ''Isn't this fun? And can you believe it? In about six months, we're going to have another one.''

Darkness had settled, dinner was over, and dessert was just a memory. They'd toasted Guthrie and Olivia's news with tea and beer, and now the evening had quieted down. Lights from the kitchen and mounted on tall poles leading out to the barn lit the yard, and music still played softly from the radio.

Easy sat on the glider, with Shay curled up at his side, and considered the evening with more than a hint of wonder. For fourteen years he'd never believed such an evening was possible. For six years he'd *known* it wasn't…that Shay would never forgive him, Guthrie would never forgive either of them. But here they sat, like old times—but better. They were older, had been through a lot and were smart enough to appreciate what they had. He wished he had more—wished his hip was in better shape and those fingers would magically reappear—but he was grateful to be alive. He was grateful as hell to have Shay at his side.

"Mr. Easy?" Emma's voice came baby-soft and hesitant from the quilt she shared with her sister. It was the first time she'd ever spoken to him, and when he turned his gaze to her, she looked as if she regretted it. But she wasn't quite as timid as Elly would have him believe. She didn't back down or run to her mother and hide. She swallowed hard and asked, "What happened to your hand?"

For a moment everything got still and stiff. Even the music seemed to fade away. Guthrie and Olivia both straightened in their chairs, and Shay reached out for a pat. Reassuring him? he wondered. Or herself?

It was Elly who broke the silence, taking her sister to task in a whisper loud enough to reach the barn. "Emma, you're not s'posed to ask personal questions."

"It's all right," Easy said, and surprisingly, it was. It was easier to deal with in a straightforward manner. He'd discovered that with Elly. "I was in an accident. My truck went off the road."

"And it hurted your hand and leg?"

He nodded.

"Our other father was in an accident. His car went off the road, and he was killed."

"I'm sorry."

She nodded vaguely, as if she wasn't entirely sure that she shared his sentiment. "Elly says you can't have horses no more. Do you want to go see my horse?"

"I—" *Would rather not. Would rather never see another horse again. Don't want to get that close to Buck. Don't want to see that paint or the gray or the chestnut or even the ponies.*

"My horse's name is Angel, and he's very gentle,"

Emma said. She got to her feet and held out her hand. "Come on. I'll show you."

He stared at her hand for a long moment—so small, so steady—and wished for some easy way to say no, but his mind was blank.

"It's late, Em," Guthrie said. "Maybe he would rather—"

"It's all right." The words came in his voice, though Easy would have sworn on his life that *It's all right* were the last words on his mind. Agreeing to limp all the way back to the corral to look at horses was definitely the last thing he wanted to do. But instead of taking the words back, he reached for his cane and got to his feet, and Emma tucked her hand into his right hand.

"I wanna come, too," Elly said, jumping up from the quilt, and her father stood up, too.

Elly raced ahead, came back and circled around them, then ran forward again. By the time they reached the corral, she was straddling the top fence rail and Cherokee was nuzzling her. Emma climbed onto the rail, too, and gave a sharp whistle. From the opposite corner of the corral, her pony trotted over.

"This is Angel," she said proudly.

Easy stood a half dozen feet back and wished it were a half dozen miles. "He's a beauty."

"He's a pinto," Emma said matter-of-factly, "and he's got good color."

He smiled faintly at hearing the technical term in that soft, little-girl voice. "You're raising two horse-smart kids," he remarked to Guthrie, standing beside him.

"El's going to be a rancher someday," Guthrie replied, his voice low enough that the kids couldn't hear. "We thought Em was going to be the prissy, spoiled wife of a rancher, but she might surprise us all and go into your business."

He didn't *have* a business, Easy thought with a lump in

his throat. He didn't have much of a future at all, except Shay.

"Would you believe, when they came here in June, Liv wouldn't go near the horses and Emma was terrified of everything? Now they act like they've lived here all their lives."

"And, of course, Elly just fit right in from the start," Easy said dryly.

"You bet. If they'd stayed in Atlanta, I can't imagine how she would have fit into the pampered Southern-belle role. Not too well, I think."

They watched the girls for a moment, identical twins petting almost identical ponies. As Elly rubbed Cherokee between the eyes, Guthrie broke the silence again. "It's a sign of complete trust for a horse to let you touch him in his blind spot. You taught me that. It's pretty much the same for Emma to make a gesture of friendship to an adult."

"I thought so." Easy hesitated before adding, "I'm honored."

"You should be." Guthrie's grin slowly faded as Buck came to the fence. "What happened to your horse?"

"My horse?"

"I assume he was with you when you had the wreck. Was he injured?"

Easy's chest grew tight. "Yeah. It—it tore up his leg— condylar and spiral fractures of the metatarsal. The first person to come along was a local rancher. He called the state police and his vet. It required a lot more effort and manpower to get Gambler out than me." The rancher had promised him they'd do their best to save the horse, and they had. He'd been so grateful.

So damn grateful—and yet he hadn't seen Gambler since. Hadn't checked on him. Hadn't helped with his care. Hadn't even called to ask how well he had recovered.

"But you didn't have to put him down."

Easy shook his head.

"Where is he now?"

"At my uncle's place down around Austin. He can't be ridden...certainly can't be used to compete anymore."

"He's living the easy life, huh?"

The easy life. He supposed that was one way of looking at it.

"What about you?" Guthrie asked.

Easy turned his head sharply to look at him. "What about me?"

"What are your plans? What are you going to do, besides make up for lost time with Shay?"

He stared hard into the darkness on the far side of the corral. "I don't have any plans. I can't ride. I can't work horses anymore. I can't do much of anything."

"How do you know?"

"The doctors said—"

"From what I understand, they also said you probably wouldn't walk again." Guthrie gestured toward Easy's legs. "It looks to me like those are your own two feet, and they get you where you're going. Besides, you don't have to ride to raise horses. Remember our plans—my cattle, your paints? I've got the cattle. Where are the paints?"

"I can't—"

"Come on, Easy," Guthrie interrupted. "I never heard you say *I can't* in your life. You always thought you could do everything—anything. What happened?"

"I got older. I damn near got killed. I got smarter."

"You got scared."

Easy turned to face him. "What is it with you people?" he demanded harshly. "I'm not scared. I'm just trying to accept reality, and for me that reality is—"

"That you're scared. There was a time when you were the only man in this entire damn state who had the nerve to get within fifty feet of Buck. Now you're afraid to walk six feet to the fence and pet him."

"I'm not afraid," Easy said flatly. It was just too damn hard getting close to something he wanted desperately and could never have. It'd be like spending time with Shay while she was happily married to someone else. It would be painful and sad, and he'd had enough pain and sadness in his life. He damn sure didn't need to go looking for more.

"Then prove it. Walk over there to that horse whose life you saved fourteen years ago and see if he remembers you. Renew your friendship."

Easy looked from Guthrie to the horse, who seemed to know that they were talking about him, then stubbornly shook his head. He started walking, all right—not toward the fence, but back to the house. "I don't have to prove anything to anyone," he muttered as he went.

Guthrie gathered the girls and caught up with him too easily. "You're right," he said conversationally. "You don't have to prove anything to me or anyone else—except yourself."

"Not even myself."

"It's just that you relate better to horses than anyone I've ever known. It seems a shame to waste that."

"It wasn't my decision. Blame whatever or whoever decided to send my truck off that road and let me survive like this."

Guthrie stopped him with his hand on his arm. "Like *this?*" he repeated. "You're alive. You're well. You've got your property. You've got Shay. Hell, you've got us. I'd say you're pretty damn lucky."

Pretty damn lucky. Easy looked at Shay, sitting in a pool of yellow light, her head tossed back in laughter at something Olivia had said. After a moment, sensing him, she looked his way, and a lovely, full-of-promise smile slowly lit her face. She was so beautiful, so special. If he lost everything in the world but her, it would be enough.

He just didn't know how to stop wanting more.

Shay was taking a break once the after-church dinner rush was over when Reese Barnett came into the café. He circled behind the counter to get himself a cup of coffee, then joined her in the booth. "You know, Sheriff," she said dryly, "this is a full-service establishment. We usually try to wait on our customers."

He made a negating gesture as he spooned sugar into the cup. "I'm perfectly capable of pouring myself a cup of coffee. Busy day?"

"The usual." With a twist—gossip about Easy. No one had come right out and asked her if Easy really had torn into Chris Taylor, or if he really did present a threat to himself or anyone else, but everyone, it seemed, had mentioned his name. "What are you doing in uniform? I thought the sheriff always got weekends off."

"That wouldn't be quite fair to the deputies, would it?"

"When they become sheriff, they'll think it's more than fair."

"I try to give everyone a weekend off now and then." He shrugged, then changed the subject. "How's Rafferty?"

"Easy's fine. Why? Have you heard different?"

"I got a call."

"Let me guess. From Inez Taylor."

"She wanted to know if we were all safe in our beds at night."

"No, she didn't," Shay said scornfully. "She wanted to stir up trouble."

Reese gave her an aggravated look. "I know that. She's just mad because you two weren't properly appreciative of Chris's concern. You know, if the Taylors really are Heartbreak's social elite, the way they claim, then I'm damn glad I was born poor trash."

Shay slapped his hand. "Reese Barnett, you were not! It would break your daddy's heart to hear you say that! Besides, the only place the Taylors are socially elite is in Inez's and Chris's own minds."

"They're so bigoted that they don't even recognize their own bigotry. Inez thought Chris was displaying such class and generosity by summoning up some pity for the poor Indian cripple.'' He shook his head in dismay.

''Neither Inez nor Chris would recognize class if it bit them on the—'' Shay broke off and managed a wry smile. ''So what else is going on in Heartbreak?''

''The same old nothin'. It's a quiet town, as you well know.''

''That I do. But it's home and we love it.''

The bell over the door rang, drawing their attention that way. ''Well, well,'' Reese said softly. ''There's someone you don't see out and about every day.''

''There's someone I've *never* seen out and about.'' Shay slid out of the booth and went to the counter as Grace Prescott stopped near the end, clutching a thermos in both hands. Her brown dress was drab and plain and gave her a more washed-out appearance than usual. The beige cardigan she wore against the afternoon chill was much too big on her thin frame, and the thick glasses that kept slipping down her nose magnified the shadows under her eyes. The poor kid never looked good, Shay thought sympathetically, but today she looked downright awful.

''Still fighting that cold, Grace?''

''C-cold? I—I—'' She pushed her glasses up, then bobbed her head and sent them sliding down again. ''Yes. Yes, I am.''

Shay gestured toward the thermos. ''You need some coffee?''

After another startled pause, Grace bobbed her head again. In her beige and brown, with her big eyes opened wide, she looked so much like a baby owl that it would be laughable, if it weren't so sad.

''Can I have the thermos?'' Shay asked gently, and Grace abruptly thrust it out, then folded her hands into the too-long sleeves of her sweater.

Reese left the booth and came to sit a few stools down. ''How's it going, Grace?''

''H-h-how is—is what g-going?''

Her response caught Reese off guard. He gave Shay a look, then shrugged. "Life. Is everything okay at the store? At home? Are you keeping busy?"

"Y-yes."

They both waited for her to elaborate, but of course she didn't. Shay tightened the lid on the thermos, then set it on the counter. "There you go."

"How m-much?"

Shay waved her hand carelessly. "No charge. Just take it."

"No, I can't—" Digging in her pocket, Grace pulled out two one-dollar bills. "My—my father..." For a moment, she seemed to be searching for words, but gave up when they wouldn't come.

Shay understood. Jed Prescott didn't take anything from anyone. He never did anyone a favor and wouldn't accept one—certainly not from a woman. If Grace went back with two dollars and free coffee, he would be furious. If she secreted the two bucks and went back with coffee and no change, he would also be furious.

She estimated how much coffee it had taken to fill the carafe, then named a price. "A buck and a quarter—is that enough?"

Grace nodded quickly and laid the money on the counter, scooped up the thermos and the change and darted out the door.

With a heavy sigh, Shay picked up the two bills. "The first—and probably last—money Jed Prescott ever spent in my café. Just touching it makes me feel dirty." She deposited it in the cash register, then returned to lean on the counter beside Reese. "Wouldn't you love to know what goes on in that family?"

"I've got my theories."

"We've all got theories, Sheriff, but none of us does anything about them."

"What can we do? Prescott's got her afraid of her own

shadow. If she doesn't come to us for help, we can't help her. And she's *never* gonna come to us for help.''

''If her life were a story, Prince Charming would come galloping up on a white steed and sweep her off to his kingdom to live happily ever after.''

''Sorry. I think Heartbreak is flat out of Prince Charmings.'' Reese paid for his coffee and left the change for a tip, then headed for the door. ''See you around, Shay.''

She waved goodbye, then went back to leaning on the counter, her chin on her hand. Reese was wrong. Heartbreak had one Prince Charming left. Well, okay, so his princely crown was a little tarnished, and he wasn't always so charming these days, but he would do for her. In fact, he was perfect for her.

He'd had a good time at the Harrises' last night. They'd gone home, put on a CD and danced in the moonlight, and then they'd made love, and afterward she'd lain in his arms and thought that she needed absolutely nothing more to be blissfully satisfied. *Nothing.* Just Easy, the moonlight and the love.

But this morning she'd awakened once again to find him standing at the window, staring out at the corral with such longing. Maybe *she* needed nothing else, but he did. He needed a purpose. Another chance. A future.

He needed a horse.

But how to convince him of that?

She heaved a great melancholy sigh and, as if in response, Geraldine came out of the kitchen. ''Why don't you go on home?'' the older woman suggested.

''We've only got an hour to close.''

''Yeah, and a dining room full of nobody. Go on. You look like you could use the rest.''

Shay straightened and fixed a chagrined look on her. ''Gee, thanks a lot.''

''Hey, I'm not the one robbing you of your sleep. I just call 'em as I see 'em.'' Geraldine's smile softened the lines of her face. "Go on. Go see that mule-headed cowboy of yours. He's all you've been thinking about all day."

"We already let Amalia leave early. What if you get busy after I'm gone?"

"There's not a crowd in this whole county that I can't handle all by my lonesome," the waitress said huffily. "Go on now. And take some food. That boy's still recuperating. He doesn't need to be subjected to your cooking until he's back to full strength."

Shay gave her a dry look as she untied the apron around her waist. "I'll have you know that Easy doesn't have any complaints about my cooking."

"'Cause he's too smart to eat it. When's he gonna come in and see us?"

"The day you all go blind," Shay said quietly, regretfully.

Geraldine clucked her tongue. "Self-conscious about his looks, huh? Like any of us care."

"Maybe we don't, but he does." She'd learned that lesson yesterday. She wished she could be strong enough to never pressure him about going out again, but she wasn't. She wanted him to be a part of her entire life, and that meant sometimes going places—to her folks' house, out to dinner, maybe to a movie once in a while. She would love for him to come by the café and have breakfast with her or maybe drink a cup of coffee while she closed up in the evening. She'd be thrilled to go with him to the Founders' Day barbecue in June or to the Christmas parade in Buffalo Plains in December, to a Heartbreak High football game in the fall or to church with her parents on Easter Sunday.

She didn't want to live two lives, one safe at home with Easy and the other encompassing everything and everyone else. It wasn't fair to him or her. It certainly wasn't fair to any children they might have.

"Hey, Earth to Shay." Geraldine gave her a shake. "Get that goofy grin off your face and get on out of here. I'll see you in the morning."

Impulsively Shay gave her a hug, then went into the kitchen to fill two foam containers with food. With a wave to Manuel, she headed out the back door and to her car.

In the hours that she'd been at work, so had Easy. The wallpaper job that they'd started in the living room the afternoon before was finished, and the trim had been painted in the dining room. He was taking a break when she arrived, stretched out on the sofa looking for something to watch on TV.

"You're home early," he said, muting the volume when she walked through the door.

Home. She liked the sound of that—liked it a lot. "After the church people, we don't have a lot of business on Sundays, so Geraldine made me leave."

"She made you, huh? Doesn't *she* work for *you?*"

"Yes."

"So doesn't that make you the boss?"

"Not with Geraldine." She put the food in the refrigerator, then came back to sit beside him. He didn't have to seriously coax to get her to lie down facing him. "You were busy. It looks good."

"I had a good teacher."

"You have a good eye and good hands. The first time I hung wallpaper, I went through an entire roll before I got it right."

"Don't look behind the couch."

She raised up to peek and saw several long rolls twisted and glued back on themselves. "Good. I'd hate to think you were that much better than me." She snuggled close to him again, and he began rubbing her neck and shoulder. "Umm, that feels good. It's been a long day."

"See anyone I know?"

She studied him through her lashes. "Reese came in."

"What did he want?"

"Just to see me." They were lying so intimately close that she could feel the tension streak through him. It made her laugh softly and practically purr as she moved closer.

"Why, Easy, you couldn't possibly be jealous of Reese, now could you?"

"Oh, hell, no. Why would I be jealous of him?"

"I can't think of a single reason."

He raised his right hand to tuck her hair behind her ear. "I can think of three offhand," he muttered.

She caught his hand, holding on tightly when he tried to pull free. "I've seen your hand before. I've touched it. It's touched me. I'm not appalled or sickened or repulsed by it."

"You should be."

"Why? Because it's not as pretty as you would like?" She gave him a chastising look. "Pretty or not, it can still do everything you need. You can get dressed, you can write, you can drive, you can cook, you can undress me." She punctuated the last with a kiss to his chin, then casually added, "You could saddle a horse. Hold the reins. Give him a good brushing."

"Don't, Shay," he said sharply.

"Tell me you don't miss the horses," she whispered. "Tell me your heart doesn't ache every time you see Cherokee or Buck. Tell me you don't stand at the bedroom window every morning looking out back at that empty corral and wish there were horses in it—wish you could go outside and feed them and talk to them and just *be* with them."

Grasping her arms, he forcibly lifted her away, then sat up and scowled at her. "I wish for a lot of things, Shay, and you know what? I can't have them. Wishes are useless. Worthless."

"Wishes *can* come true. I wished for you, and I got you."

"That proves my point," he said grimly as he struggled to his feet without the cane, took the few steps necessary to reach it, then leaned heavily on it. "You got me. Useless and worthless."

Listening to his progress through the dining room into

the kitchen, she blew out her breath, then jumped to her feet and went after him. "Listen up, cowboy—"

"Don't call me that."

"What would you prefer that I call you?" she asked flippantly. "Stubborn? Pigheaded? Mulish? How about 'O great love of my life'?"

He was standing at the sink, so all she could see was a small portion of his face, but that was enough to show the muscles in his jaw twitch to keep from smiling.

"How about Ezekiel?" She pronounced each syllable of the name he was none too fond of distinctly, with great emphasis.

"No one calls me that," he said with a scowl.

"And gets away with it? Ooh. You'd have to catch me to punish me, and I think I can outrun you." When he turned to give her the full effect of that scowl, she planted her hands on her hips. "Just for the record, one of these days we *are* going to have horses here."

"This is *my* house, *my* property. You don't have a say—"

"There's no way I'm going to raise our children in the country and deny them the thrill of having their own horses."

"We don't *have* any children."

"Not yet."

His gaze dropped to her stomach, as flat as it'd ever been. "There's no way—"

She waited, but he didn't go on. "No way what? That I'm pregnant? It only takes one time, Easy, and by my count, we have definitely made love more than once."

"What makes you think I even want kids?"

"Because that's the only future you ever wanted—you and me, this place, paints and kids. Boys who would break every record their old man had ever set, and girls who would break every heart their mother had left intact."

For a moment he looked as if he wanted to argue, then

he gave in none too graciously. "All right. When we have kids, we'll have horses."

"So we'd better start with Gambler."

He shook his head.

"Easy, you're not the only one who lost something in that accident. Gambler's career was ended, too. He went through a lot of pain, too, and he's still recovering—just like you. Only he lost *you*. The one person who trained him, rode him, took care of him, traveled with him and loved him walked out of his life."

"He doesn't miss me," he muttered.

"You don't believe that."

"He doesn't need me."

She shook her head emphatically. "You're doing the same thing to that horse that you did to us. You feel the need to punish yourself, but it's Gambler who's suffering."

"He's not suffering. He's living like a king at my uncle's place."

"He should be living like a king here. With you. With us."

He went to the back door and stared out. She remained where she was, hands clenched, her breathing shallow but steady. After a long, still moment, he spoke. "I didn't want to go shopping, but I went—for you—and look how it turned out. I don't want Gambler here, and if I bring him—for you—"

"Don't do it for me. Do it for *you*. And for him. Do it for all the years he took care of you—all the years you loved him." Deciding it was time to lighten the moment a little, she forced a smile. "Do it because, then, the next time I pressure you to go shopping, you'll have a reason not to go."

Absently he replied, "You promised yesterday that you wouldn't ask again."

"But I probably lied."

After a time he glanced at her. "What about earlier?

When you called me the great love of your life. Was that a lie?''

Solemnly she shook her head. "God's honest truth. But then, so was the stubborn and pigheaded part.''

His smile was faint and tinged with sadness. "I could say the same about you.''

"That I'm stubborn and pigheaded?''

"That,'' he agreed, then came to stand only inches in front of her. "And the rest.''

Shay felt warm and tingly, as if he'd just given her the most romantic, flowery declaration of love ever, and his gentle kiss only intensified the sensations. His next words practically made her melt into a puddle on the floor.

"No promises. But I'll think about it—about Gambler.''

"That's all I ever wanted.'' Wrapping her arms around his neck, she gave him a slow, deep, hungry kiss that curled her toes and sent shivers down his spine. When she drew back, she sighed dreamily. "Well…almost all.''

Chapter 11

Over the next few days they painted the dining room a pale peach and the living room a deeper coral shade. The new appliances were delivered, the new countertop installed, and Shay was collecting catalogs for Easy to choose furniture from. Not once did she ask him to go anywhere. Not once did she bring up the subject of Gambler.

She didn't need to. When he was alone, the horse was all he could think about.

He wasn't alone now—she was in his bed asleep—but the horse was on his mind so much that he'd dreamed about him. About loading him into the trailer. Securing the gate. Heading off down the road, even though it was late, even though he was tired. Negotiating the narrow, winding highway.

The first squeal of tires on pavement had awakened him. His eyes had popped open, and his heart had threatened to pound through his chest. His skin had been slick with sweat, and his breathing had been ragged, but beside him Shay had slept on.

Now he sat on the couch in the darkened living room, the remote in hand, a videotape in the VCR. The tape was one of the few things he'd brought from his parents' house, and he'd stored it in the back corner of the highest shelf in the bedroom closet. Parts of it had been filmed by a friend's wife, others by his folks on their rare trips to see him ride.

He'd never watched the tape—had always thought it was something he would save for when he was retired and raising his horses and kids and needed to relive a little of his former glory. He wasn't sure he had the nerve to watch it now.

But he would never know, he thought as he pushed Play, then Mute, unless he tried.

His rides were never long—out of the gate, rope the calf, truss him up, all in nine seconds or less. It took him longer to collect his rope and leave the arena with Gambler when he was done.

He didn't remember the particular rodeos, or whether he'd won or lost, but he remembered the thrill. The satisfaction when his time was good. The frustration when he'd been sloppy. The thrill no matter what. He'd loved the rodeo, loved being the best and being with Gambler.

He also remembered the ritual, caught here on tape time after time, of looking up in the stands once he'd secured the calf. He remembered how it felt to see Shay there, her worry turned to relief whether he'd won or not. He remembered how it felt in later years, when she wasn't there. It had taken away some of his pleasure in the ride—but he'd still loved it.

He watched the tape all the way to the end, rewound it and watched it again. Gambler had been so fast, and *he* had been so agile, leaping to the ground while the horse was still moving, dropping the calf to the ground, wrapping the pigging string he carried between his teeth around three of the struggling calf's hooves, throwing his hands in the air when he was finished, then remounting Gambler, putting slack in the rope and waiting to see if the calf stayed secure for at least six seconds. He was so graceful, Shay had often told him, and now he could appreciate the compliment. He *had* been graceful and quick and limber.

Now he was awkward, clumsy and slow.

He had been a champion. Now he was a loser. Afraid of his horse. Afraid of his life.

He played it one last time, going through some segments frame by frame. He had expected that seeing himself and Gambler both healthy and whole, working so well together would leave him feeling melancholy, and to some extent it did. He'd been damned good at what he did and, in an instant, he'd lost it. Unlike most cowboys, he hadn't been given the chance to slow down, to retire, but instead his career had been violently taken away from him, leaving him with nothing.

Except enough money to take care of himself. And this house. Thirty acres of good land. An ideal place to pamper a horse who'd given his best. Another shot at being friends with Guthrie. Another chance at being more than friends with Shay.

He'd lost a lot, it was true. But all in all, things could be worse. He could be dead. Alone. Unbearably lonely. And with or without the accident, it had been time for him to kiss that life goodbye. He'd had a good sixteen years, but they hadn't always been easy. Age had been creeping up on him, making it harder to compete against cowboys practically young enough to be his son. Even without the accident, he would have retired in another year or two, anyway. Instead, he had merely retired a year or two early.

Without the accident, he would have come back here to this house, bought some horses and started his next career. Now…he had the house. Down in Texas he had a horse. He just needed the career.

There was a whisper of sound from the dining room, then Shay came through the doorway. She watched the silent screen for a moment, then bent to wrap her arms around his neck. He pulled her onto his lap and held her close while they watched together.

After the last ride on the tape played—his last National Finals championship—he pushed Pause, freezing his image on the screen.

"I remember that day," she whispered. "I cried."

"So did I." A slight exaggeration, but he'd damn sure felt like crying.

"I was so happy you won."

"And I was so sad you weren't there."

"God, you were good."

"I was." It wasn't a boast, just simple agreement. For a lot of years, he'd been the best. But that part of his life was over. He'd always known it wouldn't last forever, but he'd also known it would be hard to give up. "Maybe…maybe I can be good at something else. I might be amazed at what I can accomplish if I just believe I can."

She twisted around to look at him. "Good advice. Where'd you hear it?"

"From a very wise woman."

Her smile became smug. "We Stephens women have brains and we're not afraid to use them."

"Meaning?"

When she shook her head, her hair brushed his arm and the faint, familiar fragrances that had long haunted him drifted up to him. "It's a long story about wrestling with pigs, suicide, homicide and snatching people bald. You don't want to hear it."

"Oh, I do," he disagreed. "But not at the moment."

He rewound the tape, listening to the whir until it stopped, then shut off the television, leaving them in the dark. It was cozy in the dark. "Your birthday's coming up soon. What are your plans?"

"Spending it with you."

"What are your mother's plans?"

"She mentioned a party around the pool, provided the weather holds. You should go."

"Why is that?"

"Because the last time I spent any time alone at one of those parties, I kissed my fiancé's best friend and fell in love."

"You try that now, and his wife will snatch you bald."

"I could hold my own against Olivia," she boasted.

"Hmm."

"You doubt me?"

"No. Never." She stretched lazily against him, and he held her closer, absorbing her warmth. By his reckoning, it was after three o'clock, and she had to be at work in just a few hours. He wished she would stay home with him so they could sleep in late and make love when the mid-morning sun finally woke them. But he wouldn't ask her to. The café was her job, her business. Until they were married, until she got pregnant, his advice on her hours wasn't called for.

Until she got pregnant... Last weekend when Olivia had made her announcement, Shay had been happy, no doubt, but there'd also been a wistful look in her eyes. The next day, when she'd made a reference to her own eventual pregnancy, the wistful look had been in *his* eyes. How long would it take? As she'd pointed out, it only took one time. What if one of their many times had already taken? What if she was already pregnant?

He couldn't imagine anything that could make him happier.

She sighed softly, then stirred. "You ready for bed?"

"Yeah."

She stood up and stretched, then went to the VCR, removed the tape and returned it to its box. "Be sure you put this up where nothing can happen to it. I want to watch it again."

"So do I," he remarked, surprising both her, he suspected, and himself.

They went to the bedroom, and he put the tape in his sock drawer while she climbed into bed. He stripped off his jeans, eased into bed beside her, settled his head on the pillow that smelled of her. "Shay?"

"Yeah, babe."

"I'm going to call Uncle Tony tomorrow. I'm going to ask him to send Gambler up here."

She was still for a long time, then she claimed his hand and held it tightly. "I think that's a good idea, Easy," she said, her voice husky and quavery.

"So do I," he whispered.

He hoped they were right.

The first Saturday of October was bright, with the chilly mornings and comfortable days that were typical of early fall in Oklahoma. The leaves were starting to change color, and there was a crisp, clean end-of-summer-get-ready-for-winter smell in the air.

Easy was up, dressed and outside by the time Shay woke. She pulled on jeans and a sweater, poured herself a cup of coffee and went looking for him. She found him on the front porch swing with his own cup of coffee.

She closed the screen door, then leaned against the post at the top of the steps. "Want some breakfast?"

"What would you do if I said yes?"

"Get in my car and drive down to Mom's to beg a dozen of her doughnuts."

He smiled but shook his head. "Any chance Mary can teach you to make those doughnuts? It'd be a nice tradition to carry on for her grandchildren."

"Darlin', you give her grandchildren, and she will happily come over here every single day and fix breakfast, lunch and dinner." She watched the steam rising from her coffee for a moment before asking, "What time is your uncle's foreman supposed to get here?"

"Sometime before noon."

"Are you anxious?"

His smile was shaky. "Yeah. I don't know—"

"Don't worry about it, Easy. We'll work it out."

He studied her intently for so long that she began to wonder if she'd put her clothes on inside out or sprouted an extra nose overnight. As she shifted self-consciously—brushing her hair, tugging at her clothes—he bluntly asked, "When are you going to marry me?"

Relieved that marriage was all that was on his mind, she smiled. "I've waited fourteen years to be asked."

"Will you marry me?"

It wasn't the romantic proposal girls dreamed about. There was no candlelight, no soft music, flowers or waiting diamond ring. It was simple and to the point—the straight-forward question of a man who knew what he wanted. For that reason, it meant more to her than all the hearts and flowers in the world.

She gave him the same sort of answer. "Yes, I will."

"When?"

Cupping her hands to the coffee cup, she gazed out across the pasture that fronted the house. In the timber across the road on Guthrie's property, patches of fog spread where the ground dipped lower, like thin, gray-white clouds come to ground. She watched them for a moment before turning to Easy again. "How about the day you feel comfortable standing up in church in front of our families and all our friends?"

The intensity of his gaze didn't lessen. "So you did lie—about not asking me to go anywhere."

"What kind of wedding did you have in mind? You and me, Guthrie and Olivia, Mom and Dad, with old Judge Thompson in the living room?"

"Do we really need your mom and dad?" he asked, then held up his hand before she could respond. "Just kidding. You want a real wedding."

"For a real marriage. Fancy that."

One minute passed, then another. She sipped her coffee, watched a hawk swoop from one tree to another and listened to the uneven tenor of her own quiet breathing. Finally he sighed. "No promises. But I'll think about it."

''That's what you said about Gambler—and there he is.''

A red pickup towing a horse trailer turned into the driveway. Easy set his coffee down, then spilled it as he stood up. Shay set her own cup on the rail and together they went down the steps and headed out back.

The driver came toward the house, then curved off to the left on the trail that led to the barn. By the time they reached the clearing, he'd turned the truck around so it was pointed out again, climbed out and gone to the back to open the gate and lower the ramp.

The animal he led out was magnificent. Pure black quarter horses weren't easy to come by, and they fetched a pretty penny when they sold, but Gambler had been worth double the price for sheer beauty alone. The rising sun gleamed off his coat as he took a long, steady look around his new home, then ducked his head low to delicately nibble the grass in front of him.

''Oh, Easy,'' she whispered. The horse was an awesome reminder of the dozens of times she'd seen them in the arena. They'd looked so incredible together—better matched than any other cowboy and horse she'd ever seen—and they had always performed incredibly, too. They'd been quite a sight—masculine perfection in both human and equine form.

She took a couple steps forward before it registered that Easy hadn't moved. Hesitating, she looked back and saw that he was staring at the horse as if it were his worst nightmare come to life. In spite of the cool temperature, sweat beaded across his forehead, and his knuckles were white where they clutched the cane.

Her heart sank as she returned to him. ''Easy?''

''This was a mistake,'' he said, his jaw clenched so tightly that his mouth barely moved. ''Tell him to take him back to Texas.''

''Easy, please—''

''*Tell him.*'' Spinning around so quickly that he nearly stumbled, he headed back to the house.

She watched him a moment, then looked back at Gambler, debating which one she should see to first. The horse won. Crossing to him, she held out her hand so he could sniff it, then stroked his neck. "Oh, Gambler, you're a beauty," she whispered. "I'd forgotten just how handsome you are. It's been a long time. You probably don't even remember me."

"Give him lots of attention, and it don't matter to him whether he remembers you," the foreman said, then flushed. "No offense, ma'am."

"None taken. How was your trip?"

"Uneventful. The best kind. You want him in there?" He nodded toward the corral. Guthrie had come over the day before, and he and Easy had replaced the broken boards and oiled the gate. Guthrie had brought a small stock tank, a fifty-gallon barrel and a bag of feed to fill it and fresh hay. Everything was ready.

Except Easy.

"Not yet. He looks good. Does he require any special care?"

The man shook his head. "Just feed and attention. His leg's about as healed as it's ever gonna get. They had to do surgery—put some pins in."

Like Easy. Still perfectly matched. "He hardly limps."

"Just a bit. It gets more noticeable when he's tired. He's pretty much okay. He's just not going to be doing any fast or fancy maneuvers."

Again, like Easy. Shay walked around the horse, noticing the sheen of his coat, the fine line of muscle and ligament, the obvious impression of power. When she reached the foreman again, she gave him a heartfelt smile. "He's beautiful."

"That he is. It's a shame he can't do what he trained for—a shame he can't be bred." He looked toward the house, where Easy was just walking around the corner. "It's a shame *he* can't do what he trained for."

"No, but he can be bred," Shay said slyly.

The man looked startled, as if he didn't know whether to be amused or embarrassed. He settled on both with an disconcerted chuckle. "You have everything you need?"

"We're all set. I'd invite you in for breakfast, but my culinary skills are well-known and well-mocked around here. Would you like a cup of coffee? I didn't make it."

"No, thanks. I'll stop in town on my way back."

"Go to the Heartbreak Café. Tell 'em Shay said to set you up right."

"I'll do that." He handed her the reins, then closed up the ramp and locked the gate. "Tell Mr. Rafferty that his aunt and uncle send their regards and they'd like to hear from him sometime."

"I will." Shay led Gambler away from the truck, then watched as the man drove off. When he was gone, she turned the horse loose in the corral, put out feed and checked the water, then leaned on the fence and simply watched him for a time.

Finally, with a shiver, she returned to the house. She collected her mug from the porch rail, picked up Easy's where it'd fallen under the swing, then went inside.

He was working in the front bedroom—the room farthest from the corral, with nothing out the windows but empty pasture. She stopped in the doorway, leaned against the frame and folded her arms over her chest. "He's gone."

He stopped sanding the window frame to face her. "Thank you."

His expression was so heavy with relief that she knew he'd misunderstood. It almost made her hate what she had to say next. "Gambler's out back."

His features grew hard and dark. "Why?"

"Because you sent for him."

"I told you—"

"And I ignored you."

His eyes glinted dangerously. "Get him out of here. I don't want him here."

She took a deep breath, seeking patience, and blew it out

slowly as she moved farther into the room. "He's not a package that you can just toss on the first truck headed out of here. This is a horse who's made a long trip at your request. He's tired, he's settling in, and he's not going anywhere."

"I hauled him all over the damn country. He's used to long trips. Head toward town, catch the foreman, and have him take him back."

"No."

"Then I will." He dropped the sandpaper to the windowsill, grabbed his cane and started toward the door.

She waited until he passed her to speak. "Easy, if you send that horse back, then I'm leaving, too."

Her words stopped him in his tracks. For a long moment the room was utterly still. Hell, the entire world had gone utterly still. No birds sang, no planes flew overhead, no one even breathed. There was just silence—cold, stunned silence.

Then he moved. The floor creaked. The rubber cane tip squeaked on the wood plank as he turned. Slowly she turned, too, to face his anger.

"What did you say?" His question was deadly quiet, his dark eyes made darker by scorn.

"There's nothing wrong with your hearing. I said if you send Gambler away, I'm leaving, too."

"Don't threaten me, Shay."

"It's not a threat."

"What happened to you love me, you want to marry me? What happened to 'Don't worry about it, we'll work it out'?"

She knotted her hands together as she approached him. "Easy, I'm willing to make all the concessions in the world if you'll just make one. I'll be a damn recluse. I'll live out here with you and we'll never go anywhere, never see anybody, never do anything. I'll do all the things couples are supposed to do together by myself. I'll even marry you with no one but Mom and Dad and Guthrie and Olivia and old

Judge Thompson in the living room. But you have to give
me something in return.''

He stared at her for a time, then gave a stunned shake
of his head as he turned away. ''Jeez, I guess I got stupid
somewhere along the way. I thought that marrying you,
having a relationship with you, that I was giving you—
Well, hell, I don't know. *Me*. Obviously you don't agree.
You see marrying me as some great sacrifice that you're
willing to make for—for *what?* If I'm not giving you anything, why in the hell would you want to marry me?''

Heat flushed her face and made her voice unsteady.
''That's not what I meant, Easy, you know—''

''What do you get out of being with me? Do the people
in town think more highly of you for your kindness to the
poor Indian cripple? Are you just stroking your own ego—
proving that even though I left you six years ago, you've
still got what it takes to bring me to my knees? Are you
that eager to get married, afraid those kids won't come if
you wait much longer? What the hell is it, Shay?''

He shouted the last words, and they vibrated between
them, making her flinch. Still, when she spoke, her voice
was quiet, steady. ''You know I love you, Easy. I've loved
you so long and so much that I wouldn't know how to stop
if I wanted. I loved you when you were brash and bold,
and I still love you now that you're not. Just being with
you makes my life complete. But I can't make your life
complete. I can't give meaning or purpose to your life. But
that horse can. That horse can make the difference between
your living or merely surviving.''

''*You* could have done it, Shay. I thought you *had* done
it.'' He shook his head bleakly. ''Like I said, I must've
gotten stupid somewhere.'' His limp was more pronounced
than usual as he walked to the door, where he paused.
''Make whatever arrangements you have to, but I want the
horse out of here.''

He was in the hall before she found the courage to ask,
''What about me?''

This time he didn't turn back. He stopped, and for an instant his shoulders rounded. Then he lifted his head, straightened his spine and coolly said, "I want you out of here, too."

It was a lie.

Not five seconds after the screen door had closed behind Shay, Easy had wanted to run after her and tell her that he'd lied. But he couldn't run, and even if he could have, he couldn't have asked her to stay.

She had come back that night, pulling her car right up to the barn, using the headlights to see while she fed Gambler and checked his water. Easy had watched from the kitchen window, hiding in the dark, and he'd wondered whether she would come to the house to talk to him.

She hadn't.

She'd come back Sunday morning, too, before dawn, repeated the routine and left again. This time she *had* stopped by the house, but she hadn't knocked at the door. She hadn't wanted to see him. She'd just left a note, trapped between the screen door and the frame, saying that her father had agreed to keep Gambler at his place and she would be over to pick him up as soon as Jim returned from a buying trip with the horse trailer.

In the meantime he worked. The front bedroom was ready for papering and painting. So was the hallway, and he was about half-done with the preparatory work in the bathroom. He didn't know *why* he worked. He didn't have the paper or the paint, and he damn well wasn't going to go into town to get them. He just needed something to keep him busy, to stop him from brooding.

Something to keep him away from the back windows.

He'd made a point of not looking at Gambler. That instant's glance when the horse had come out of the trailer had been enough—enough to see the limp, to notice the foot-long scar on his leg, to know he couldn't do this. Gambler was the best horse any cowboy had ever had—loyal, smart, talented as hell—and now he was reduced to living the rest of his life as a cripple.

And he had Easy to thank for it. Or hate for it.

He damn well hated himself.

He was sitting in the dark Sunday evening, nothing but the television, a bowl of popcorn and a beer for company, when headlights cut across the yard. Shifting his gaze to the side window, he watched as a pickup drove past—a pickup without a trailer—then turned back to the television.

Fifteen minutes later footsteps sounded heavily on the porch, then a knock at the door. He didn't respond, but Guthrie had never waited for an invitation before entering this house.

He hesitated in the doorway, glanced around, then settled his gaze on the beer. "Mind if I join you in a drink?"

"It's in the refrigerator."

Guthrie went to the kitchen, returning with a bottle of beer. He hung his jacket on the back of the rocker, then sat down, and in silence they watched television until a commercial break. "Well?"

Easy didn't look at him. "Well what?"

"What went wrong?"

"What makes you think anything's wrong?"

"Let's see… Shay came by the house, and she'd obviously been crying. She's taking care of your horse while you sit here in the dark and drink. What's up?"

"Nothing," Easy said with a harsh scowl.

The commercial break ended, the movie came back on, and Guthrie fell silent again. Easy stared at the screen, though he didn't have a clue what the story was about. He wished Guthrie would go home and was glad he didn't— wished his visitor had been Shay instead and was glad it wasn't.

"You know," Guthrie said, his tone as casual as if he were about to comment on the weather, "I don't envy the people who had to take care of you after the wreck. In spite of your name, you're not an easy person."

"What the hell does that mean?"

"You're pretty damn difficult to deal with. I don't get you. You know what I would've done if I'd been in your boots fourteen years ago? I would have dragged Shay straight to the nearest justice of the peace. I would have married her, settled down with her, had kids with her, and I never would have given another thought to the poor sap she left behind."

"Bull," Easy said flatly. "If you'd been in my boots, you would have gone and stayed the hell away from her."

"You're wrong. If I had loved her that much, I would have knocked myself out trying to make her happy. I would have proven it to her and the entire damn world. I wouldn't have wasted our time feeling guilty because she loved me and not someone else."

Easy didn't bother to point out that Guthrie had never been just "someone else." Betraying someone else wouldn't have been a problem. Betraying the other person you loved dearly… *That* was a problem.

Instead, he focused on another part of his words. "And just how did you have to prove that you loved Olivia?"

"I was ready to sell the ranch and move to Atlanta."

Easy snorted scornfully. "What the hell would you do in Atlanta?"

"Damned if I know—but as long as I was with Liv and the girls, what did it matter?"

Easy stared at the television screen. Guthrie had been willing to give up everything and move halfway across the country to be with the woman he loved. All Shay had asked of *him* was that he keep his horse here. So Guthrie was a better man. Well, hell, no one had had any doubts about that in their whole damn lives. Guthrie had *always* been better—smarter, more responsible, more reliable, more respected.

But Shay had loved *him*.

Did love him now.

Would always love him. He knew it, because he would always love her.

"What's the problem with the horse?" Guthrie asked quietly.

Seeking the words to explain, Easy stared into the past, barely noticing when Guthrie got up to turn down the volume on the TV. His friend was in the rocker again before he found anything to say. "He was—he was the best. From the first time I ever saw him, I knew…I knew he was mine." Like the first time he'd kissed Shay. It'd been that immediate, that certain. He'd *known*.

"I loved that horse. He made me what I am—what I was. When we worked together, it was like—he knew what I was thinking. I knew what he was thinking. I've never connected like that with anyone in my life."

"Except Shay."

Except Shay, Easy silently agreed. "When the guy unloaded Gambler from the trailer, all Shay saw was this beautiful horse. All I saw was this champion, this best horse I'd ever known, with a limp and a scar and a leg that's not much good for anything, and it's my fault. I did that to him."

"Yes, you did," Guthrie agreed. "And even though you didn't mean to, it's something you're going to have to live with. *Live with,* Easy. Not hide from. And that's the problem, isn't it? As long as he's here, you *can't* hide from it. You can't forget for one minute that he's in that corral out back. You can't forget what you did to him. You can't forget what you did to yourself."

"This isn't about me—"

"Yes, it is. If you forgive yourself for Gambler's injuries, then you're gonna have to forgive yourself for your own injuries. You're gonna have to accept that there are things you can do."

"You mean, *can't* do," Easy said bitterly.

"No, you've got that part down pat. You've got to learn that there's plenty left that you *can* do. You can't throw a rope with your right hand…learn to do it with your left. You can't gentle wild horses…train the gentle ones. The doctors say you can't ride…prove 'em right. Or prove 'em wrong. Just prove something, damn it.''

Getting to his feet, Easy paced to the front door, then back to the dining room door. "It's not that easy! I ca—''

"If you say 'I can't' one more time, I'm gonna punch you.''

The threat startled him. He blinked, then asked dryly, "You'd hit a cripple?''

"No, but I'd hit *you*.''

Meaning that he wasn't a cripple—unless he wanted to be one. He didn't. God help him, he didn't. But if he wasn't, then what *was* he?

Good question. Now he needed a good answer.

"Get your jacket. We're going to go out and see your horse.'' Guthrie surged out of the rocker and grabbed his own coat, walked to the front door, then turned back and gestured. "Oh, and you might want to grab that cane. You didn't even notice that you'd walked across the room without it, did you?''

Abruptly Easy realized that he was standing on his feet and only his feet. The cane was propped against the couch where he'd left it when he'd sat down two hours ago.

"You know, Olivia was concerned when you first came back that if this was all you had accomplished in five months, then you might not get any better. But you didn't even try in those five months, did you? You checked yourself out of rehab long before they were ready to let you go, and you moved in with your mom, who babied you even when you were in the best of health.'' Guthrie shook his head in dismay. "God only knows what you could do if you had a reason to try—and I can think of two off the top of my head. So, come on. I want to see this horse again.''

She had never felt less like celebrating a birthday in her life, Shay thought as she stared at herself in the bathroom mirror. Her makeup was exquisitely done and covered the shadows under her eyes. Her hair looked better than it did on the best of days. The rich, dark gold of her sweater made the brown of her eyes appear richer and darker.

She looked great. And felt like hell.

A rumble of thunder made the windowpanes vibrate, drawing her gaze that way. It had been pouring since before dawn—fitting, she thought. There would be no party around the pool. Any party at all was unwanted, but that would have been a reminder she couldn't bear.

"Shay?" Olivia knocked at the door. "You can't stay in there all day."

"Why not?" she grumbled. "I've got everything I need in here."

Olivia opened the door and gave her a sympathetic smile. "Come on. Everyone's waiting."

"Not everyone." Easy wasn't out there. She hadn't seen or heard from him in the week since he'd told her to get out. He'd stayed out of sight the two times she'd gone to feed Gambler. After that, Guthrie had volunteered to care for the horse, and she'd let him. Instead, she'd hung around the café and her house, hoping—praying—that Easy would come looking for her.

He hadn't.

"This is the first birthday party your mama's given you in fourteen years," Olivia said. "Try to look like your world isn't falling apart, would you?"

Shay pasted on a phony smile. "How's that?"

"Pretty pathetic. Come on. Let's go get some food."

Arms linked, they walked down the hall into her mother's family room. Her father gave her a kiss and a cup of fruit punch. Shay would have given a lot for something stronger, but to get that, she would have to find someone concealing a flask, and she wasn't up to figuring out who that might be.

Olivia went to help Mary in the kitchen, leaving Shay to face half the town. Though she'd rather cry, she smiled at jokes about getting older and gray hair, about creaking joints and biological clocks. She didn't have to worry about hearing Easy's name, though. It was almost as if he'd never come back, except for the discomfort. Folks were making an effort to not mention his name, and it increased her own discomfort. She wasn't sure she could stand another minute of it when Reese appeared at her side and drew her off to a quiet corner of the island that separated family room from kitchen.

"Thank you," she murmured as she slid onto a bar stool.

"You looked like you just might strangle Mrs. Davis. I'd hate like hell to have to arrest you on your birthday."

"But you'd do it, wouldn't you?" Her smile was mirthless as she gazed over the crowd. "Give me another hour here, and jail might look *real* appealing."

"Every party needs a pooper—" When she glared at him, he broke off. Looking properly chastened, he said, "You look damn good for thirty-five, Shay."

"It's the miracle of cosmetics."

"Right. If cosmetics could make all women look like you, then all men would be happier."

Not all of them. There was one who was none too eager to gaze on her face.

"I hear Olivia Harris is pregnant. It won't be long before you will be, too, will it?"

Her narrowed gaze settled on his face. "It takes two, darlin'. You volunteering?"

"No way. I imagine Rafferty could do some serious damage with that cane of his."

She swallowed hard, trying to ignore the pain that tightened her chest. "I don't imagine Rafferty would care."

"Oh, yeah, right. I don't imagine that there's been a day gone by in the last fourteen years when he didn't care."

"If this is your way of trying to confirm whether the gossip is true and he's dumped me again, Sheriff, then your investigative techniques leave a little to be desired." She finished her punch, set the glass down and took a look around. Her mother was deep in conversation with the pastor's wife, her father was talking livestock, no doubt, with her uncle, and Olivia was occupied with the kids. There was no sign of Guthrie. "Do me a favor, Reese," she said as she slid to her feet. "If anyone asks where I am, tell them I went to the bathroom."

"It won't work. You've already hidden in there twice. Since most folks here know you're not the hiding type—at least, not normally—they'll assume that you must be pregnant. You know how pregnant women have to go all the time." He grinned slyly. "You wouldn't want to start that sort of rumor, would you?"

"Fine," she said huffily. "Tell them I had to get something out of my car."

"In this pouring rain? What kind of gentleman would I be if I stayed dry and cozy and let the birthday girl go out in this nasty weather?"

"Whoever considered you a gentleman?" she retorted darkly.

Patience, she counseled herself. All she had to do was open the presents on the hearth and blow out the candles on the cake, and then she could escape on her own. It wouldn't be long. Her mother would clap her hands for everyone's attention and say—

"All right, everyone. The kids are anxious to get that cake cut, so, Shay, let's open the packages first, and then we can all eat."

With everyone's eyes on her, Shay smiled as if she couldn't think of ten million things she'd rather do than open presents. She moved to the hearth, seated herself on the cool stone and, with help from the kids in attendance, began opening gifts. She made all the right faces, said all the right things and wished to God she could be anywhere else in the world. Alone. So she could cry.

Only one package remained. She opened it, admired it without even noticing what it was and started to rise just as Guthrie and Reese set a cardboard box in front of her. Sinking back down, she studied it.

It was a cumbersome box, heavy enough to require two men to move it. There was no tag on it, though a worn place on top showed where one might have been torn off, and it was splattered with rain. It wasn't taped. Instead the flaps were folded to secure them. She pulled the first one loose, the others lifting easily, and leaned forward to look inside.

It was a saddle—and not just any saddle. It was a fine one, not too showy, custom-made by one of the best saddle makers in the business. She'd been there the day it was ordered and the day it was picked up, and she'd traveled thousands of miles with it.

She stared at it—just stared—then reached inside to gently dry a raindrop that'd fallen from the flaps. The leather was worn smooth, and it smelled like—well, like good, worn leather. It was a familiar scent, one that she associated with ranches and rodeos and cowboys—one cowboy in particular.

Slowly she lifted her head. Everyone who had gathered around earlier had now backed away, clearing a path across the room to the entrance.

To Easy.

Without thinking, she stood up, stepped around the box and walked right up to him. "I told you I would borrow Dad's trailer and come get Gambler." Her voice was low, shaky, heavy with tears.

"Stealing a man's horse is a hanging offense," he murmured.

"Even if he doesn't want that horse?"

"How could any man not want a horse like that? She's beautiful."

Tears filling her eyes, she smiled unsteadily. "He. Gambler's a *he*."

His gaze searched her face, then slowly his mouth curved up. "Yeah. He's beautiful, too."

"The saddle—" She gestured, and he caught her hand, holding it tightly in his.

"The only way I'm ever going to know what I can do is if I try. What's the worst that can happen? I could get thrown."

"You've been thrown before," she said encouragingly.

"And you'd be there to help me get back up. Wouldn't you?"

"Always," she promised.

As if he couldn't wait any longer, he gently touched her jaw. "I love you, Shay. I haven't always shown it, and I'm sorry, but I'll work on that. But I've always loved you, and no matter how stupid I get, that's not going to change."

"I love you, too," she whispered and reached for him, but he took a step back, holding her at arm's length.

"Will you marry me? Will you stand up in church in front of our families and all our friends and become my wife? A real wedding. For a real marriage. For always."

When she took a breath, the tightness in her chest eased. The ache around her heart disappeared. For the first time in a week, she smiled a real smile, a big, bright one that lit her face and her eyes and her whole world. She knew, because she saw it reflected in *his* face, in *his* eyes.

"Yes, Easy," she said loudly enough for everyone to hear. "I'll marry you."

Finally he pulled her into his arms and kissed her—a deep, hungry, full-of-promise kiss that was interrupted when, from somewhere nearby, Elly Harris gave a great sigh. "Whew. I thought he'd never ask. Now how about that cake, Miss Mary?"

As everyone began moving toward the kitchen, Easy brushed a chaste kiss across her lips, then for one sweet moment he simply held her. Once the candles on the cake were lit, they joined the others at the island. Amid jokes about the smoke detector and the fire department, and with help from the kids, Shay blew out all thirty-five candles.

"What'd you wish for?" Elly asked as she licked frosting from the candle she'd pulled out.

"You know she can't tell you!" Emma admonished her twin. "Else it might not come true."

"What *did* you wish for?" Easy asked late that night when they lay in their moonlit bed, watching Gambler in the corral.

She glanced at him over her shoulder. His long, lean body was snug against hers, and he held her with his left arm as if he might never let her go. He was handsome and sleepy and loved her dearly—but she loved him more.

When she opened her mouth to answer, he suddenly hushed her. "If you tell, it might not come true."

"I can tell you." Turning to lie on her back, she gazed up at him and solemnly answered, "You. I wished for you."

"Then your wish came true. You got me."

His kiss was gentle and tender and touched her heart, making it difficult for her to go on. She managed, though. "And for more horses. And for babies. Boys who will break every record their old man ever set, and girls who will break every heart their mother left intact."

"We'll go see Jeff Hendrix tomorrow. I hear he's got some paints for sale. As for the rest—" Rising over her, he nudged her legs apart, then slid easily, snugly, inside her.

"What are you doing?" she asked with a laugh that faded into a low moan as he stroked her in just the right way, as he kissed her in just the right place. That quickly he took her from already well-satisfied to needy again, desperate again.

"I'm making your wishes come true," he replied.

And he did.

Epilogue

It was a bright November Saturday. The temperature hovered in the low fifties, but the wind gusting out of the west made it feel a good ten degrees colder, maybe more. Easy ignored the chill, though, as he made his way to the barn where Guthrie waited.

A month had passed since Shay's birthday. The wedding had taken place the following weekend—in church, with all their families and friends—and he'd spent much of the three weeks since preparing to make good on his promise to try to ride again. He'd worked practically every day with the physical and occupational therapists in Tulsa that his Houston doctor had recommended. He worked harder and pushed harder than ever before.

But never before had he wanted something so damn much...except Shay.

He was stronger and healthier than he'd been since the accident. This afternoon he was going to find out if he was strong and healthy enough. The idea that he was, with all its promise, dazzled him. The possibility that he wasn't—that he might never be—frightened him.

"Are you ready?"

He drew a deep breath, then dried his palms on his jeans before facing Guthrie. "I guess so."

"Where's Shay?"

"She had to run into town. She'll be back later."

"Want to wait for her?"

He considered it as he watched the paint in the corral, the first of what he hoped would be many purchases. Her name was Suzy Q—short, Elly had announced when she and her dad had brought her over by trailer, for Suzy Cute, and she was the cutest girl horse Elly had ever seen. She was also gentle, even-tempered and well-suited to this afternoon's experiment. Chances that she would react unfavorably to a bumbling novice on her back were somewhere between slim and none, which meant that Easy had pretty good odds of walking away no more damaged than he already was.

Still, horses had been known to surprise a man. If Suzy Q was going to take him for a wild ride or toss him face first in the dirt, he'd rather not have Shay around to watch. Even when he was fit, she'd worried too much. Now....

"Nah," he replied. "I don't need an audience." At least, not yet.

Guthrie went into the corral to lead the mare out. When they stopped in front of him, Easy traded his cane for the reins, then reached up, grabbing hold of the saddle horn with one hand, the cantle with the other. His undamaged right leg provided strong support while, with minimal help from Guthrie, he worked his left foot into the stirrup, then pulled himself up into the saddle.

It wasn't until he was settled, until he felt the familiar form of his favorite old saddle underneath him, that he realized he was holding his breath. He let it out in a slow rush, then let that old sweet feeling of homecoming wrap around him. This was where he'd spent much of his life, and he'd missed it more than he'd let himself admit. The world looked better from astride a horse. Life was easier, brighter, far more pleasurable.

"You okay?" Guthrie asked, backing off a few feet, but staying close enough to help if needed.

Easy shifted. There was a slight discomfort in his hip from this new position, but there was always a slight discomfort there. Even though he was right-handed, the reins felt natural in his left hand. Of course, for a right-handed roper—or ex-roper—that was where they belonged. "Yeah," he murmured. "I'm okay." Hell, right this moment, he felt damn near perfect.

Guthrie moved farther away, and Easy urged the mare into a sedate walk along the trail that led to the driveway. Her pace was slow and steady, the ride smooth and easy. It wouldn't win him any prizes, but that was all right. The biggest prize of all was simply taking the ride.

Reaching the driveway, they followed it to the road, then turned and headed back. He remembered the day not too long ago when he'd walked that distance with Elly and thought he might not make it back. He'd thought that about a lot of places, but here he was, back where he'd always wanted to be, where all his dreams had started, where they were finally coming true. *Home.*

Suzy Q meandered back to the barn. After he reined her in, he turned to find Guthrie watching. "You've got the same look on your face that Elly had the first time she rode Buck by herself," he remarked. "The same look we both wore our first times."

"I don't know how people live without horses."

"They manage, but they're sadder for it." Guthrie's gaze moved past him, and he gestured to the driveway. "There's Shay."

Easy tracked her little car from the road to its parking spot beside the truck, then watched her climb out in that incredibly graceful, sensual way of hers. He'd been wrong a few minutes ago when he'd thought that being able to ride again was the biggest prize of all. It was wonderful, but it couldn't begin to compare to Shay. There were plenty of things he could live without—a career, fingers, horses if he had to—but not her. Never her. She made life worth living.

She was smiling as she approached them—not in a big, surprised, oh-my-God-look-at-you sort of way, but just her usual cut-him-off-at-the-knees-and-make-him-glad-he-was-alive smile. "Hi, Guthrie."

Guthrie tipped his hat. "Miz Rafferty."

She tilted her head back to meet Easy's gaze. "Hey, cowboy."

"Hey. Want to go for a ride?" His voice came out huskier than it should have, but emotion could do that to a man. Looking at Shay did it to him. And even being able to offer her a ride.... He had plenty of excuses for the tightness in his throat.

"Ooh, how many chances to ride off into the sunset with a handsome cowboy does a woman get?" With help from Guthrie, she swung onto the horse behind Easy, then wrapped her arms snugly around his middle.

"Unless you want me to stick around," Guthrie said, "I'm gonna head home. I'll see you guys later."

They both said their goodbyes and Easy added his thanks before guiding Suzy Q through an open gate into empty pasture. There they picked up the ranch road that sixteen years' disuse had almost obliterated and followed it at an easy pace toward the timber. After a time, she broke the silence, leaning forward so that her mouth was close to his ear. "How's the world look from Suzy Q's back?"

"Pretty damn fine," he replied. But he wasn't looking at the world. He was looking at *her*. *His* world.

And it *was* pretty damn fine.

* * * * *

Watch for another HEARTBREAK CANYON *book,
coming soon from Marilyn Pappano and
Silhouette Intimate Moments.*

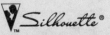